Other books by the author:

Pit Bull

Starlight

The Angel of the Garden

Overgrown with Love

Pulpwood (Livingston Press)

Eating Mississippi (Livingston Press)

A Song
for
Alice Loom

Scott Ely

Livingston Press
University of West Alabama

Library of Congress Control Number 2006927022
Printed on acid-free paper.
Printed in the United States of America,
Publishers Graphics
Hardcover binding by: Heckman Bindery
Typesetting and page layout: Angela Brown
Proofreading: Margaret Walburn, Tricia Taylor,
Lauren Snoddy, Tina Jones, Angela Brown,
Jennifer Brown

The author wishes to thank the National Endowment for the
Arts and the Rockefeller Foundation for the support they gave
in the writing of this novel.

Cover Design: Angela Brown
Cover Layout: Angela Brown
Cover Photos: Angela Brown

This is a work of fiction.
Surely you know the rest: any resemblance
to persons living or dead is coincidental.

Livingston Press
is part of The University of West Alabama,
at Livingston, ALabama.
It thereby has non-profit status, and all
donations are tax-deductible:
brothers and sisters, we need 'em.

first edition
6 5 4 3 3 2 1

Always for Susan

A Song
for
Alice Loom

Chapter 1

My name is Louis Sabine. Once I blew a mean saxophone. When I played the sax, I blew doo-wah, doo-wah, wah, wah and those cats would dig it, you know. Then I joined the Marines and became a cool cat with an M-1. Right now the only thing I'm digging is the volcanic ash of Iwo Jima.

But enough of that hep cat talk. No kind of talk will stop those Japanese from digging me up. They're working just over the rise with their metal detectors, sweeping that black ash, sweating up their polyester shirts. Death was a big surprise to me. That naval shell, a fourteen-incher at least, fell right on my head. I like to think, for some reason, that it came from the Nevada. But it could have been the Tennessee or the Idaho. Why that should make any difference I don't know. They always told me I'd never hear the one that got me, but that's not the way it was. I heard it all right, sounding like somebody was driving a locomotive down out of the sky over my head. We were pinned down by machine gun fire, so even if I'd had time to run, I couldn't. I just lay there, my face in that hot ash. It didn't hurt at all, and the next thing I know I'm buried in the ash and looking down at what's left of me. I call it the field. What I'm in. It's not big but I'm comfortable.

It's those Japs I'm worried about, digging away and probably every now and then resting on their shovels and looking off at Mt. Suribachi. For lunch they'll cook noodles or maybe rice and fish over an alcohol stove and squat there in the ash and work those chopsticks. I bear them no ill will. Looking for their dead, that's all they're doing.

I know what happens when they dig up the dead. They stop talking. No one knows where they go or what happens to them and that scares the shit out of the rest of us. Right now there're three of us: me and Saki, who's about twenty-five yards away up the slope, and Ernie, who's from Iowa, lying under twenty feet of water. A bad trick to play on an Iowa farmboy who'd never even seen the ocean until he joined the Corps. But Ernie is cool, very cool. Saki talks about living in Tokyo and the girl he was going to marry. He describes her tiny feet and hands. He tells us about taking her to see the cherry blossoms in the spring. He talks about cherry blossoms all the time. With Ernie it's always hunting pheasants in Iowa, walking through the corn on a drive and the birds getting up at the end of the field, cackling like Ernie says they do, their wings beating frantically and those long tail feathers sticking out. Ernie says he shot lots of tail feathers out of pheasants. I talk about my music, hum out rhythms for them. But they don't understand, don't dig much of it. What really surprises me is the romantic turn everyone's conversation takes. You'd think no one would be more cynical than a dead Marine. They trained us to act, to do something even if it turned out wrong. And now we can't act; we can only lie curled up in our fields and talk. There're others, but these are the two I'm able to talk with right now.

Over the years I've talked with Japanese and Americans on the island and people all over the world. I've talked with my dead kin. For a few minutes, just after they're dead. As they die, I know. And I've talked with one live person, Alice Loom, who I love. I guess I couldn't stand talking with all the unburied dead in the whole world. I'd go crazy trying to sort out that babble of voices. Not a

Scott Ely

single one of my people hasn't been given a proper burial. I'm the only one. Imagine what the odds on that have to be.

Just as long as they haven't been buried properly we can talk. I started talking with plenty of Americans in Laos during the Vietnam war. Soldiers lost in that jungle. Their bones lying white amid all that green. They're lucky. Nobody is ever going to find them, no Japanese showing up on bone-hunting vacations. Not a single American I talked to in Laos knew anything about jazz. Rock and roll. Rock and roll, that's all I heard. And after a couple of them sang some of it for me, I'd heard enough. Didn't want to hear any more. Nothing interesting. Like a kid beating something out on a tin can.

I talk to them all the time. They come and go. It's like I'm a short-wave set and some days I can't talk to someone across the street, but on others I can talk to the whole damn world, feel as if I can ride those radio waves to the end of the universe. It's funny that in all this time there's not a single person I've talked with who's known anything about jazz. Do all jazz musicians get burials? It seems like at least one could get himself drowned in the middle of the Pacific where three miles down he'd rest comfortable in his field and we'd talk. Anyway, I'm better at this than I ever was at the saxophone. No one else has talked to anyone off the island. It's my gift.

I talk to Alice Loom. Sweet Alice. She is one fine woman. Love lets me talk with her. It's important, I think, that I'm even concerned with love when I'm dead.

I talked to her that first time right after I got killed, and I thought it was easy. But then I discovered that I couldn't always do it. When I talk and she doesn't answer, Ernie calls it talking to the volcano. But when she hears and talks back, Ernie and Saki are amazed.

Talking to her makes me feel good and warm like when there was something of me to feel warm. I hope she doesn't think she's

A Song For Alice Loom

going crazy. Talking has got its dangers for me too. It makes the field unstable, causes sparks and flashes to kind of play around the edges, and we all worry about what would happen if one collapsed. Those that have had theirs collapsed by the Japs aren't saying anything. So I'm careful how much I talk to her. But what I've got to say is important.

Never mind what Looms did to Sabines. It didn't take long before it was hard to tell who was Loom and who was Sabine. Even if I knew she could never hear me, I'd still talk. Maybe that's a way of explaining what love is when no one knows what it is, not even after you're dead and have got no way of expressing it. Alice and I talked of love plenty of times, the way you do in bed, but she wouldn't marry me, and all the time I thought it was her not wanting to bring more Sabine blood back into the family. But now I know that was not it at all. With her it was like something was missing. Sometimes, even then, I thought she didn't really love Hudson and wouldn't be able to love any child we had. It was like there was some hard little place in her, that nobody knew about. I hope by now she hasn't become like a pecan whose meat has dried up.

I liked lying in the air above my body and watching it melt away. It was like looking at one of those films of flowers growing up out of the ground from seed except that in my case it was as if I was watching it in reverse. There wasn't even a bad smell. I like it here, don't want anyone to come dig up my bones. I'm not cold or hot or hungry and except for not having my saxophone I feel fine. There's nothing to do but talk and tell stories. Japanese to Americans and Americans to Japanese. Like I said, that little cat Saki has some stories to tell. And that Marine from Iowa. He can tell a story. I would've liked to harvest wheat with him and then at noon sit under the shade of a wagon, half the field shaved clean and the rest waiting, and listened to him tell a story. He has a real gift.

Scott Ely

When I talk about the crimes of the Looms, which were not unusual but the ordinary abuses of people owning slaves, my field jumps and sparkles. Mostly, though, I talk of love. What was done happened in such a short space of time. I wonder what I'll think of it if I still lie in my field in a thousand years, in a million years. My kin live lives of confusion. Maybe not being able to love was the penalty the Looms paid for what they did to the Sabines, because I sure thought Alice wanted to love me but she couldn't, at least not when I was alive. Now she says she loves me. I talk about that a lot with Saki.

The past is a strange thing. Before I left I looked at the picture of my grandfather Leonidas Sabine standing with his platoon in the Negro regiment he joined. He has his drum slung from a strap around his neck, the sticks raised, as if he's preparing to beat out an advance on a rebel position. He looks like a white man among those dark faces. He may have been almost as white as the white officers, but none of them are in the picture. If they'd given him a rifle, it would have been almost as tall as he is. The bayonets on those soldiers' rifles were long enough to kill an elephant. Those Japs were good with the bayonet. And my father was no bigger than my grandfather. So I didn't get my size from him. It must have come from my mother Anna. She was Swedish and blond and three inches taller than my father.

Saki keeps worrying about those Japanese over the ridge with their metal detectors. But they've swept this part of the island before and found nothing. There's plenty of metal buried here, and I think it confuses them. But those damn metal detectors keep getting better and better. And they've had more than forty years to perfect them. So I tell Saki to relax. Pretty soon I'm going to start trying to talk with Alice again. They like that, Saki and Ernie. They lie in their fields and listen and after I'm finished—usually when my field begins to spit sparks and kind of lose its definition around the edges—we talk about what she's said. Ernie says I must be scaring her half to death. But Saki doesn't think so. The Japs are big on ancestors. I've found that out from Saki. If I'd have known the things I know now about Japs, I would've looked on those landings, all those firefights and those banzai charges—that's when they'd get drunk on that Japanese whiskey they make and try to punch a hole right through our lines—differently. I would still have killed them, but it would have been different. I can't say exactly how. At least I would've known who I was killing.

What I have to say, I learned from being dead. Love is what I learned. Once a soldier over in Laos told me that all of us have the oracle of our ashes. I'm not sure I know what that means, but I like the sound of it. It's true that I can look down anytime I want and see what's left of me. Does that mean that I've avoided the confusion of the living?

Saki thinks I should put it all into poetry, but I don't know anything about poetry. I think, though, I might be able to blow it on my horn. I think I could do that.

I wish I could feel that horn again, moving my fingers over the keys, the reed vibrating against my lips, the mouthpiece slick and wet. But I can't. Saki wants me to start talking, but Ernie advises, as he puts it, for us to lay low until those Japs get out of here. What I do is to start counting all the junk that's buried on this beach: a tank tread, ammo boxes, a jeep transmission, frags (we worry about them because if they blow spontaneously they can disrupt a field), shell fragments, boots, fatigues, a sword, helmets, and over where the Japs are poking around, a ten dollar gold piece some Marine carried as a lucky charm. So I go through all that junk and it's like a prayer, a kind of now I lay me down to sleep sort of thing which you know can't really do any good but makes you feel better.

Once they're gone I'll let the field settle down and then see if conditions are right for talking with Alice. But I know if I had the

Scott Ely

sax I could play it all to her. She'd hear me every single time. Saki could write a song about love, and he could sing it as I play. Yes, I'd play about love, a kind of dark, smoky sound, moving slow and easy, wrapping that music all around her so she'd understand. Alice would like that. She always thought I played better than I really did, and I can see her bobbing her head and swinging her crossed leg in time to the music, letting it fill her. A song for Alice Loom. A song for all of them.

Chapter 2

Larue Sabine couldn't sleep. It was too hot, the sweat not drying on his chest, the air thick and clayey in his lungs. He lay naked and wide awake in the bed with Miss Ella. She was asleep, breathing slowly in and out, her breath making a faint whistling sound like a pot of water getting ready to boil. She sounded that way, he imagined, because she was so old, all her insides dried up and hard with sharp edges, and when her wind moved around them they whistled. A mosquito buzzed in his ear. He slapped at it. It had flown in through a hole a dog had made in the screen that morning. Larue had filled the smaller holes with wads of cotton, creating clusters of fuzzy white galaxies against the darkness of the screen.

Miss Ella was a thin, tiny woman, not much taller than Larue, who was ten years old. She held herself very straight, and she didn't use a cane. Her hair was white. Dark spots stippled her high cheekbones; her nose was thin. She claimed some Choctaw blood. Larue was glad he was dark, that his skin wasn't going to ever have those splotches on it. He complained when his mother called him her beautiful boy but liked it at the same time.

Miss Ella was his Aunt Sabine, not a real aunt but a cousin many times removed who bore the same name as his mother, a maiden aunt who (he had heard his father say it once) had never been touched by a man. She was a voodoo woman. Men and women came to buy love potions and charms for protection against spells. On a set of unfinished pine shelves in her bedroom were ranged jars with powders, colored sand, the skeleton of a snake, a stuffed black cat, bundles of herbs and bird feathers tied up with rubber bands, a rag doll Virgin Mary, and the wing bones of an owl; but the object Larue liked best was the skull of a mad dog. It had been shot right out on the street in front of the house. Larue liked to stick his finger in the bullet hole, a jagged gash, not the perfect sort of hole he imagined a bullet would make. Miss Ella used the teeth for charms, so they were mostly gone except for the eyeteeth, which she said she was saving for something special. She had boiled the flesh off the skull in a black kettle set over an open fire in the back yard and then laid it on a fire ant bed to finish the job.

The Virgin had eyes made of blue glass and a mouth of red thread, not curving up in a rag doll smile but instead running straight across. She wore a pair of tiny gold high-heeled shoes on her feet and a gold thread halo around her head. A belt, braided of green feathers, encircled her waist. She had been one of Miss Ella's main charms in New Orleans when they had lived across the river in Algiers; and he went to sleep listening to the deep horns of the freighters as they slipped their moorings and went downriver, carried on the brown water flowing higher than his bedroom, stack and superstructure and running lights floating away in the darkness. Now here in Pine, where the river ran below and not above, the Virgin seemed to have lost her power amid all the Baptists. Larue sometimes turned the dog skull toward her and thought she looked frightened, ready to jump off the shelf. Skulls were what they wanted in Mississippi, not rag doll Virgins.

But it wasn't the Virgin who made him feel safe nor that white skull; it was Miss Ella who commanded the power in these things. He slept well with her, knew no man would dare wander into that back bedroom.

Mr. Hone at the corner store had asked after Miss Ella. He was worried about her and the heat. It had been over a hundred every day for a week now. Every afternoon, Larue sat on the porch and watched the clouds pile up over the swamp land across the river, white puffy clouds shot through with black, like oysters gone bad, but it never rained. Mr. Hone had a fan going in the store, moving the thick air from one place to another.

"Boy, you watch after Miss Ella," he said. "Old folks can't tolerate this heat."

And one of those old men—as much a part of the store as the popcorn machine or the sign outside: BOILED P—NUTS GUARANTEED WORST IN TOWN—mentioned the name of someone who had died from it. Larue had told Mr. Hone he would watch out for her. He laughed to himself at the thought of lying awake and Miss Ella sound asleep under both a sheet and a wool blanket. At least tonight there were no men about. His sister Tiffany was asleep in the next room with his mother. He liked it when the house was quiet.

The four-room house was built in 1917 by Marion Loom—the founder of the Pine lumber mill—to put up workers from a munitions plant. He used number three yellow pine and studs six feet apart. The houses had been hastily thrown up in a section of the city known as French Town. After the war the plant closed and the white workers moved on. The houses were left to decay, their miserly frames inadequate to the task of keeping walls plumb or their roofs from sagging.

The house was set up on decaying brick piers. Larue liked to lie under the house, listening to the people moving about overhead. But he didn't like to listen to his mother and her clients: their laughter and the creak of the bed and afterwards the sound of the men's big feet on the floor. He didn't like it, yet he lay there motionless in the cool darkness and listened.

The men often joked with him as they sat in the outer room on the old brown sofa, sometimes settling a loose cock back inside their underwear. His mother scolded them and threw them a bathrobe. They laughed, pulling her down on their laps.

When they did that, put their hands on his mother, Larue brought up his father.

"He jumps out of airplanes," Larue told them. "He's an airborne ranger."

And he thought of his father floating down under a white canopy. He had three 101st Airborne T-shirts with screaming eagles on them. Also a fatigue jacket with the eagle done on the sleeve in black stitching. Larue liked to run his long graceful fingers over the pattern

Scott Ely

as he lay in bed in the dark. There was also his father's night jump parachute, the canopy black nylon, the shroud lines thin braided black nylon. It lay carefully folded under Miss Ella's bed, making a smooth black mound in the darkness. Solid looking but really light and airy, like a piece of the night sky you could shake out when you wished. You jumped at night with it, floating down on the enemy. When they saw you, they were dead. Much of the day he lay under the house and thought about his father, who was working on a shrimp boat in Biloxi. After the season was over, he was going to come home with plenty of money to spend. They'd buy a color TV.

Sometimes the men laughed at this and sometimes they regarded the boy gravely, who stood before them with his eyes cast at the floor, his fists clenched at his sides. The men thought he was thirteen or fourteen. Some of them considered how angry a boy of that age would be with them. These men treated him gently.

"He's coming back," Larue said.

"Boy, a man like that don't come back," one of the men said.

Larue looked him in the eye.

"He's coming back," Larue said.

Then the ones who treated him gently might lower their eyes, but the others always laughed.

Tonight there had been no TV because the electricity was gone. The water and plumbing had been gone for almost a week. The last time a man was there his mother had filled the front bedroom with candles, and after he was gone she had let Larue blow them out, the room smelling of bayberry and smoke. The smell made Larue ache in some way he couldn't understand, mixing as it did with the smell of the man on her; and he was glad when he heard her washing herself, squatting over a pail of water set in the tub, the water making a rasping sound as one handful after another was sucked down the drain.

His mother complained to Mr. Wendell Loom, the son of Marion, about the power and water. Mr. Wendell was old but not as old as Miss Ella. He had white hair and blue eyes and a nose that looked like someone had taken a piece of clay, rolled it into a ball, and stuck it on his face. His ears were covered with white hairs. Larue always wondered why he didn't get the hairs cut off at the barber shop. Mr. Wendell said she should use the outdoor privy and said she had sold the toilet bowl.

Larue had gone along with her when Mr. Wendell had come by in his big car. The white man blew the horn, and she went out to the curb to speak with him. The automatic window, tinted dark, slid down with a whirr, and suddenly there was that white man's face, looking like the belly of a dead catfish. Usually Anse Carter drove the car, a thin little man with short arms. Everyone knew he carried a .38 in the pocket of that blue suit coat he wore winter and summer. He could shoot dragonflies out of the air with it. Even Miss Ella's charms were no protection against Anse Carter.

"Ruth, I can't have you hauling off my toilet bowls," Mr. Wendell said.

"I ain't been selling no bowls," she said. "That one bowl cracked. I told you that. We put it out for you to see. Then it was gone. Children made off with it. Wild children nobody's watching."

Mr. Wendell ignored her. It was like she was talking to the big hackberry tree across the street at the entrance to the city garbage department. Beyond the tree was the main office and then sheds and a parking lot for the trucks. Finally there was the levee and beyond that the river, the feathery tops of the cypresses looking to Larue like they had been spun with green cotton candy.

"You get some of your men friends to help you out," he said. "I expect one of the big ones broke that bowl. Got wild on cocaine and took his meanness out on my property."

Larue, who had moved closer, felt the cool air coming out of the window, smelled Mr. Wendell's cigarette smoke, which got sucked out into the heat in a thin blue spiral, smelled the perfume his mother had put on before she walked down to Mr. Hone's store.

"I won't have no money for you," she said.

Mr. Wendell didn't get mad. He just grinned.

"I'll be moving some folks in. Lots of people need a place to live."

The window went up with that nice whirring sound, and the car drove slowly off. His mother stood and watched until it disappeared.

"That man thinks he owns this whole town," his mother said.

"Does he?" Larue asked.

"Hush, child," she said.

The next day, lights and water gone, they had started drinking

Scott Ely

from the well. Larue pulled them up a bucket of water and brought it into the house. They had never used the well, and when he lowered the bucket into it, he'd been surprised by the splash and realized there was a lake, a river right under their feet. The stove was bottled gas so they could still cook.

He hauled enough for Tiffany's bath, the water sloshing out of the bucket onto the kitchen floor when he filled it too full. He filled a big pot with the last bucket. His mother dipped a glass in it and gave Tiffany a drink. Then she drank.

"Pure spring water," his mother said. "I ain't never had pure water. Grandmother used to tell us about how good it tasted out of the well. She was right."

She offered him a glass, and he drank a little but didn't like the taste. He wasn't going to drink water as long as he had enough money for a cold drink at Mr. Hone's store.

"I'm gonna get me a drink at Mr. Hone's," he said.

She laughed.

"Where you getting money for drinks?" she asked.

And then before he could answer she said, "You bring Miss Ella a cold drink."

She put two quarters in his hand.

"Spending the last of my money on cold drinks," she said and sighed.

Then she had laughed again, a strange sort of high-pitched laugh.

Larue closed his eyes, Miss Ella's whistling sound bearing him off to sleep.

He woke to the sound of Tiffany crying, a muffled sort of sobbing like she had the pillow over her head. He slipped out of bed and crept out of the room and across the hall, the boards cool and smooth against his feet, the one weak one bowed under his weight like always. Then he smelled it and understood what had happened. Tiffany was scared of the dark and had refused to go to the privy by herself. So she had done it in the bed and that was why she was crying, because his mother had hit her for ruining the bed.

Miss Ella sat on the bed holding his mother's hand in the dark. The half moon was up so Larue saw the scene clearly. Tiffany was a still lump on the bed, hiding under the covers. As the crying, a low wail, started again, Larue realized it was coming from his mother.

"Boy, you go run to the Adams' house," Miss Ella said. "Tell 'em call a doctor."

"Can't you?" Larue asked.

She shook her head.

"I done made a tea," she said. "I can't do no more than that. Runs through 'em fast as I put it in. You go quick."

Larue bolted out of the room, wanting to get away from the smell and his mother's wailing. He ran along the street, past the liquor store, and up on the porch of the Adams' house, which was made of brick and had a low chain link fence all around it and flowers in the yard instead of just bare dirt. It belonged to them instead of Mr. Wendell. That was one thing in French Town Larue was sure Mr. Wendell didn't own.

He banged on the door until a light came on. Then the door opened, and there was Mrs. Adams in a robe and slippers, curlers in her hair.

"Boy, don't you know it's time for sleeping?" she said.

"Yes, ma'am," he said. "Mama's sick, Tiffany's sick. Miss Ella said for you to call a doctor."

"Miss Ella don't hold with no doctors," she said.

Mr. Adams now stood behind his wife dressed in a pair of overalls. He worked for the garbage department as a truck driver. Larue liked the way he drove his truck fast down the hill into the lot every afternoon, one hand on the wheel and the other hanging out the window using his cap to cover the number painted on the door so that Mr. Guess, who stood in the doorway of the office with a pair of field glasses and a clipboard, couldn't read his number.

"One of those men cut up Ruth?" Mr. Adams asked.

"Hush, Tom," she said.

"Is the man gone?" she asked.

"Gone," Larue said. "Just mamma and Tiffany and Miss Ella."

She opened the door and let him in. He sat on the sofa and watched her call the doctor. A child came out of a bedroom dressed in only a pair of blue underpants, rubbing her eyes. Larue started out of the house.

"You wait 'til the doctor comes," she said. "You want a Coke-a-

Cola?"

Larue sat on the sofa and drank the coke while Mr. Adams sat beside him. The room was full of furniture. They had two reclining chairs in front of the TV, a round shag rug, pictures of kin over the old coal scuttle, a table with chairs that all matched, and green curtains on the windows. Mr. Adams turned on the TV, and they watched football. Mrs. Adams came into the living room dressed, the curlers out of her hair. As she started out the door, Larue gulped down the rest of his drink and stood up.

"You stay here, boy," Mr. Adams said. "They 'bout to score a touchdown."

So Larue sat on the sofa with the empty Coke bottle in his hands and watched football.

Ella sat on the bed and held Ruth's hand. She'd tried everything, but they were melting away before her eyes. What was inside them was now outside. She hadn't seen anyone die that way in a long time. It was an old sickness. Beyond the reach of any healing tea, not even a tea made of a bluejay's tongue, a caterpillar still in its cocoon, and Johnny the Conqueror root.

Ruth moaned, too weak now to thrash about in the bed. Ella's shoulders hurt from wrestling with her.

"Lay still, honey," she said.

She no longer expected that Ruth could even hear.

"Not even a wet cloth for the fever," she said. "It ain't right. It ain't right."

Ruth was gasping for breath, soon to be another lump in the bed just like Tiffany.

"*They're gonna be all right,*" the voice said. "*All right.*"

It was a soft voice that came to her out of the darkness.

"Oh, Lord!" Miss Ella cried. "Sweet Jesus!"

"*Don't worry,*" the voice said. "*Dying's nothing at all.*"

"Who are you?" Miss Ella asked. "Are you the devil?"

She heard laughter.

"*No ma'am, I'm Louis Sabine,*" the voice said.

"Leonidas' boy?"

"*That's me.*"

"You're dead."

"*On Iwo Jima. Don't you come dig me up.*"

"I won't dig nobody up."

I wonder what I'm doing talking to a living person who isn't Alice. It makes me feel uneasy. But I look at the field and it's stable. Nothing unusual seems to be going on. Maybe after you've been dead long enough you can talk with the living, I tell myself. Maybe it's a certain number of years and then it happens. Like puberty. A predictable change.

For the moment I leave Miss Ella alone and talk with Tiffany. She's not scared. The others are listening too, although they can't talk to her.

"Where will I go?" she asks.

"*A safe place,*" *I say.* "*You tell Miss Ella not to let those Japs dig me up. Not to let them dig my friends up*"

"Don't be afraid," she says.

"Who are you talking to, my baby?" Ruth asks.

I say my name. She doesn't know the family history like Miss Ella Does. I mean nothing to her.

"Who you talking with?" Miss Ella asks.

"*Ruth and Tiffany,*" *I say.*

"I can't hear them," she says.

"*I can. I don't know why you can't.*

"You know who's gonna die."

"*I don't know anything.*"

"Who are you?" Ruth asks.

"*Your kin,*" *I say.*

"My father?" Tiffany asks.

"*No, a cousin.*

"Like Miss Ella?"

"*Yes.*"

Then I lose them. Maybe, I think, the undertaker has come? I try to talk with Miss Ella, but I can't reach her either.

I tell Saki and Ernie what has happened, that some of my kin are dead. A mother and her little girl. And that I'm talking with a living person. They find that strange and worry about what it means. But I tell them to be cool.

"*Our fields are fine,*" *I say.*

Scott Ely

"Mine too," Saki says.

"And mine," Ernie says.

They're easy to convince, although talking to live people I don't know, even though they're kin, makes me uneasy.

"They're gonna be buried," Ernie says.

"They will know what we know," Saki says.

And we lie in our fields and talk about what it means to be dead. It's easy to talk about as long as those Japs aren't around with their metal detectors. Saki and I lie in that black sand. Ernie in the blue sea. And I stretch myself out through the world, talking to the dead.

Ella found she couldn't even cry over them. She was too exhausted. A ghost had talked to her. An ancestor from the grave. She knew what Iwo Jima was and that Louis Sabine had been killed there. She carried that story in her head.

Now, she thought, Larue had no mother and a father gone off to do no good somewhere. And Mr. Wendell Loom still driving up and down the street in his big car. Mr. Wendell who had denied them even water to wash their dead.

"Miss Ella?" the voice asked.

"Yes," she said.

She liked the sound of Louis Sabine's voice. It was soft and comforting.

"How did they die?"

So she told him. He didn't interrupt her. She could sense his displeasure.

I tell Saki and Ernie that Looms are still killing Sabines. I wonder when it's going to stop.

"What you gonna do?" she asked.

"Nothing," I said. "I can't do nothing. But you've got to do something. The Looms are our blood. Make them be responsible."

"Responsible?"

"Yes, for their kin. For what Wendell did. Him or one of them. It makes no difference."

Then the voice was gone, and although she called out for Louis Sabine, he wouldn't answer.

I tell Ernie and Saki what I told Miss Ella. Both of them think it's a good idea, to make the Looms responsible. Saki worries that my people will come and dig us up, like his are trying to do. Americans aren't like the Japanese in that way, I tell him. That seems to satisfy him, and we all settle comfortably in our fields.

When they heard the sirens, Larue guessed it was going to be all right. They would take his mama and Tiffany to the hospital.

Mr. Adams turned off the TV, and they went out of the house together. Larue saw the red light on the ambulance going round and round along with the blue lights of two police cars. People were standing about on the sidewalk watching.

Miss Ella was looking into the back of the ambulance like she was waiting for someone to invite her to climb in. The ambulance had been at the house one time before when a man got cut in the front yard. Larue had watched the doctor work on him. As the ambulance pulled away the doctor, his hands clenched together, was mashing up and down on the man's chest.

The doors closed and the ambulance drove slowly down the street.

Miss Ella put her arms around him. She smelled like soap, her rose soap which she used every Sunday.

"They're both gone," she said. "Gone to Jesus. They'll be happy there."

Larue felt her body heaving and thought of all those sharp insides clanking around together. He started to cry too because he didn't want Jesus to get his mother and Tiffany. He imagined Jesus looking down on them as they drifted up to heaven.

"They ain't gone," he said.

"They gone, boy," she said.

She looked down at the boy who had buried his face in her skirts.

"You ain't gonna leave?" Larue asked.

"No, child," she said. "I'm staying right here."

"Where will you go when you die?"

"I won't die."

"You'll conjure Mama and Tiffany back?"

"Ain't got no spells to make who's dead alive."

She thought of her kin, the voice of the spirit. He was dead yet was alive in a way.

Scott Ely

"But you—"

"Don't need no spells. I'll fly up in the sky. Go kick that dog star out of the way to make room for me. I'll be the brightest one."

She'd shown him the star, the brightest star in the sky, coming with the rising and setting of the sun, taking their attention away from the Venus star. Miss Ella called Venus the love star. Larue repeated the words: "love" and "dog," "love" and "dog" over and over under his breath. There was a sound they had in common. He liked that. It could be a code, a spell, and if you said it over and over enough times some secret might be revealed.

"Don't you leave," Larue said.

He began to cry.

"I ain't going nowhere," she said.

Miss Ella led him into the dark house. They went to bed together. She kept waiting for the voice to come out of the darkness again. All those years she'd tried through spells and charms to talk with the dead but never had. And now that voice had come out of nowhere, when she wasn't even expecting it. She tried to calm herself; she tried to sleep.

Beside her in the bed, her body as rigid as if it were a piece of iron, the rose smell fading away, Larue waited for her to begin to breathe like sleep again. For what seemed like hours he listened to her breathing in quick jerky gasps as if she had just finished a race. So he abandoned any hope of sleep and waited for the light, heard a rooster crow, and then he slept.

Chapter 3

Alice Loom heard Lou Sabine whisper to her, the dead man's voice floating through the house, up and down the stairs and through the high-ceilinged rooms, a murmur she could identify but not understand, like a familiar voice from across a big lawn. Sometimes his voice was like that, but at other times it was clear, as if he were standing next to her. And she wished that he would run his hands through her hair. She didn't think that he would speak clearly to her today. But the sound of his voice was soothing, like falling water.

She listened as she counted the knives and forks, making sure each place setting was correct. Once a month the family had dinner together. She wanted it to be perfect.

Then she walked through the big house her father Marion had built just before the Crash. It had pocket doors between all the downstairs rooms, paintings on the ceilings, and carvings on the cornices. It had taken a year to build and Italian artisans had done the painting and carving, chattering to each other in their musical language. She loved the house, loved the way it creaked in the night and the smell of the hardwood floors, loved the big oaks and pines which covered the lawn. Because the house had been there waiting, her brother Wendell womanless and childless, it had been easy to come home to Pine from New York. She'd felt at the time she had little choice, although occasionally she thought of the men she had been seeing, those goodbyes in restaurants and apartments, those offers of marriage. But then or now she wasn't interested in marriage. She had her music and the house. At first they had all lived there together. She and her children, Hudson and Rosalind, and her brother Wendell. But now Hudson had his own house and Wendell lived in an apartment attached to his office. Wendell always came for the evening meal.

She'd stopped hoping for grandchildren. She was sorry for that. Her plan from the first had been that once she had the children she would have no need for men, music and children all she desired. Now things had changed and she longed for Lou Sabine, the longing, the love, like stopping a passage of music at mid-stroke of the bow, her fingers and brain feeling it ready to unroll, but the notes hanging there in a void, giving her an empty feeling. But sometimes she wondered if she should have given herself over to that voice. When she realized she loved him he was already dead: perhaps she should have found another man to love.

She started up the big marble staircase to the second floor to call her daughter Rosalind, the voice of Lou Sabine still in her ear, the tone going up and down like his saxophone. She remembered descending for young men, her shoes clicking on the smooth stone, her gloved hand running lightly on the wrought iron banister. She remembered playing her viola in the music room upstairs. Now her hands were crippled with arthritis, and her right hip ached at the thought of going up the stairs. She hesitated—a tall woman with big hips, who even after the addition of middle-aged fat looked elegant and graceful— and returned to the dining room with its crystal chandelier. She sat at the head of the table under her father's picture.

Lou's voice had been coming to her ever since that day in 1945 when, pregnant with Rosalind, she sat in a New York subway seat, her viola beside her, the warmth of the car a relief from the February cold. Her son Hudson, five years old then, was at the sitter's. A young soldier sat next to her, and at first she thought it was he who had spoken. But it was not, the soldier was concentrating on his newspaper. He was reading about German setbacks on the Russian front, a picture of tanks in the snow on the front page. So she knew Lou was dead. Not even her legal husband. But he had claimed her as his wife, and she had been receiving her allotment and later the telegram along with the insurance. That day the orchestra had practiced Beethoven's Ninth. The hall was cold, and she wore a sweater as she cradled the viola against her neck, the chorus singing Schiller's "Ode to Joy."

"Alice," Lou said.

"Lou," she whispered.

The young soldier was concentrating on the sports page.

"It's me."

"How?"

"I'm dead."

She sucked in her breath, and the soldier had turned his head to look at her. She smiled at him.

"No, Lou," she said. "Where are you?"

Now the soldier had known she was having a conversation with herself but had decided to ignore her. Alice had been thankful for that.

"On Iwo Jima," he said.

And he'd gone on to describe where he was and the two soldiers he talked with, Ernie and Saki.

"Don't come here," he said. "After the war don't come here and look for me. Graves registration found O'Brien and he stopped talking to us. I'm scared of that happening to me. I don't want to ever stop talking."

"You won't stop," she said. "You won't ever stop."

The soldier had gotten up and moved to another seat.

"I'm fine," he said. "Just keep talking to me."

"I love you, Lou," she said, that word, the feeling she had for him, coming as a surprise.

But she received no answer. She sat and listened to the sound of the wheels on the rails and wondered if she were going mad. Then the telegram had come and he'd spoken to her again, and she knew she was perfectly sane.

The voice, during those times when she could hear but couldn't make out the words, had taken on characteristics of other senses. Sometimes it was like a warm blanket. Today it was like a smell of mahogany veneer, gone crazy on the huge armoire in the upstairs hall.

Rosalind's father, Lou Sabine, had been talking to Alice since she lay still in bed early in the morning. Lou had said something, a whisper, like the rustle of lace curtains.

The Looms and Sabines were related, one family servants of the

Scott Ely

other in the beginning, at least in the beginning in America. What the Sabines had been in Africa and by what name no one knew. They could just as easily have been kings as slaves. From the beginning Looms had slept with their slaves. Alice liked to consider herself as much of a Sabine as a Loom.

Now the individuals were sorted out by color even though the same blood flowed in black and white veins. After the war a Loom slave, one who'd been taught to read and knew the classics, had taken the Sabine name. No one knew why.

Lou was a beautiful man, the Sabine blood showing faintly in his curly brown hair, his black eyes. Seeing him was like suddenly hearing a piece of music never heard before, and so you wanted to hear it over and over, knowing that you'd never tire of it.

When he heard her name, he had laughed as if he had been expecting it to happen for years and now here she was. He told her he had been passing for white. She remembered pausing and considering how that might make him feel, caught at some shifting point between the two races, never able to belong completely to either one. But even at the time she'd been out of the South long enough to realize some might look at the ambiguity as a positive quality, an advantage, not a disadvantage.

"Mama?" she heard her son Hudson say.

She looked up and saw him standing over her. There was a burning smell in the air.

"My roast!" she said.

Alice ran for the kitchen and with Hudson's help got the roast out of the oven.

Instead of worrying about the roast she kept listening for the sound of Lou Sabine's voice.

"It's hardly burned," Hudson said.

Hudson watched Alice cut away the burned part. He preferred to stay out of the house. He hated his uncle Wendell.

"Did you put up your usual hundred signs today?" she asked.

Hudson laughed.

"Just a few, Mama," he said.

Hudson, the manager of the city sanitation department, had been putting out signs for the coming mayoral election. Maurice

Longstreet had been mayor for almost thirty years, and Hudson put up a few Longstreet signs every day.

Alice looked at Hudson. He resembled Henry in the face. But who would have thought the son of Henry, a delicate man with small bones, would be so big. He had inherited her hips and long arms. She had a picture of Henry upstairs. He had been killed in 1940 while playing in a ship's orchestra, the passenger liner torpedoed. Now he was on the bottom of the North Atlantic. He never talked to her, nor did she think of him very often. She didn't think she had ever loved him and had intended not to love him or Lou. Her love for Lou Sabine was a surprise, discovered on that subway in 1945. Too late. She and the Germans, she thought, surprised at the same time. That very day she went to a jewelry store and bought a ring, began to wear it for Lou.

Wendell came in the kitchen door. Last night he'd slept at his office in town. Alice was ten years older. She remembered Wendell getting caught stealing milk bottles off the neighbor's porches and selling them.

"Burned roast," Wendell said as he sniffed the air.

Alice started to rub her hands. The arthritis always flared up at times like this.

"Sister, the Sabines are going to be the end of this family," Wendell said. "I just had the water and electricity of a whole tribe of'em cut off. Destroyed my property. I try to treat those people right. I put up screens and put in new plumbing. They tear it out faster than I can build."

Alice wondered if these Sabines were kin. But she was only mildly curious about them. She couldn't get excited over every person in Mississippi named Sabine. It was Lou's voice she wanted to hear.

"Mama, you make the gravy," Hudson said. "I'll carve the roast."

Alice went to the stove and started to work on the gravy. Hudson began to carve the roast.

"Least you're cooking," Wendell said. "With Rosalind it's always tofu and bean sprouts. I'd just as soon go out on the front lawn and eat the crab grass."

Wendell poured himself a drink.

"Daddy spent all that money on music lessons," Wendell said. "She

Scott Ely

don't even play that thing anymore."

One of Wendell's favorite games was complaining about Rosalind. Hudson decided to ignore him.

"She's a good teacher," Alice said.

Wendell laughed.

"Part time at the University don't count," he said. "Why, I made more off my investments riding to work this morning then she has in the last ten years. How can somebody without a real job spend all their time having niggers talk into a tape recorder? She's making people laugh at this family. She hasn't missed a Braves' game in years. Sits right there in front of the TV while other people are working. Wish I had time to watch baseball."

Hudson hoped Wendell wouldn't start talking about the shooting. He liked to tell of the day their father Marion shot a drunken black man, who turned out to be a Sabine, as he stumbled through the hedge into the garden where Alice was giving a recital. It was true that the man was carrying a butcher knife, but he had threatened no one with it.

Wendell had a hold on them. Their grandfather had left the house and the money in Wendell's name. He had orders to give Alice an allowance. He always paid it promptly on the first of the month and then spent the rest of the month complaining about household expenses.

"Go tell Rosalind that dinner is ready, Hudson," Alice said.

Hudson went up the marble stairs. He hated the house with its ornate furnishings. Even the doorknobs had fancy carvings on them.

At the bedroom, the turret room at the end of the hall, he knocked on Rosalind's door. Mozart was playing inside.

"It's Hudson," he said.

Rosalind told him to come in. He pushed open the door. One thing Hudson did like about the house was the workmanship on the doors and windows. You could raise a window anywhere in the house with one hand; the doors swung open like bank vaults.

She sat at a table in the center of the room writing in a notebook. She looked up at him and smiled, a pretty woman, very thin. Only the lines on her face betrayed her age. She had none of her mother's big features. Her bones were delicate.

Hudson looked around the room. The walls were lined with books. Rosalind taught history. She had been trying to finish her dissertation for years. It was about the early history of Pine. Music posters were on the wall. There was a photograph of her giving her first recital, the viola almost as big as she was. There were pictures of her friends at Julliard. And Braves' pennants and autographed baseballs. Sometimes Hudson and Rosalind drove over to Atlanta for a game.

On the wall above Rosalind's unmade bed was a framed picture of her. She held a guitar, her dark hair falling long down her back, and wore tight, bell-bottomed jeans topped by an olive drab army t-shirt. Rosalind had quit Julliard in the late sixties. She'd formed an all-girl band and had gone to Vietnam to entertain the troops. During a rocket attack on a base camp she suffered a head wound. She'd come home and recovered quickly, but instead of taking up music again she had studied history.

"Mama says come to dinner," he said.

"I'm not hungry," she said. "I've got work to do."

"You know what these dinners mean to Mama."

"Oh, all right."

They went downstairs. Wendell and Alice were waiting at the table. Rosalind sat down across from Hudson, Alice and Wendell at either end. Alice asked the blessing. Rosalind and Wendell worked hard ignoring each other.

"Be sure to save a little out for Anse," Wendell said.

Anse Carter was Wendell's collector of rents. Wendell allowed him to live in the small cabin in the back yard which had once been the cook's house. Anse reminded Hudson of one of those white grubs he found under rotten logs and used for fishbait.

"I wish you'd pay him enough so he could find his own place," Alice said.

Alice would not allow Anse in the house. Wendell called Anse his reclamation project because Anse had been in prison.

"He needs to be around family life," Wendell said.

"A disgusting little man," Rosalind said.

"You people up at the University think you're better than the rest of us," Wendell said. "Anse does good work for me."

"Collecting rents from those who can't afford to pay," Rosalind said. "Those people live like animals."

"They tear it up soon as I fix it," Wendell said. "You wouldn't do any better at taking care of those rent houses."

"I wouldn't have them," Rosalind said.

"That cabin is not fit for humans to live in," Alice said. "Let Mr. Carter rent an apartment or live at a boarding house if he wants family life so much."

"Just save some out for Anse," Wendell said softly. "I'll take him a plate."

Alice found the relationship between Wendell and Anse Carter a strange one. It was more like that between a falconer and a falcon. Anse and Wendell were not friends. Anse always addressed him as Mr. Loom. Yet the clothes on Anse's back were old boyhood clothes of Hudson's that Wendell got from Alice, and it was always Wendell who took Anse a plate after dinner. She could imagine Wendell staying up night after night to watch him tame. So in some strange sort of way if Wendell loved anyone it was Anse, the kind of love a person might give to a favorite dog. Wendell had never married either, as if when children she and Wendell had made a pact between them. She almost smiled when she thought that she was in love with a dead man and the only thing Wendell appeared to love could hardly be classified as human. Now the Looms were going to die out. She had some hope for Hudson, but he had all the signs of a perpetual bachelor. It wasn't that he didn't like women. There was hardly a good-looking woman in town that he hadn't taken out. His former girl friends all spoke highly of Hudson; their mothers spoke highly of Hudson. It was dangerous getting used to living alone, she thought. You passed a certain point and it became too easy.

They began to eat. Wendell started telling about how he had been buying up oil leases.

"A-rabs is crazy," he said. "Sooner or later they'll do something to make the price go up. Maybe the Jews will drop a bomb on 'em."

"Why do you love war?" Rosalind asked. "How can a man who fought in France love war so much?"

"Please," Alice said.

"You wouldn't know anything about it," Wendell said. "I do. And Vietnam don't count. That wasn't even a real war. You got yourself hit on the head and think you've been in combat."

"You don't care who dies," Rosalind said. "As long as you make money."

"How long have you been home from Vietnam?" Wendell asked. "Those boys who did the fighting are working at real jobs. You can't even finish a term paper."

Rosalind didn't reply but shook her head.

"She's been depressed," Alice said.

"Mother!" Rosalind said.

"Damn it, I get depressed," Wendell shouted. "We all get depressed." Then Wendell lowered his voice. "You come go to work for me."

"And cheat people," Rosalind said. "Put ten people in a four-room house with a leaky roof and one bathroom. You think I'd do that?"

"You'd do it," Wendell said. "If you had to pay taxes and make a payroll, you'd do it."

"Someday, Uncle Wendell, those people are going to get tired of what you're doing. They'll drag you out of that big car. And even that dirty little Anse won't be able to save you."

Wendell started to rise. Hudson reached out and took his arm, which felt thin and frail beneath his jacket. He'd never laid hands on his uncle before.

"Stop it," Hudson said.

Wendell sat down. Hudson released him.

"Yes, stop," Alice said. "Both of you. I will no longer tolerate this at my dinner table."

Wendell apologized to Alice. Rosalind left the table, walking fast with quick short steps.

"That's my bad arm you grabbed," Wendell complained.

"Sorry," Hudson said.

Wendell was rubbing his arm.

Hudson thought of the signs he was going to put out. This was exactly why he avoided coming to the house. Wendell and Rosalind were constantly in conflict.

"Have some more roast, Hudson," Alice said.

Hudson took some more even though he wasn't hungry. His mother was trying to reestablish the ritual of the meal. Meals were important to her. Wendell and Rosalind ruined most of them. Wendell had returned to talking about oil again.

Hudson thought of Holly Matthews. He'd met her at the country club. She was a lawyer from Texas who'd just moved to town. They'd go over to Atlanta for a Braves game. Make a weekend of it. Instead of sleeping in the camper they'd stay at the best hotel in town. Have champagne for breakfast.

"I've watched you fight for years," Alice said. "This will be the last time or you will no longer eat at my table."

"I said I was sorry," Wendell protested.

"The last time," Alice said. "I will speak to Rosalind so that she will understand."

Alice chewed a piece of partially burned roast and listened hard for Lou Sabine's voice to filter through the tinkle of the silverware. She thought she heard it, imagined him lying deep in that black volcanic sand, while above palm fronds were splayed against the blue sky. She pictured his bones as white and very clean.

Chapter 4

Hudson went up the steps from Myrtle Street and across the big lawn, the birds singing their morning songs. It was still early morning but already hot, even on the shaded walk, the heat almost a living presence as it hovered about him.

The big houses looked like they would be there forever, the streets tree-lined, the yards filled with azaleas. It had a combination of smells, freshly cut grass mixing with that of pine straw. The cicadas hummed from the big pines. Going up the walk always brought back memories of his boyhood.

The yard was filled with signs supporting Maurice Longstreet for mayor. Maurice looked good for a man of sixty-five. He still had all his hair, and the face on the sign with those square features was strong and confident. Maurice should be confident, having been mayor all those years. YOUR MAYOR FOR THE NINETIES the signs read. Hudson had seen better slogans in past elections. Since before sunrise he'd been putting up signs on lawns, and there was still a stack of them in the back seat of his car. He thought how he'd measured out his life and Maurice's too by those signs, Maurice's hair progressively turning whiter from its jet black, and Hudson putting on weight, so the thought of pounding those signs into hard, sun-baked lawns in the heat was not something he looked forward to. No longer did he park the car at the end of the street and, carrying a bundle of signs over his shoulder and a sledge hammer in his hand, stride confidently on the asphalt between the rows of houses. Now he parked at each individual house, leaving the air conditioning running and returning even from these short trips dripping with sweat.

With the election only a few weeks away, Joe Wallace Hollins, the young smartass assistant to Maurice, had been down to the Sanitation Department almost every day worried about rumors there was going to be a strike and a union was being formed. Hudson had told him he thought he could head off a strike until after the election. He'd secretly stockpiled fifty thousand plastic trash bags which he planned to hand out to customers. There'd been strikes before and he had handled them, and there was still no garbagemen's union. But Joe Wallace had been hard to calm down. So Hudson lied to him and told Joe Wallace he had a spy in the union organizers' camp and knew every move they were going to make. This seemed to satisfy Joe Wallace.

"But of course it's August," Hudson said as Joe Wallace opened the door. "Time for revolutions."

Joe Wallace had stopped in his tracks.

"You hear about any revolution, you let me know," he said. "Maurice will want to know."

Hudson had waved him out of the office. Joe Wallace hurried away in his button-down shirt and pleated pants. Hudson couldn't understand how Maurice could stand to have that frantic, deadly serious young man hovering about him. It would be like having one of those small dogs that barked constantly and pissed on the furniture.

He was more worried about a persistent underground fire in the landfill than he was about a strike. There had been no rain for two weeks, and the fire still smoldered, feeding off pockets of methane and god knows what else. If you got within thirty yards of the smoke, you could feel the heat even through the soles of your shoes.

Hudson had also made a secret contribution to the campaign of Sydney Cable. But that was not unusual either. He had made secret contributions to every candidate who had run against Maurice. That way, if Maurice should lose, Hudson could go to the winner and wave the photocopy of the check in his face. Politicians understood contributions and didn't forget. Over the years he'd gotten by with smaller and smaller contributions. Now the amount had gone back up again, and he remembered looking at what he had written on the check as if someone else's hand had done the writing. But it was a close race and he had to protect himself. The funny thing was that Sydney was even more conservative than Maurice. Sydney had said he wanted to privatize the garbage department and other municipal services. But even if it went private someone would have to run the place. Hudson knew they'd have a hard time finding anyone who could do it better than he could.

As he went up on the porch steps, he felt a twinge in one of his knees, an old injury from high school football. He'd been more interested in baseball, but he never could learn to hit a curve ball. He was carrying too much weight, he thought, too much weight, and the doctor had warned him his blood pressure was not looking good. He was going to have to start jogging and watch his diet. If he wasn't careful, he wouldn't be able to keep up with the dogs when he started bird hunting in November.

He tried to think of the times he'd been seriously in love. Probably three or four. Something always happened. He preferred younger women. But most of them were interested in having babies. He wanted no part of children. Now he saw two of those women from time to time as he drove about the city. They both had babies and walked with them in the early morning and late afternoon on the streets near his mother's house.

Nancy Patterson jogged as she strolled a pair of twins, the gleaming metal stroller with its huge spoked tires gliding effortlessly over the sidewalk, the twins buckled in with sunhats on their heads. She'd be covered with sweat and looking good in her lycra shorts. He'd stop the car and admire the twins. She'd talk of inviting him and a friend to dinner; sometimes she'd suggest someone.

He had already started to push open the door when he noticed Wendell's car was not in the driveway.

Hudson opened the door and smelled only biscuits and coffee. He found his mother in the kitchen. She was sitting at the table with the morning paper spread open.

"Where's Wendell?" he asked.

"Gone to the TV station to see if he can keep this out of the news," she said.

Her hands were shaking when she gave him the paper, and she

Scott Ely

looked as if she were about to cry.

"It's a disgrace," she said. "A disgrace for this family. And for this town that allowed it to happen."

Hudson looked at the paper. There on the front page was a picture of a young black woman and a little girl. FAMILY DIES FROM CHOLERA the headline read. Hudson started reading the news story. They lived on River Street in one of the shacks owned by Wendell. Then Hudson remembered. It was the Sabine family, the ones Wendell had been talking about at dinner. Wendell had had the water and power turned off after they had refused to pay their rent. And the paper said they had contracted the cholera drinking from a well. The mother was survived by her ten-year-old son Larue Sabine and an elderly cousin, Ella Sabine.

"Damn him," Hudson said.

She started to cry. He put his hand on her shoulder, her body feeling fragile. But she quickly recovered and dried her eyes. She was a tough, strong woman, qualities he'd always admired.

"Wendell won't care about them at all," she said.

"I don't imagine he will," Hudson said.

Wendell had spent his life doing things that made them all wish he was not a member of the family, his rapacity famous throughout the town and the state.

As his mother got up and poured them both a cup of coffee, he finished reading the article. It went on to describe how quickly cholera can kill, children succumbing in a few hours from dehydration because of their slight body weight. The article concluded by saying there was no danger from an epidemic because the source was the contaminated well. The city water supply was not affected in any way.

Hudson thought of the woman and that little child dying in the night with not a light in the house, too weak to make it to the privy. Thinking about it made the coffee taste like muddy river water. He drove past the houses several times a day and wondered now how many times he had seen that little girl playing in the yard. He thought of Wendell's arm in his, how frail it felt. And how much power Wendell had over so many people. It made Hudson sick to think of it. Rosalind was right about Wendell.

A Song For Alice Loom

"Wendell should let 'em pay their own utilities," he said. "He won't have any luck with the TV station. It won't matter how well he knows Ed Luck. Unless he's got something on Ed and even then it might not be enough. Oh, I'll bet Maurice has been calling Ed all morning. Sydney will make a campaign issue out of this."

And like always, Hudson thought, everything: the deaths, his mother's grief, the grief of the survivors, was going to be swept away in the campaign, submerged beneath the political rhetoric of Maurice Longstreet and Sydney Cable.

Hudson thought with satisfaction of the contribution he had made to Sydney's campaign. This could blow up in Maurice's face. Everyone knew that Maurice and Wendell were in business together. It could turn out looking bad for Maurice, very bad.

He was glad he no longer had any ties with Wendell. He'd gone to work for Wendell when he graduated from college. And he'd discovered that Wendell had been paying bribes to state legislators. Hudson had been making the deliveries, not knowing what was inside those brown envelopes. The state police were investigating and Wendell suggested that Hudson take the blame. After all, the money came from the rent on Wendell's property that had passed though Hudson's hands. Wendell told him that he thought Hudson would get at most a year in prison. Wendell promised rewards at the end of the year. He said he thought he could get Hudson a job in the prison library. Instead Hudson had quit. The investigation turned up nothing and Hudson realized that Wendell had bribed someone. His Uncle Wendell would have had him go to prison rather than pay a bribe.

Then Maurice had asked Hudson to take over the garbage department as superintendent. Wendell had not been happy about that. Twenty-five years later Hudson was still there.

His mother took the paper from him and read the article again. Every now and then he saw her lips move.

"Mama, Wendell won't be coming to breakfast," Hudson said.

Hudson was glad she didn't have a big breakfast: ham, grits, biscuits, melons laid out, because now he didn't feel like eating.

"I should go live with my cousins in Memphis," his mother said.

"Mama, this is your house too," Hudson said. "Don't you let Wendell run you out of it. Grandpappy intended for you to stay. Wendell can sleep at the office. He won't come here for awhile."

"He better not come in my kitchen today."

As Hudson looked at her determined face, he imagined that if he were Wendell, he too would stay clear of the house for a few days. It was going to be a long time before things were comfortable for him there again.

"I've got signs to put up and then I've got to get to work," he said. "Maurice is worried about a garbage strike."

"This may give it to him," his mother said.

"Let's hope not."

Hudson realized his mother might be right. He was relieved no Sabine worked for him. He was struck by his cynicism and kept telling himself that those people, yesterday alive and laughing, were now dead. It was important they be mourned, their deaths paid attention to. But now consideration for them as people was beginning to fade, and he felt mostly anger at Wendell for letting it happen. And he was angry at himself for letting it fade, telling himself that this was what it meant to be living at the end of the twentieth century; but that was not enough, and he felt ashamed. He told himself he had to be practical and think about the strike, not get diverted by worrying about people who were already dead. Anything could set off a strike. He'd been working overtime to make sure the department was running smoothly.

Alice was glad Hudson had paused, standing there before her looking out the kitchen window. She would let him continue to think whatever it was he was thinking. She thought she'd heard the murmur of Lou Sabine. She listened hard, hearing only the hum of the refrigerator and a car passing on the street, and realized it was nothing. She'd been listening for Lou Sabine all morning, but there had been nothing, the old house still and quiet. So she'd stayed calm and waited, rubbing her aching hands.

Rosalind, dressed in jeans and an army fatigue jacket with "Rosalind" printed on it, came into the kitchen.

"Well, Wendell is now murdering people," Rosalind said. "His own kin."

"Just because they have your father's name doesn't make them kin," Hudson said.

No one outside the family knew about Lou Sabine. Hudson could imagine what the newspapers would make out of it.

"A Sabine was my father," Rosalind began.

"None of that concerns us," Hudson said.

"It's important," Rosalind said.

"They are kin, Hudson," Alice said. "You can't ignore that they're kin. Or that Wendell is responsible for their dying."

Usually it was Rosalind who went on and on about the Sabines. Now he was going to have to listen to both of them.

"I'm sorry they're dead," Hudson said.

Hudson tried to think of some way of steering the conversation in another direction but knew it was hopeless. In a stack of notebooks Rosalind had transcribed everything she could get her mother to tell her about her father and family history. Rosalind also sought out Sabines and interviewed them. It seemed to Hudson that she spent half her time roaming about French Town with a tape recorder and her notebook.

Alice looked at her big middle-aged son. She wondered what he and Rosalind would say if she told them about Lou talking with her. She thought of Wendell. He was just like his father. She remembered the day of her recital, how she heard the ladies gasp and then turned her head, the viola in one hand and the bow in the other; and the man came stumbling through the hedge, fell against a table scattering teacups, staggered to his feet, and then her father had shot him, the pistol in his hand not seeming big enough to topple the man. But it did, the man falling a different way this time, heavy and final. The ladies screamed and turned their heads. She had neither screamed nor turned her head.

Alice considered that Rosalind had named the crime directly while she and Hudson skirted around it, talked about "maybes" and "responsibility."

"Rosalind is right," Alice said. "Wendell murdered them."

"He murdered no one," Hudson said. "He's partly to blame, but it's not murder."

"It's time for the news, Mama," Rosalind said.

She poured herself a glass of orange juice and left. They heard the

Scott Ely

news come on.

Hudson took a handful of biscuits out of the oven.

His mother went to join Rosalind.

Hudson decided to give up and go to work. Rosalind was going to spend the day with the deaths of the Sabines. Before it was over she would probably drag down all her notebooks from upstairs and read to her mother. If she'd spent as much time on her dissertation as on the history of the family, she'd have had it done years ago. He poured himself a cup of coffee.

Rosalind came back into the kitchen as he was doing it.

"She could be related to us," Rosalind said. "You know I didn't even get a chance to interview them."

"Why do you want to know so much?" Hudson asked.

"You say that because you don't care about your father."

"Henry the piano player who went down with his ship?"

"You can be so insensitive. Your father wasn't a Sabine. I'm both Loom and Sabine."

Hudson supposed he might be interested in the past too if his father had been a Sabine, passing for white in the Marine Corps.

"I live in the present," Hudson said. "Right now I've got a landfill fire to worry about."

"I'm worried about Mother. You know how two or three times a year she gets so strange. She's acting like that now."

"She'll be all right."

"It's always been difficult for her. She took her viola and her talent and got herself out of Pine. Do you realize how hard it was for a woman to do that then?"

"I know that."

"No, you don't know. And can't understand."

"I do the best I can."

"You're going to have to do more."

She turned and walked away.

He went out of the house eating a biscuit. There was time to plant a few more signs before he was due at the office. He could come in anytime he wanted, but since he demanded that the drivers complete their routes on time, he had to set a good example and generally was at work by seven.

Hudson drove down Myrtle and turned left onto Jackson. Yardmen were already at work cutting grass and mulching plants with pine straw. They were also cutting limbs and trimming hedges. They piled the stuff out on the street, making more work for the garbage department. It wouldn't be long before leaf season was upon them, the streets lined with heaps of leaves.

He was halfway down Jackson before he remembered why he was there. Someone had stolen two of Phil Butler's signs, and Hudson had promised to replace them. He had not passed the Butler's house yet and started to look for it. He liked the town this time of day, the streets empty and shaded by the big oaks, the green cans and plastic bags set out waiting for pickup.

Chapter 5

Hudson drove around the courthouse and on Market toward River Street. Four blocks later, the land sloping toward the river, he hit French Town. It was an area of unpainted houses, a labyrinth of alleys and small streets, of quick-growing trees like locust and ginkgo that turned vacant lots into jungles and pushed their way up through the broken sidewalks, of sagging chain-link fences covered with honeysuckle and trumpet creeper, of the smell of bare earth and broken wine bottles and garbage. The French Town stray dogs evaded the animal control truck with ease, and waiting for night to come they casually overturned garbage cans to feast on the remains of pigs' feet, fish, and ham hocks.

The town had originally been established as a fur trading outpost—the location of the building itself forever lost and at its best probably no better than the present day shacks—by a Frenchman who came up the river from the Gulf; but the French soon discovered the area was prone to flooding. People who lived there caught yellow fever. They relocated to the bluffs where city hall now stood, abandoning the settlement to whores and saloons and river men. Then the Baptists got rid of the whores and most of the saloons, the remaining ones done in by Prohibition, which lingered on in Pine into the 1970s.

The yellow fever was gone, but flooding was still a danger. The levee along the river had controlled it for the last ten years, but Hudson would not be surprised if one day he had to go to work in a skiff. Then they would have to shovel out the mud and chase the snakes out of the filing cabinets again.

Those inhabitants of French Town who worked as maids and yard men on Jackson Avenue or Myrtle Drive could still walk to work. Those blacks who lived along the railroad tracks in a larger section where federally funded housing projects had been built took city buses that only blacks rode to their jobs. There was no federal housing in French Town because no one wanted to put any money into a section which was sure, sooner or later, to be underwater. So French Town was much the same as it had been in the 1940s or 50s. There was a housing development on the other side of town for middle class blacks called Sunlight Estates. Hudson had a supervisor who lived there. There were mixed neighborhoods, but they were looked upon by whites as "going down," the property values plummeting.

He drove past the frame houses, most of them surrounded by chain link fences and trees like chinaberry and mimosa in the yards. The mimosa were in bloom, their pink blossoms fallen into the street, forming rose-colored pools on the asphalt, the passage of the car scattering the flowers.

Hudson turned onto River Street and drove along the line of houses set up on brick piers. He tried to pick out the one belonging to Ruth Sabine. Then he saw a concrete truck backing into a yard. That was it all right. The city was sealing up the contaminated well. The shack had curtains in the windows and the screens were in place. But the door was ajar, giving the house a deserted, uninhabited look as if the people had left in a hurry and were not planning on returning.

Off to his left was the garbage department yard. Hudson could never bring himself to call it the sanitation department. He liked garbage. It was a good honest word. That was what their trucks hauled to the landfill.

He drove past the big hackberry tree, all spread out because the mules that used to pull the garbage wagons had eaten the top out of it. He turned the car into the entrance. Most of the trucks were already gone, the sun glinting on the roof of the shop, and beyond that the line of willows which marked the river.

Then the woman was in front of the car with a large portrait photo in either hand so that Hudson had to step on the brakes hard to avoid

Scott Ely

hitting her. Where had she come from so fast? he thought. She was having a hard time holding the portraits in their imitation gilt frames. A small boy, dressed in a 101st Airborne T-shirt with an eagle's head on the front, stood beside her with an umbrella. All the shade from the umbrella was on the woman, the boy seemingly unconcerned about the heat.

The woman spoke to the boy, who exchanged the umbrella for the photos and held them up for Hudson to see. One was of a woman and the other a little girl. He knew immediately who they were. He rolled down the window, the heat slipping into the car, despite the fact that he had the air conditioner on high, the vents trained on his face.

"When you gonna make it right, white man?" she asked.

She was a tiny old woman but held herself erect and straight. Her hair was white, and on her head was a black straw hat with a green ribbon, which he imagined she must wear to church. She wore a black dress and heels. The morning breeze made the ribbon and the thin dress flutter. She looked like a bird getting ready to launch itself into flight.

"Yes, ma'am?" Hudson said, not knowing what else to say.

Anyone older than he was, except for those working for him, he addressed as "sir" and "ma'am."

"What you gonna do?"

Then it struck him. Ella Sabine had mistaken him for Wendell.

"I'm Hudson Loom," he said. "You want Wendell."

But then he was sorry he had said it. Wendell would not be polite to her. No use sending her to him.

"What can I do?" he asked.

Maybe the woman needed some money. He started to reach for his billfold. He thought she should save those pictures for the funeral.

"You a Loom," she said.

"Hudson Loom," he said.

Hudson spoke the words loudly and slowly. He was beginning to suspect she was hard of hearing.

"They dead," she said.

It was getting intolerably hot in the car, and Hudson was losing his patience with the woman.

"Yes, ma'am, I know," he said. "I'm sorry."

He had his billfold out and was reaching into it for a twenty. As he took out the bill he noticed the woman was shaking her head.

"Don't want no money," she said. "This boy got to be schooled, looked after. I not long for this world."

"You get in touch with social services," Hudson said. "I'll call them for you. They'll look after that boy, find him a foster home."

A truck went past, the scent of rotting garbage trailing after it. The black driver gave the old woman a long look. So, Hudson thought, the trouble from the Sabines was staring him right in the face, the whole affair the trigger needed to start a strike. He imagined the narrow streets and alleys of French Town filling up with garbage, swarms of flies hovering above the stinking heaps with an insistent perpetual hum louder than he would have thought possible.

"You got a big house," she said.

He heard the words but tried hard not to acknowledge them.

"The State of Mississippi will take care of that boy," he said.

He liked the sound of the phrase. It had an official ring to it the woman would be compelled to pay attention to.

"Don't need no state of Mississippi to tend to Larue," the woman said.

Hudson took a close look at the boy for the first time. He was black instead of light like the old woman. His head was oval, no hint of the round Loom face.

"Miss Ella, you stay out of the sun," Hudson said. "I'll call social services."

The woman made no reply. She glared at him. Hudson started to roll up the window.

"You a Loom," the woman said.

Hudson almost suggested she go talk with Rosalind. She would appreciate Miss Ella's views on the history of the two families. But instead he kept cranking and then the glass was up. The boy had gotten out of the sun at last and was standing in the shade of the hackberry tree. The old woman was saying something, but Hudson couldn't hear it through the glass.

Although it was hard not looking back at the woman as he went inside, he forced himself. Once in his office he looked out through the blinds. She was still in the sun but had the umbrella over her head.

Scott Ely

The boy was standing by the tree, the pictures cradled in his arms, his hands around the outside of the frames and the bottom of the frames running along his forearms. It was as if the boy had turned himself into a triptych: the dead on the wings, the center still alive like a tree that had lost its outer branches. He displayed the pictures to the passing cars. Hudson was now reminded of a peacock. He closed the blinds.

Hudson looked at the large-scale map of the city which covered the entire wall. The supervisors' areas were marked by the shading of different colored ink, the city divided up into five areas. When he had taken over there was chaos. He had restored order to the department. Black workers had been confined to garbage and white workers to trash. Trash workers made more than garbage workers. He'd corrected that long before the other departments had been forced to by the federal government. Maurice had been grateful for that.

He checked his appointment book: the landfill fire, a trip to Vicksburg, and plastic bags were on the list. He wrote *call social services* on the page. Then he picked up the supervisors' reports from his in-box. Sam Roberts had one of the new diesel garbage trucks down, and had taken one of the five old gasoline trucks Hudson kept in reserve. He went through all the reports. All the other trucks were running; only one driver and four workers had called in sick. The ice machine was down. Tom Guess, Hudson's assistant, had gone to the ice house and brought over a load of ice for the big Igloo cans they kept on every truck. He filed the reports and, since it was eight-thirty, decided to give social services a try.

As he picked up the phone Joe Wallace walked through the door.

"Hudson, I hope you're calling the police," Joe Wallace said.

Hudson never liked the way Joe Wallace, who until recently was not old enough to order a glass of whiskey, called him by his first name.

"Somebody steal a garbage truck?" Hudson asked.

"You know what I mean," Joe Wallace said.

He pulled open the blinds a crack and looked out.

"She's interfering with the operations of this public service," Joe Wallace said.

A Song For Alice Loom

Joe Wallace was so full of himself, Hudson thought. He was going to law school at night while working for Maurice. Hudson suspected Joe Wallace had flunked out of the Ole Miss law school. "Theory," Joe Wallace liked to say of the Ole Miss school. "Theory is all they teach up there. Won't do you a bit of good in court."

"Sydney Cable don't think it's a necessary public service at all," Hudson said. "Police and fire. That's about it."

"Sydney doesn't have a chance," Joe Wallace said.

But Hudson knew he had started Joe Wallace thinking about not working for the city any more. Whenever Joe Wallace got nervous, his brown eyes started shifting back and forth, like a ball in a pinball machine. His eyes were doing it right now. Hudson was pleased.

"Maurice wants you to get that nigger woman off city property," Joe Wallace said.

"Ain't any more niggers in this city," Hudson said.

"Now, Hudson, we both know how things are," Joe Wallace said. "That election is coming up, and we can't have a Negro woman parading around with pictures of the dead. It's like she's holding the city responsible. Maurice had that well filled up."

Hudson wondered just what Wendell had on Maurice. Probably city money paid for the concrete truck when it should have been Wendell paying. But it seemed like Wendell never paid for things he did. It was always somebody else.

"She's got me mixed up with Wendell," Hudson said. "She'll get tired and go away. She's an old woman, grieving for her kin. Just let her be."

"I'll tell Maurice how you look at it," Joe Wallace said.

His eyes had stopped moving now. They were staring straight at Hudson.

"Tell him anything you want," Hudson said. "I've got work to do. You probably do too."

"Suit yourself, Hudson."

Joe Wallace always said his name like he didn't think much of it. The boy went out the door and Hudson heard his car start. He opened the blinds. Joe Wallace didn't even slow down or look at Miss Ella when he drove past. The old woman stood motionless with the umbrella in that heat as if she was cast in bronze. Hudson thought he

Scott Ely

might have made a mistake about her. She looked like she could stand out there for a long time.

Hudson picked up the phone and started to call social services. But first he called the shop and had them carry an extra cooler full of water and some paper cups out to Miss Ella.

All the social services case workers were busy. He left a message to return his call. Then he opened the blinds a slit, a shaft of sunlight shooting into the office and illuminating the dancing motes of dust. She was still there, the water cooler under the tree by the boy who was filling a cup. The boy took it to the old woman, who drank it slowly and gravely and handed the used cup back to the boy. He retreated to the shade. Hudson hoped Joe Wallace would come by soon and see the cooler. Miss Ella was back to looking like a bronze statue beneath the black umbrella. Hudson closed the blinds.

Chapter 6

Hudson worked on specifications for a new landfill scraper but couldn't concentrate. The image of the old woman kept popping into his mind, standing there and asking him over and over again what he was going to do about the boy. Sooner or later she'd figure out Wendell was the one responsible and leave him alone. He decided to drive to the landfill and take a look at the fire. At ten he had to drive to Vicksburg for a demonstration of a tire shredder.

She was at her post when Hudson drove out of the yard in the white sanitation car, the air conditioner laboring to flush out the hot air. He had expected to have trouble with her, but she was being distracted by a crew from the TV station, the reporters in a half circle about her, all of them out in the sun, the light flashing off the camera lenses. The whole pack of them was going to end up with sun stroke. Yet even with the crew about her, a microphone thrust in her face by an eager reporter, she noticed him. She followed the car with her eyes, and he felt himself involuntarily shrinking down in the seat. Hudson expected Wendell would be raising hell with Ed Luck about the TV coverage. While Miss Ella talked with a reporter, she pointed in the direction of the row of shacks. The boy, who was sitting on top of the water cooler in the shade of the hackberry, grinned at him and waved. Hudson waved back as he took a left on River Street.

Hudson drove along River Street and past the Roosevelt Bridge, condemned a few years ago and a new one built downstream. He crossed the new bridge, which didn't have a name, and followed the highway, running perfectly straight through low land the city had designated as an industrial park where there were a few sheet metal buildings: a truck warehouse, a chicken plant, but not the kind of development Maurice had promised. No computer companies, no high tech. Then he turned and drove parallel to the river. On either side were fields planted with rows of waist-high pines, pieces of white paper caught up in them, as if they had been crudely and hastily decorated for Christmas by a group of children. A flock of crows swooped low over the trees along the river. Ahead was the gate to the landfill.

"Charlene's hot again," Moses said as he came out of his gatekeeper's shack to raise the gate.

Charlene was the name Moses had given to the landfill fire. Hudson's gatekeeper named all the fires with women's names. Moses' greatest day was when he discovered a newly born baby someone had left at the edge of the landfill wrapped in a plastic garbage bag, and the doctors at the hospital had allowed him to name it. Moses still kept the newspaper article about that thumbtacked to the wall of his shack. Rose Cherry Moses he had named the child. For the rest of that child's life, as long as she stayed in the South, she'd be called RC. Because Moses liked to take a drink, he didn't work out as a truck driver, but for ten years he'd proven to be an excellent gatekeeper.

Behind the shack was a mountain of tires. Part of Moses' job was making sure tires didn't end up in the landfill. They seemed to have a life of their own, working their way to the surface no matter how deeply they were buried, and leaving holes in the landfill. Hudson suspected that was what Charlene was feeding on, a load of tires someone had slipped past Moses.

The landfill was deserted except for John driving the big scraper used to cover the garbage with dirt. The trucks were all still out on their morning routes collecting garbage and trash. When Hudson had taken over the landfills, which were called dumps then, they had been filled with scavengers like in some third world country. He'd posted guards and gotten rid of them.

Hudson got out of the car, stepping into the heat and dust. The landfill buzzed with flies, but he'd grown used to them. Bits of paper

A Song For Alice Loom

were tumbled across the dirt by the morning breeze. The gang of crows swooped down over the trees next to the river, looking like pieces of black paper blown by the wind. They were waiting for the arrival of the first garbage trucks. There wasn't much space left in this one, and Hudson had been searching for new sites. Two old landfill sites had been turned into baseball fields. He was proud of the way they'd reclaimed the useless swampland.

He cautiously approached the fire, the landfill spongy beneath his feet. It would be several years before it settled and was firm. Ten years later you'd still be able to smell the gas from the decomposing garbage. Hudson had had the fire roped off with barrier tape borrowed from the police department. He stopped at the yellow tape and felt the ground. It was hot. Off in the center of the roped-in space was a fissure from which dark smoke swirled, like the vent of a volcano. That oily-looking black smoke caused him to think he must be right about the tires. Being so close to the fire made him nervous. He wondered who Charlene had been. Moses claimed he named them after old girlfriends. Charlene, he thought, a tall woman in a red dress with dangling earrings and purple eye shadow. That was Charlene.

He had decided that if the fire was still going next week he'd start pumping water up from the river. But that caused cave-ins and sometimes did no good at all. Sooner or later the fire would burn itself out.

On the way back to his car, thinking of how good the air conditioning was going to feel, Hudson saw another car come into the landfill. Private vehicles were allowed past the gate with a permit, after Moses had inspected their cargo. But this was not a pickup but a big sedan. It was moving fast, white and heavy looking, the dust smoking beneath the tires. It was Wendell.

The car stopped by his, the tinted glass on the window so dark he couldn't see the occupants. Hudson sighed. He supposed this was as good a place as any to argue with Wendell over Miss Ella.

Wendell got out of the passenger side, so that meant Anse Carter was driving.

"That nigger of yours made me buy a permit," Wendell said. "You owe me ten dollars."

Hudson pulled ten dollars out of his billfold and handed it to

Scott Ely

Wendell. The flies buzzed about Wendell's face; he slapped at them. His uncle always reminded Hudson of a dirt dauber, those wasps who built mud nests for their young on the rafters of his garage. Like the wasps, his body was constantly quivering, always in motion, thin legs and arms moving. Wendell slapped at the flies again, a few scraps of paper sailing by his wingtip lawyer shoes. Hudson thought Joe Wallace and Wendell must buy their clothes at the same store.

"Dammit, Hudson," Wendell said. "Let's talk in the car."

Hudson got in the back seat. It was cool in the car, the sun blocked out by the tinted windows.

"Morning, Mr. Loom," Anse said.

Anse Carter was always polite, his manners perfect. When he shot you he probably said, "Now if you don't mind I'm going to shoot you, sir." Hudson didn't bother to reply and watched with satisfaction the back of Anse's neck get red.

"You got to do something about that nigger woman," Wendell said.

"You were the one who cut off her water," Hudson said. "Why me?"

Hudson considered how sweet it was going to be to deny Wendell something he wanted.

"Because she's looking to you to make it right," Wendell said.

Hudson wondered how Wendell had gotten so much information so quickly.

"I got that well sealed up. Now all you got to do is get her to shut up. It'll be easy."

Hudson thought of the boy sitting on the water cooler.

"She thinks we're kin," Wendell said. "Just like Rosalind."

Hudson thought he heard Anse start to chuckle. Wendell looked at him too. Anse cleared his throat, put down the window, and spat.

"Somehow I think that's Rosalind's doing. Spending all her time in French Town with that tape recorder. Once we could've just had her put in the state hospital. Out there with the other crazies. She could interview them."

"It really doesn't matter who put the idea in her head," Hudson said. "She believes it."

"Good, then you understand how it is," Wendell said.

A Song For Alice Loom   49

The car had filled with the smell of garbage. Wendell was going to have to drive around in the heat with the windows down to get rid of it.

"You got plenty of room at home," Hudson said. "You take him in."

"I'd tell that nigger—" Anse began.

"Be still," Wendell said.

"You can clean up your own mess," Hudson said.

Wendell smiled.

"I would," he said. "I'd even take that boy home myself until after the election. I'm a practical man. But she don't want him to go there. She wants you to take him. Just you. His blood kin. Maurice says he would appreciate it if you would. He'll be calling you in to talk."

No matter what Maurice said or Wendell said Hudson was going to stand firm. They'd have to find some other way to satisfy Ella Sabine.

"If Sydney wins I might retire," Hudson said. "Sell the house and live at the lake."

Hudson had surprised himself. The words were out the instant the thoughts formed in his mind.

"Cabin is under water every other year," Wendell said.

Hudson ignored him.

"Listen, Hudson," Wendell said. "That woman has got that boy out there with a Sydney Cable sign. You'll be having a garbagemen's strike before the week is out."

Hudson thought Sydney Cable's slogan, A NEW START, was not so good either.

Hudson laughed at the thought of the boy with the sign, and Wendell and Maurice getting worked up about that.

"It ain't funny," Wendell said. "They had that woman on TV. Ed Luck's going to be sorry about that."

"Like I told you," Hudson said. "You're the one who cut off her power. Wouldn't fix her plumbing. Look, I called social services. They'll get a foster family for the boy. Make sure he gets to his kin or wherever it is she wants him to go."

"No goddamn social services department is going to solve this," Wendell said.

Anse was making some sort of sucking sound deep in his throat.

Wendell gave him a look.

"It stinks in here," Anse said.

"Then go stand outside," Wendell said.

"Can't, the doctor says I've got to keep out of the sun."

Anse was sensitive to the heat. He'd been in prison at Parchman. That was for shooting three men in a barroom brawl. The first two had been clear self-defense. But when Anse had shot the third outside the club as the man was trying to open the door of his truck, they'd given him two years for manslaughter. They'd tried him at farmwork, but he kept passing out from the heat. He had ended up working in the prison ice house. The day he came home he had started driving Wendell's car and wearing the old suit and a straw cowboy hat. That was the reason for the tinted glass, Anse's aversion to light and heat. Hudson had heard Wendell complain that it made his car look like a hearse. His uncle called Anse his rehabilitation project, but Hudson knew the reason Wendell employed Anse was that scrawny, sunken-chested Anse would do whatever Wendell asked. And Anse preferred to do most of Wendell's errands after the sun had set. He could walk down the narrowest alley in French Town with impunity. It was said he could see in the dark like a cat.

"That boy can move in with me," Anse said and laughed.

Hudson thought Wendell looked like he was getting ready to tear open the door and run screaming across the landfill. He gave Anse a hard look.

"You take him in until the election," Wendell said. "It's only a few weeks. Give social services time to find him a foster home."

"Why don't *you* give Miss Ella a place to live," Hudson said. "I mean after social services takes care of the boy."

Right away he was sorry he said it. It was really dumb stirring Wendell up when he was already mad enough. Wendell could cause him trouble. Hudson looked out on the desolate landfill, covered with dust and paper and a million flies, and thought of watching Murphy hit one out of the park. He pictured himself lying in bed with Holly Matthews.

"Look, dammit!" Wendell said.

Wendell reached back and grabbed Hudson's wrist with his fingers, which were too short and stubby for his thin arms. Hudson noticed his uncle was sweating, his face beaded.

"Me and Maurice have got business plans," Wendell said. "He has to stay mayor. Sydney Cable can't win."

Hudson started to say that yes, Sydney Cable could win, but thought better of it. It was strange that Wendell, a little man almost twenty years his senior, could make him afraid. Especially after Hudson had forced Wendell to sit down at the dinner table. Frailness didn't count for much if you were mean. Hudson supposed it was like stepping on a cottonmouth. It didn't matter how big you were, you were always scared.

"You take in that boy. Get that old woman off the street."

Hudson opened the car door, the hot air coming in with a rush along with the smell of garbage. A piece of paper blew in and swirled about Anse Carter's head. He cursed and swatted at it as if it were a yellow jacket.

"Those people died of cholera on your property," Hudson said. "You make it right. I won't do it for you."

Then he shut the door.

In his car it was very hot, but there were no flies and no smell of the garbage. Being hot was worth not having the flies and the smell.

Wendell's car went off fast across the landfill, the only way Anse Carter knew how to drive. It was a testimony to Wendell's power in the city that Anse had never received a speeding ticket and that no one had ever questioned his right to carry the .38. The pistol was to protect the rent money he collected at night in French Town and other places.

Hudson started his engine but waited until their car was out of sight before he followed. He'd call social services again when he returned and settle the matter of the boy. He looked forward to the trip to Vicksburg for no other reason than it would get him out of the city.

He imagined taking Holly Matthews to Atlanta. It would be good to go to a double-header and forget about garbage strikes and Miss Ella. He'd take Holly to a French restaurant he knew about. They'd eat wild boar and drink good wine. While back in Pine Anse Carter was preparing to prowl the streets of the poor sections after late rent payments and Wendell was huddling with Maurice trying to make

Scott Ely

sure they won the election and Miss Ella and Larue were standing out on the street holding pictures of their dead, he and Holly Matthews would sit in the stands and drink beer and watch Murphy make those catches on the warning track look easy.

Chapter 7

Hudson turned onto River Street. There by the hackberry, her figure dancing amid the heat waves, was Miss Ella, seated in a rocking chair. He came closer. Her figure was no long mirage-like. He clearly saw the hat and the ribbons and the way she kept her legs pressed tightly together. She sat very straight with the umbrella held over her head, rocking back and forth. The media had deserted her, her image on video tape and negative and her story in storage in a newspaper computer. The water cooler was still by the tree, but the boy was gone, probably sent for food or cold drinks. Again she fastened her eyes on him as he drove past. Although he had made up his mind about her and was resolved to stand firm, Hudson felt himself shrink under her gaze.

Tom Guess met Hudson at the door.

"She's on city property," Tom said.

"I've already talked to Joe Wallace and Wendell," Hudson said.

"Mayor Longstreet called," Connie said.

Tom took the pink message slip out of the secretary's hand and handed it to Hudson.

"What about social services?" Hudson asked.

Connie shook her head.

"He's called three times," Tom said.

Hudson had long ago given up trying to get much work out of

Tom, who, just like his father Grafton, spent much of his time going to funerals. Hudson supposed he would be at Ruth and Tiffany Sabine's.

"That old woman is gonna cause a strike," Tom said. "You'll be taking that boy in?"

"There's not going to be a strike," Hudson said.

He went into the office before Tom could ask another question. Tom lingered out in the hall, watching Miss Ella through the window. Hudson called social services again and left another message.

Just as he put down the phone a big man in a white cowboy hat came into the building. Hudson guessed this was Mr. McWill who was to drive him to Vicksburg for a demonstration of the tire shredder. Connie ushered Mr. McWill into the office. McWill was an inch or two taller than Hudson. As they made their introductions the phone rang. Hudson was afraid it was Maurice, so he didn't touch it.

When they got in Bill McWill's car, a blue Mercedes, Hudson saw the boy had returned to his seat on the water cooler. Miss Ella was still in the same position in the rocking chair. She was still holding the umbrella, but there was no hamburger or cold drink in her free hand. Hudson went back inside and gave Connie a twenty-dollar bill, instructing her to make sure the old woman and the boy had some lunch. Tom Guess was at his desk, pretending to be hard at work.

Back in the car McWill handed him a picture of the Tire Gator. The machine, about the size of a small U-Haul trailer, was painted green and on the side was a picture of an alligator taking a big bite out of a tire. A skinny young man in a white t-shirt knelt in front of it.

"That Spence boy is a genius," McWill said. "Been over in Arabia working for them A-rabs. Do anything with a milling machine. Turn you a steel dick in a minute flat."

McWill laughed. Hudson managed a chuckle. He knew it was going to be a long trip to Vicksburg, but at least he would be away from Miss Ella and Wendell. Perhaps social services would have it all cleared up by the time he returned. Yet he knew social services was dragging their feet. Wendell and Maurice were behind it. They were waiting for him to take the boy into his home, satisfy Miss Ella. Well, he wasn't going to do it.

They went up out of the yard. Hudson looked up from the Tire

Gator literature. The boy was holding the umbrella over Miss Ella. She was asleep, her head thrown back and her mouth open, giving everyone a good look at her dentures. That comforted him, the look at her unguarded self. She might actually get tired or hot like any ordinary old woman and give up.

All the way over, McWill, who was from Fairview, Texas, talked about raising acid-free tomatoes on account of his sensitive stomach.

"You gotta get the pH right," McWill said. "Don't and that acid will eat the lining right out of your stomach. You grow tomatoes?"

"Just eat," Hudson said.

"I wouldn't take a chance on those grocery store ones. You know. The kind they grow in Florida. But Mexican tomatoes ain't bad. You ate any of them?"

"No."

"Best tomatoes I ever had were grown out at the Harrison, Arkansas sewage plant. Grew right in the sludge. No acid in them. But if you don't do it just right you'll get poisoned. Those boys in Harrison ain't saying how."

McWill went on and on about tomatoes. The Texan was an entrepreneur who wanted to raise money to manufacture the Tire Gator if they could get enough people interested. They were going to a rubber recycling plant where McWill and the Spence boy (Hudson had not learned his first name) were to give a demonstration for the rubber people.

Hudson looked at his watch. It was eleven. Maybe right now Miss Ella and Larue were eating hamburgers and drinking milkshakes under the hackberry.

The plant was located below Vicksburg on the banks of the Mississippi. Their guide had them put on hardhats and ear protectors. The tires were broken up under huge hammers and the fragments run through electromagnets to lift out the pieces of steel cord. A coating of rubber dust lay everywhere. The workers who tended the machines reminded Hudson of coal miners, their eyes staring out at him through begrimed faces. The noise of the hammers was deafening.

But even amid all the din, Hudson wondered what Miss Ella and

Scott Ely

the boy were doing. It was hot in the plant but not as hot as out in the sun. He had a mental picture of the old woman lying crumpled on the gravel, the boy pouring water over her face. He realized he was just frightening himself. Miss Ella had shade and plenty of water to drink. She'd probably live to be a hundred.

Outside they watched the Spence boy give a demonstration of the Tire Gator. A conveyer belt took tires up to the top of the machine where they tumbled in to fall on sharp disks which neatly sliced them into slivers.

"Do an airplane tire, boy," McWill said.

The skinny young man, dressed in jeans and a spotless white T-shirt, pulled an airplane tire out of the pile and dropped it on the belt. It fell onto the blades and with the sound of a knife going through a piece of hoop cheese, the tire was sliced neatly into slivers.

"See that," McWill said. "Tire's full of steel belts. Gator chomped it right up."

Spence grinned. Hudson had seen enough.

On the way back to Pine, Hudson had to endure more lectures on the art of growing acid-free tomatoes. But during the time when McWill was not talking about tomatoes, Hudson agreed to have the Tire Gator brought to Pine to see how it worked on the mountain of tires at the landfill. Once the tires were chewed up they could either be put into the landfill or sold for recycling, whatever was cheaper.

It was a relief when McWill turned onto River Street, the figure of Miss Ella in her chair along with the boy and another person, snapping into view, all of them dancing on the heat waves. Hudson wished the old woman would remain that insubstantial looking, airy and only fleetingly rooted to the ground, but he knew that in another hundred yards she'd become more corporeal and solid than the hackberry.

Then Hudson recognized the third figure. It was Rosalind who stood by Miss Ella, holding a microphone up to the old woman's mouth. The boy held the umbrella over them. McWill swung the car into the yard, spinning the wheel with a couple of fingers as he lay back against the leather-covered seat. Drink cups were scattered about. Larue had probably blown it all on Cokes and milkshakes.

McWill let him out and promised to have the Tire Gator delivered for a week's trial. Hudson took another look at Rosalind as he pushed open the door.

"Hudson, you've had six calls from the mayor," Tom Guess said. "Maurice even called twice himself."

Connie handed Hudson a collection of pink slips.

"None from social services?" Hudson asked.

"No, sir," she said. "You want me to call them?"

Hudson told her he'd call and went into the office and closed the door. Now Tom was watching Rosalind and the old woman. Hudson thought about calling social services again but with his hand on the phone changed his mind. Instead he sat and leaned back in his chair and like a chess player tried to work out the moves he or Maurice or Wendell could make. Tom returned to his desk. When Hudson got up and cracked the blinds to see what was happening, he saw Rosalind walking down the hill.

Hudson returned to his desk and watched her come into the building, speaking with Tom Guess at the door. She had her notebook open and wrote something in it. Then she came in and sat in front of him, her blue workshirt shirt stained with sweat. Hudson went to the machine and bought her a cold drink, which she downed in a couple of gulps.

"Hot out there," Hudson said.

"I got plenty from her," Rosalind said. "She tells the same stories Mama does."

Rosalind turned on the tape recorder. After considerable time spent running the tape back and forth, she found the place she wanted. She pushed the play button.

"Why do you want Larue to live with my brother?" she asked.

And Miss Ella, "He's good kin. Mr. Wendell is bad kin. Larue is a smart boy. Mr. Hudson can send him to school. Just get the boy settled and I'm ready for Jesus. Go be where Ruth and Tiffany are sitting at his feet."

"See," Rosalind said.

"No, I don't see," Hudson said. "We could be kin. I'm not saying we couldn't. But that boy is Wendell's responsibility, not mine."

"They could come stay with you for a while," Rosalind said.

"No," Hudson said. "Don't you bother Miss Ella anymore." Then he paused and carefully considered what he was going to say.

Scott Ely

"Why don't you take her home?" he asked. "Mother would like that."

"I asked," Rosalind said. "But Ella won't. Mother sent me out here to give Ella some money so she can take a room at a boarding house. I was going to drive her there. But she wouldn't go."

"Then leave her alone. You're just stirring up things."

"Ella Sabine knows things. She knows about my father. The whole family."

"You should be trying to convince her and the boy to go home with you. If you can make Miss Ella believe that you're the one to take her on, then I'll bet Wendell will put you back in his will. He can stay at the office until social services decides what to do about her and the boy. Mother will be happy about that."

"I told you. Ella won't budge. Why won't you do it?"

"She is Wendell's responsibility."

"You're just being stubborn."

"She's gonna cause a garbage strike."

He realized he'd raised his voice, only when she took a step back from the desk.

"Then do it. Avoid the strike."

"I'm not cleaning up Wendell's mess." Hudson thought of the year Wendell would have been willing for him to spend in prison. He remembered how Wendell had pointed out all the business opportunities the family would lose if he himself went to prison. "Just think of it as a hitch in the army," Wendell had said. "You missed your chance to go to Vietnam."

"It belongs to all of us," Rosalind said.

Hudson felt as if, while walking through the river swamp, he'd stepped in a pool of quicksand. He decided he'd quit his job before giving in to Wendell.

"Did Miss Ella get something to eat?"

"I ate the extra hamburger," Rosalind said.

"That's ok," Hudson said softly. "I just don't want that old woman to die of heat stroke on city property."

"She's not going to die," Rosalind said. "I think she's going to be out there a long time."

She went out of the office. Through the blinds Hudson watched her walk back up the hill and sit down under the tree by Larue.

He picked up the phone and dialed Maurice's office. It would be easier to get through the rest of the day once he had gotten that over with.

Chapter 8

Hudson sat in the waiting room outside Maurice's office and listened to Mrs. Sims type. Over Mrs. Sims' desk was the head of an elk, one of Maurice's trophies from his yearly hunting trips in Colorado. At his home a brown bear stood snarling in the entrance hall. There was some sort of kinship between bovine Mrs. Sims and the head. Its black glass eyes could have been exchanged for hers and no one would've noticed the difference. She constantly worried about Hudson tracking in dirt from the landfill onto the carpet. And now, as Hudson sat before her, she kept sneaking glances at his feet.

Maurice had served the longest term of any mayor in the history of Pine. During reconstruction a newly elected mayor had lasted only one day, shot by his disgruntled opponent in the street. Hudson had read about that in the copy of council proceedings the city published for its 200th anniversary. They counted the time it had been a French fur trading outpost and so came up with the figure. Not long after the outpost was established there were Looms in Mississippi. It had always surprised Hudson that Maurice, a non-Mississippian, had been so successful as a politician. He'd come down to Pine during World War II as an aviation cadet. Maurice was from Minnesota.

Mrs. Sims told him he could go in. Hudson felt the thick carpet give under his shoes. She always made him feel like he had manure on his feet.

Maurice was seated behind his desk, a bad sign. But there was a bottle on the desk and two glasses, and that was a good sign.

"You got Wendell all upset," Maurice said.

Underneath his accent was a trace of that flat Minnesotan speech. Maurice never tried to hide it. Hudson thought the people who voted for him liked it, thought Maurice could do things an ordinary person from Mississippi couldn't.

"You heard any complaints about trash and garbage?" Hudson asked.

Maurice laughed.

"No, Wendell's gets picked up every day," Maurice said. "But he liked it better when your boys came around to the back of the house."

Over much opposition Hudson had persuaded Maurice that customers could put their cans out by the curb. In this way he could give better service with fewer men. There was part of Maurice that liked those extra workers, potential votes for him.

"What are you going to do about Ella Sabine and that boy?" Maurice asked.

Hudson was getting tired of people asking him that question.

"Joe Wallace asked me the very same thing," Hudson said.

Hudson found himself thinking of Murphy hitting a triple off the wall as he sipped Maurice's whiskey.

"I should have asked you myself," Maurice said.

"It's a matter for social services," Hudson said.

"I'd rather keep them out of this. Ella Sabine is looking for you to take in that boy."

Hudson stared down at his glass. He wanted to drink it quick but forced himself to be cool. He took a sip.

"Wendell can take him in," Hudson said.

"You could be kin," Maurice said.

Hudson marveled at how casually they could talk of miscegenation, no longer a crime in the State Code but still one in the minds of most of the citizens, white and black, and then wondered where Maurice had gotten his information. When Maurice had been elected mayor that first time, they wouldn't have been talking about it like this.

"I believe one of my ancestors once owned a slave who took the name of Sabine. That old woman is crazy. And I'm not going to be responsible for making things smell all right again for Wendell. We could be related to that boy. We could not be related. We're probably about as much kin as you and me."

Maurice grinned and said, "I don't think so."

Hudson looked carefully at Maurice, his face framed with white hair that looked just as good behind the desk as on the poster. Maurice was one of those men who, when their hair turned white, looked better than before. It grew thick and vigorous like the pelt of some wild animal Maurice had nailed up on his wall at home.

"I've had my fill of Wendell," Hudson said.

"Think of what's gonna happen when Sydney turns your department over to a private company," Maurice said. "You'll be spending your time watching the Braves."

All Hudson's whiskey was gone now and Maurice, who had the bottle by his glass on the other side of the big desk, was not offering him more.

"That's right," Hudson said. "I could retire."

Now the thought of watching baseball had an insistent physical appeal, like a thirst that needed to be quenched.

"When the strike starts it's your responsibility," Maurice said.

"I've got bags stockpiled," Hudson said. "I'm ready."

Maurice poured himself another drink.

"You do something about that boy," Maurice said. "Satisfy that woman."

"I'll call social services again," Hudson said.

Maurice studied the whiskey in his glass.

"You call me back when she's satisfied," he said.

Hudson got up to leave. Maurice took a drink of the whiskey.

"That's good stuff," Hudson said.

Hudson started for the door.

"Hudson."

Maurice had stood up and was looking out the window at the city hall gardens where a couple of trustees from the city jail, dressed in blue jumpsuits, were clipping the hedge.

"You see Joe Wallace, you tell him to get himself back up here," Maurice said. "That boy is smart but undependable lately. He must have himself a girlfriend. Sleeping with a girl on city time. I'll skin him alive."

Maurice grinned.

Hudson, who was careful not to grin back, nodded in agreement and went out of the office.

The mayor's office was downstairs; the three councilmen had offices upstairs. Hudson went past the city clerk's office and up the stairs. He never liked to do much business with Jack Tisdale, the councilman in charge of the Sanitation Department, but he had the requisition Connie had prepared for the pump and plastic pipe in his pocket, and it needed Jack's signature.

Hudson went by the other two councilmen's offices and into Jack's outer office. There was Joe Wallace with a plastic cup to the door. Joe Wallace saw him and put a finger to his mouth for quiet but didn't remove his ear from the cup. Joe Wallace was taking advantage of the fact that Jack had fired his secretary.

"He's reading his Bible again," Joe Wallace said.

Joe Wallace offered Hudson the cup. Hudson refused it. Hudson didn't need the cup. He could hear something out of the *Book of Job*. Jack must have been shouting, because it was a thick door.

"The mayor is looking for you," Hudson said.

Joe Wallace scuttled off down the hallway. And Hudson thought that was the right word, "scuttle," like some kind of bug that lived in the walls.

Hudson knocked on the door. Jack opened it, Bible in hand.

"I need a pump," Hudson said. "Landfill fire."

It was always best to keep things simple and direct when dealing with Jack.

Jack plucked the requisition out of his hand and studied it.

"Surprised there's enough water in the river," Jack said.

Jack sat down at his desk and studied the requisition. He was a little crazy with religion but had always supported Hudson.

"Joe Wallace is doing Bible study with you," Hudson said.

Jack grinned.

"Listening at the door again with that cup."

Jack signed the requisition but kept it on his desk.

"Wendell came by today," Jack said.

Scott Ely

Hudson started to protest, but Jack raised his hand for silence.

"What you do about Ella Sabine and that boy is your affair," he said. "That's what I told Wendell."

At last someone understood. Too bad Jack didn't count. A little religion in a political campaign was all right, but Hudson suspected that when Jack came up for reelection next year he'd lose. With that prospect at his back, if a strike started Jack could change his mind quick when his phone started ringing with complaints from the voters.

Jack pushed the paper across the desk to Wendell.

"Just don't let things get out of hand down there," Jack said. "That landfill fire. Has it been burning long?"

"Can't get it put out."

"What do you think it means, that fire?"

"That someone put tires in the landfill."

"You don't think it's a sign of something? The Lord's sign?"

"No."

Jack stared at him for a moment.

"I guess you're right. You should know."

Hudson went out of the office. That was Jack all right. It was as if Jack had transported himself back to a time when the whole world lay spread out before man, full of symbols and signs from God. It seemed to Hudson as if this day everyone in town was a little crazy. Jack was not the only one.

He walked by the city clerk's office. Joe Wallace was leaning on the counter talking to one of the clerks. Joe Wallace waved and smiled as if the matter of the cup was now some secret they shared, which made them friends.

Out on the city hall steps Hudson saw that the trustees, two blacks and one white man, had finished the hedge and were putting the clippings in plastic bags. The hedge would end up in the landfill to provide more potential fuel for Charlene.

Hudson got in the car and drove down Lamar Street until it intersected with Magnolia, the street that was the northernmost boundary of French Town. Magnolia took him to River, and Miss Ella and Larue came into view again, their figures shimmering on the asphalt, she rocking in her chair and the boy holding the umbrella over her. He drove past. She was asleep again. The boy's hair was wet, the sunlight caught up in the beads, and Hudson supposed he'd put his head under a faucet. Larue didn't look at him, as if he were lost in a daydream, his eyes unfocused, waiting patiently for the old woman to wake up and tell him what to do next.

Chapter 9

Hudson swiveled his desk chair about, turning himself toward the window. The afternoon sun beat against the closed blinds, like some animal clawing to get in. He thought of Ella Sabine sitting in the circle of shade from her umbrella, thought of her folding the umbrella and facing the afternoon sun as it dropped down over the shacks, and thought of her staring full into it, the light and heat falling off her like a slip off a pretty woman. The air conditioner set in the window hummed and groaned. He got up and adjusted it, directing the flow of air toward his desk. He resisted the impulse to open the blinds and look at her. The phone rang.

It was a Ms. Russell from social services. She told him she was sorry she had been so late in returning his call but that she had a very busy day, lots of problems. He could imagine her sitting at her desk with that stack of pink message slips she'd been told by Maurice or Wendell to ignore. But she had called. Maybe she wasn't that sure about Maurice winning and wanted to hedge her bets with Sydney Cable too. The election had put everyone off balance, made people hard to read. He patiently listened to her make excuses. Then she asked him what surely she already knew.

"How may I help you, Mr. Loom?"

He wondered how that made her feel: superior, embarrassed; it was hard to say.

"I've got this problem with a little boy and his cousin," he said.

"Are you related to them?" she asked.

Hudson felt like slamming down the phone. Damn woman, he thought. She knew the entire story. Probably Rosalind had told her. He vaguely remembered seeing her at the house.

"A black little boy and his cousin," he said.

"I'm sorry, Mr. Loom," she said.

He thought he heard laughter in her voice and paused, considering how to proceed. Then he told her about Larue and Miss Ella, getting madder and madder at the woman's shameless prevarication as he did it. Ms. Russell sighed and cooed and clucked her tongue.

"Mr. Loom, I don't want to sound unsympathetic," she said. "If you knew what we deal with on a daily basis. There's just no imagining if you're not here. Little Larue is being cared for by a responsible adult relative and unless there's a complaint, a documented complaint, we can't interfere. We can't deal with rumor. If we dealt with rumor, God only knows where we'd be. I have to tell my case workers that every day, and they are professionals."

"That adult guardian has been sitting in a rocking chair in the sun all afternoon right outside my window," Hudson said. "That boy has been there holding an umbrella over her head. Goddamit! Does that sound responsible?"

"Mr. Loom, I know your family and will not take abuse over the phone," Ms. Russell said, her voice hard and controlled. "I went to school with your sister. I have been in her home."

Hudson felt exhausted, like in high school after the coach had made them run wind sprints. He thought about his heart, the doctor's concerns about his blood pressure. He picked up his free hand. It had made a wet print against his khaki trouser leg.

"I'm just concerned about that boy, Ms. Russell," he said. "Rosalind has spoken of you many times."

"You are a sweet man, Mr. Loom," she said. "I have to talk to abusive people on a daily basis. You are not one of them. Oh, wait. I have another call. Remember, documentation, Mr. Loom. Goodbye."

She hung up and Hudson sat holding the phone in his hand. He looked up and noticed Tom Guess staring at him through the door window to the hall. Hudson wondered how long he had been standing

Scott Ely

out there, if Tom Guess had seen him wipe his sweaty palm on his shirt front. Then Hudson saw the top of a head covered with curly black hair.

Hudson went to the door. There in the hall was Larue with two cans of Coke.

"I let him use the machine," Tom said. "He had his own money."

What Hudson could not understand was why Tom was standing with the boy. He supposed Guess was showing him to the door and had been so arrested by his outburst at Ms. Russell that he had stopped. Larue had been content to stand in the air-conditioned office and stare at a blank wall while Tom stared at Hudson in the office making a fool of himself with Ms. Russell.

Larue took a sip of one of the cokes and started for the door.

"Wait a minute," Hudson said.

Larue stopped and looked up at him warily. Hudson wondered if Miss Ella had told the boy she wanted him to become his guardian.

"Come in to my office and sit in the cool air," Hudson said.

He took one of the cans of Coke from the boy and gave it to Guess with instructions to have Connie take it to Miss Ella.

In the office the boy backed up against the air conditioner and spread out his arms. He moved with the grace of a child. He'd turn awkward as he got his growth. His high-top tennis shoes were new. The airborne shirt looked like it hadn't been washed in a long time. Not much documentation of distress for Ms. Russell.

"It's hot," Larue said.

Now that he had him alone Hudson was unsure how to proceed and realized he had no idea what he was going to say to the boy.

"Miss Ella must be hot," Hudson said while out of the corner of his eye he watched Connie go out the door with the Coke.

"No, sir, she don't get hot," Larue said. "Don't feel the heat at all."

Larue was not surprised that Miss Ella stood the heat so well. He imagined she had some kind of charm against the heat. She'd told him he was going to live with this white man. Mr. Hudson was big, but Larue didn't feel afraid of him. He wondered what Mr. Hudson's house was like and did it have air conditioning. Then he thought of his father working on the shrimp boat in Biloxi. He made up his mind that he was not going to live with anyone but his father. Larue looked around the office and saw the models of bulldozers and there among them a garbage truck. It was painted white instead of green like the ones belonging to the city.

Then the image of his mother and Tiffany intruded. They were going in the ground, he thought. How could they fly up to Jesus if they were going in the ground? He discovered that by focusing on the truck, those images of his mother and Tiffany, lumpy and rigid in the bed, became light and airy, their bedclothes fluttering in the breeze, rising up right through the roof of the house.

Hudson thought that probably tomorrow or the next day they would bury the mother and the sister. The boy had not even had time to mourn them, caught up as he was in Miss Ella's scheme.

"Well, you be sure she stays under that umbrella," Hudson said.

The boy was looking at something in the office, his eyes fixed on one point.

"You may think she can stand the heat," Hudson said. "But she can't. Old people can't—"

The boy's eyes had gone from Connie coming back into the office to the same spot in the room again. Hudson realized it was the models that drew the boy's eyes. On a shelf on one wall along with stacks of forms and magazines were a model of a garbage truck sent him by the Peterbilt people, a model of a Terex scraper, and a couple more of D-6 Caterpillar tractors.

"Go get the one you like," Hudson said.

Larue took them down from the shelf. It didn't take the boy a minute to decide on the garbage truck. Hudson approved of the choice. The truck, a cab over, was a scale model. You could detach the cab and look at the engine. The garbage bin tilted open just like on the real trucks.

The boy returned with the truck to stand in front of the air conditioner, the mechanical wind rippling his T-shirt.

"Mr. Wendell gonna let us stay for a month," the boy said.

Larue liked the heavy feel of the truck, not like the plastic models he'd occasionally been allowed to buy at the store. It was heavy, he thought, heavy as opposed to how light his mother and Tiffany were as they floated up into the sky.

So that was it, Hudson thought. The boy's mother and sister dead and Wendell was going to make it all right by giving them a month's free rent.

"Then we're going to Biloxi," the boy said.

"You got kin there?" Hudson asked.

"They got shrimp boats in Biloxi," the boy said.

Hudson wondered if Larue imagined himself working on one of those shrimp boats, going out in the blue Gulf with nets draped from the masts on a boat with a name like Miss Lucy or Diamond Sue.

"Your father's people?" Hudson asked.

Maybe they were fishermen and had a boat and a thriving business and could take good care of Larue and Miss Ella.

"My papa has a shrimp boat," Larue said.

Larue thought again of his father, the bow of the boat cutting a wake in the blue water. He flipped the cab of the truck open and snapped it back.

"Works on a shrimp boat?" Hudson asked.

"I got to go," Larue said.

Larue looked at the truck in his hands and then at Hudson. He wanted it but didn't want to ask. His mother and Tiffany intruded again. Once they were in the ground how could they fly up to Jesus. It didn't make any sense. He thought of asking Mr. Hudson about it but changed his mind.

"It's yours," Hudson said.

Larue picked up his Coke off the air-conditioner and darted out the door with the truck in his other hand.

Hudson looked at his watch. It was almost four and in a half-hour the trucks would be returning from their routes, the yard filled with drivers. And every truck would drive by Miss Ella. Maybe Maurice was right to worry about a strike. But he had handled strikes before and there was still no union because he saw to it that his people were paid well over minimum wage.

Soon they would bury them. The old woman might get so caught up in the mourning she'd abandon her post or at least be diverted until after the election.

Hudson looked up and saw Tom Guess at the window, who quickly looked away and pretended he was on his way out the door. It was irritating to Hudson to think his fretting over Miss Ella had made him such an interesting subject to Guess.

He opened the blinds, the afternoon sun flooding the office. The first truck came down the hill. Miss Ella was in her chair and the boy was under the tree playing with the truck. At the bottom of the hill stood Tom Guess, a clipboard in his hand, looking from Miss Ella to the boy and then back again. Guess then went off down to the parking lot to check in the trucks for his report.

Hudson stood in the light for another few seconds, shading his eyes with one hand, the other hand on the cord to the blinds, as he watched Larue run the truck in circles around the top of the water cooler, his cheeks puffed out as he no doubt was making engine noises to accompany his play. A slight tug on the cord snapped the blinds shut, leaving Hudson in dark coolness again, the sweat already beginning to bead on his face. He sat down at the desk and, taking out a map of the landfill, began to plot the death of Charlene.

Chapter 10

Larue did not want to spend another day holding the umbrella for his aunt, but when she woke him at dawn he realized that was what they were going to do. He carried out the rocking chair and once she was in it, Larue sat beneath the hackberry playing with the garbage truck, waiting for her to call for the umbrella. Today she'd left her church hat at home, the one with the green ribbon, and wore a straw hat with a green visor. She wore that whenever she went out. It could be night, and if she was going to walk down to Mr. Hone's store, she'd put on that hat. He watched a pickup come down the hill pulling a machine behind it on a trailer. The machine was painted green and had the picture of an alligator on it taking a bite out of a tire. TIRE GATOR was printed in big red letters under the picture. They unhooked the trailer and chained the machine to a telephone pole at the side of the shop. Then the pickup drove out of the yard and up the hill again.

He steered the truck over the hills and valleys formed by the roots of the tree, making engine noises. Then he looked up and she was there above him, her wrinkled old lady's face staring down at him.

"You steal that truck?" she asked.

"Nome," he said.

"Where'd it come from?"

"From Mr. Hudson."

"Ah."

She reached out her hand, and he placed the truck in it. Larue expected she was going to take it back to Mr. Hudson and ask him if he stole it. She'd done the same thing when he came home with a model airplane from the drugstore. They'd gone back to the store. She'd made him hand it over and apologize to the owner.

But instead of walking down the hill to the office, she returned to the chair. Larue stayed in the shade and looked in wonder at her rocking back and forth holding the umbrella with one hand, the other hand resting on the truck in her lap.

Ella felt comfortable in the chair. She believed she was going to win. How could she lose when the spirits were on her side?

"Miss Ella?" the voice said.

"You rest easy," she said. "I doing what you asked."

And she told him about the demand she'd placed upon Mr. Hudson.

I tell Ernie and Saki that I'm talking to Miss Ella. It surprises me that I'm able to do it again. Right now my field is calm. I believe that I can talk with her forever. Then I try to talk with Alice, but she doesn't answer. Maybe, I think, I can talk with just one living person at a time. I decide to concentrate on Miss Ella. She's the one who needs me.

"I don't know if I can do it," she said. "I'm an old woman."

"You can," I say. "Make him listen to you. Make him take responsibility."

"You keep talking to me."

But then there was no more of the voice. She looked out over the tin-roofed buildings below, as if she expected to see Louis Sabine perched on one of them. But there was nothing, only the glint of the sun off the metal.

I can't hear her any longer. Ernie says to keep trying, just as long as my field's stable. Saki says to be careful. So I talk calmly, trying not to get excited.

Ella heard a murmuring in her ears that she couldn't understand, but she knew it was Louis Sabine. She rocked back and forth in the chair, lulled by the sound of his voice. Hudson Loom was going to take Larue into his house and raise him as his son.

She took a red pen out of her purse and began to put markings on the truck: wavy lines and numbers. She finished. She looked down at the office where the blinds were drawn and then across the roof of the shop which was catching the morning sun and at the garbage trucks parked in neat rows in the lot. The office blinds opened, then closed. The toy truck felt heavy across her legs. The sun rose higher over the cypresses along the river, a sluggish red ball, the light falling on her face. Now the men would be coming to work

"You get over here and hold this umbrella," she said.

Larue took up his station by her as the men began to come in to work in cars and pickups, some with body panels painted in different colors but most unpainted, the rust bleeding the color away, the metal full of rust-gnawed holes. They drove down the hill slowly, looking carefully at Miss Ella, who sat rocking back and forth, her eyes fixed on the truck in her lap.

The men stood around in a crowd in the truck lot like they always did. Then a driver got in a garbage truck and drove up the hill. Larue knew him. He was one of Mr. Adams' friends, a thin, light-skinned man with a red bandana around his head. He turned his head when he drove past as if Miss Ella and Larue were a sight that might make him go blind. Pretty soon Mr. Hudson came out of the office and without looking up to him and Miss Ella on the hill, Mr. Hudson walked down to the lot.

"What he doing?" Larue asked.

"Just be patient, child," Miss Ella said.

Ella watched Hudson walk over to the group of drivers and their crews, the man walking stiffly, as if his clothes were metal.

Hudson felt Ella Sabine's eyes on him as he approached the drivers, the day already so hot that he felt relief when he walked out of the sunlight into the shade cast by the shop. He saw their eyes not on him but turned toward her. He'd sat in the office since before sunrise, thinking of what he was going to do about the old woman if she resumed her post again. But he hadn't counted on what had happened.

"Mr. Wilson, you don't feel like driving today?" Hudson asked his best driver.

Louis Wilson looked up at Ella Sabine and then back at Hudson.

"You get her back in her house, Mr. Loom. Make her take the spell off."

Hudson noticed Louis had lowered his eyes when he said the part about the spell.

"Mr. Peavy just drove out to run his route," Hudson said.

"Mr. Peavy like to take a drink," Wilson said.

The men laughed.

Wilson continued, "He's a good driver but everybody know he like to take a drink."

"Peavy would drive that truck right past the devil himself," Mr. Adams said.

The men all laughed.

"You do what she wants, Mr. Loom," Adams said. "Then we'll drive."

Hudson turned and started up the hill. No one had mentioned the word *voodoo*. He wasn't sure he wanted even to think it. But there it was. That woman was sitting in the chair with a model truck in her lap and only one driver dared to drive past her.

Larue watched as Mr. Hudson slowly walked up the hill toward them. Then he stood before them, his face covered with sweat.

"Miss Ella, I gave the boy that truck," Mr. Hudson said.

She said nothing, just kept rocking back and forth, the rockers making crunching sounds on the gravel. Mr. Hudson looked mad and Larue wanted to run, except he was holding the umbrella and somehow he could not separate himself from her as long as he was holding it.

"Miss Ella, that boy probably wants his truck back," Mr. Hudson said.

The voice of Louis Sabine murmured in her ears. Then suddenly it was gone. She sat upright in the chair. And for a moment she felt panic. She forced herself to be calm.

"That boy is here to hold my umbrella," she said. "Not to be fooling with no toy truck."

"I'll have a tarp put up," Mr. Hudson said. "Be nice and cool under it."

"Larue can play with this truck in your house," she said.

Larue tried to imagine Mr. Hudson's house, if it had a swimming pool. He wasn't sure how he felt about going to live with Mr. Hudson,

Scott Ely

especially now that Mr. Hudson looked like he was mad.

"I don't own those houses," Mr. Hudson said, waving his arm in the direction of the street.

"You a Loom," she said.

She had begun to rock a little faster. Larue imagined her rocking faster and faster, finally the chair tipping forward and spilling her onto the asphalt. He imagined her, as light and frail as she was, making no sound when she hit, like a gas-filled balloon bouncing down the hill.

"Miss Ella, I guess I'll have to take that truck back," Mr. Hudson said.

The man opened his hand and there was a knife lying in his big palm. Larue had seen him sitting on the edge of his boat by the river using the knife to clean fish.

"This'll be for the boy," he said.

"Don't want him having no knives," she said.

Larue wanted the knife, would have been willing to trade ten trucks for it.

"I been wanting me—" Larue began.

"Don't be worrying about what you ain't gonna have," she said.

Mr. Hudson sighed and slipped the knife into his pocket.

Below the men were gathered together by the shed. Most watched, but there were a few who looked the other way: at the willows by the river, at the rows of trucks, at the sky. Larue knew he wouldn't look away, miss a chance to see who was going to win.

The truck lay in her lap, making a sag in her dress. Mr. Hudson looked at the truck and she at him.

"You give it to the boy," she said.

Hudson, who had taken a half step forward, now stepped back. He looked at the truck, covered with the strange markings. Below, the group of men drifted out of the sun into the shade of the shed, all of them watching.

"I did," Hudson said. "I—"

She stopped rocking, the chair motionless. It was like that moment in the morning between darkness and daybreak when Larue imagined he could hear the mockingbird begin to sing before it began and as he was thinking the song the first notes broke through and the sky lightened, song and light washing over him together, joined so that

A Song For Alice Loom

the two different things became the same. Eye heard and ear saw. She picked up the truck.

"You let him play with this in your house," she said.

"No, dammit!" Hudson said.

Larue saw the men eddy like floodwater in the river, some spreading out toward the office where there were faces at the door and windows.

Mr. Hudson turned to look at the men, like he was trying to force them with that look, his stare, to get in their trucks and drive out of the yard. Larue imagined Mr. Hudson's eyes connected to them by fine wires so he could move them like puppets. The men eddied and swirled about the yard, but no one got in a truck.

The white man clenched and unclenched his big hands. Larue wondered why he just didn't pick her up, chair and all, and carry her into the office.

"I won't take him in," Mr. Hudson said.

She rested one finger on the cab of the truck. Larue thought of telling her that she could swing the cab open if she wished and look at the engine.

"Loom blood in him," she said.

Ella felt the sun now, even though she was in the shade. The heat of it pressed on her like a weight on her chest, made it hard for her to breathe. She wished Louis Sabine would speak to her but he was silent.

I lie still as my field pulses. Saki and Ernie are scared because theirs are doing the same.

You be careful, Lou, Ernie says. You be careful.

I say I will. I lie still in my field. But I feel good because I know that Miss Ella is a strong woman. She'll make the Looms be responsible for that boy Larue.

Hudson swayed before her eyes, his face shiny with sweat. She had moved this big man from office to shop and now here before her. She was winning. She fought hard to maintain her concentration.

Larue wondered how it would feel to be big like Mr. Hudson.

Mr. Hudson looked at the men again.

"This is foolishness, Miss Ella," he said. "Those men are going to lose their jobs over you. Some have got families to feed. Little children like your boy."

"You feed Larue," she said.

Then Mr. Hudson had the truck, his big hand moving faster than Larue would have thought possible. He smiled as he looked down at the men again.

"What you gonna do with it?" she asked.

Ella felt good again, calm now that he'd made his move. She had him. Of all the things he could have done this was the worst.

Larue hoped he was going to give him the knife in exchange.

"This is going back in the office where it belongs."

"Put it in the office," she said. "Bury it in the dump. Throw it in the river. Won't make no difference."

"It's going back in the office," he said.

Hudson walked down the hill.

"He forgot the knife," Larue said.

He wanted to run after Mr. Hudson but was afraid of Miss Ella.

"Hush, child," she said. "You live in his house you'll get all you want. Get yourself educated."

Ella felt cool, as if she'd just dusted herself with rose powder after her bath.

Larue didn't want to go live with this white man. He didn't want to live with Miss Ella who always talked about dying. He wanted to go to Biloxi and live with his father.

"You stay close," she said. "Won't be no trucks going out today. Tonight you'll be sleeping in a Loom's bed."

Larue looked at the men, still standing about in the yard and at Mr. Hudson disappearing into the office. The faces had vanished from the windows.

"He'll bring me that truck back," she said. "You'll go home with him."

Larue held the umbrella over her head and waited for Mr. Hudson to come out of the office. The men huddled about in a strip of shade by the shop. No one went in or out of the office. Once Larue thought he saw the blinds open but it was only for an instant, a sudden narrow slit in one of them which disappeared immediately, leaving that smooth, unbroken surface again.

The morning dragged on as Larue watched the sun slowly climb above the feathery-leaved river cypresses. She kept rocking, the same slow beat. The men lolled in the shade, smoking and talking. They had lost that flowing water urgency when she had held the truck in her lap. Now they were like one of those shallow pools left after high water in which small fish and frogs swam, the sun shrinking it day by day until there was nothing left but a cracked pattern of mud.

Larue had gone half-asleep, already scolded by her for letting the umbrella droop, when suddenly there was Mr. Hudson crossing the yard with the truck in one of his big hands. Immediately the men reverted to their swirling and eddying pattern. Mr. Hudson talked to them, occasionally pointing up the hill to where Larue and Miss Ella were stationed. Finally he held the truck up before them. Most of them took a step back farther into the shade along the wall.

For a moment Larue thought Mr. Hudson was going to throw the truck at them or tear it apart before their eyes. But instead he lowered his head and started up the hill. The men remained in the shade. As the white man drew closer Larue stood up straight and made sure Miss Ella was in the circle of shade.

"Take it off," Hudson said, his voice flat and tired sounding.

He dropped the truck in her lap.

"Take in this boy," she said.

"Take it off," he said.

"You don't believe in none of it," she said. "But they do."

She gestured toward the men with one hand.

"I don't know what I believe," he said. "You make them believe it's safe to drive."

"Ain't easy undoing things," she said.

"I ain't going with him," Larue said.

The words burst out of him before he knew he was going to say them,

"You see," Hudson said. "This boy wants to stay with you. We're arguing about something that can't happen. The social services people won't let it happen."

"I want to live on a shrimp boat," Larue said.

Larue watched them both pause. Mr. Hudson grinned. Miss Ella began to rock fast again, the rockers crunching on the gravel.

"You ain't gonna be riding about on no shrimp boat," she said.

"You gonna get yourself an education."

She got up out of the chair, holding the truck in both hands as if she was afraid it was going to break. Then she slowly stooped down and placed it on the asphalt. For a moment the truck hesitated. It began to roll. Larue stepped forward but she stopped him, her skinny fingers around his arm. Mr. Hudson took one step, then stopped. They all watched the truck roll down the incline, bouncing in the rough places so that several times Larue thought it was going to turn over, but it didn't. Finally one of the front wheels hit a pebble, and the truck flipped and tumbled end over end, coming to rest at the bottom of the slope with the doors open and the cab broken away from the engine.

The men came out of the shade into the sunlight. Hudson walked down the slope to the truck. He knelt and picked it up, closing the doors and swinging the cab back into place. But the cab was broken and wouldn't stay closed.

"You take Larue home with you, I'll fix it fine," the old woman said.

Ella felt tired but triumphant. She looked forward to watching Hudson walk off with Larue by his side.

Hudson glanced up at her. Then he looked at the men who had left the shade, some drifting towards their cars while others had edged forward for a better look at the truck. Hudson walked up the hill, holding the truck loosely in his hand. One of the doors popped open again, but he didn't bother to close it. He stopped in front of them. She thought he was going to put the truck back in her lap, but instead he reached out and pressed it into Larue's hand.

"You go back under that tree and play with this," Hudson said. "I'll hold the umbrella."

Larue looked at her to see what she wanted him to do. But she said nothing, the beginning of a smile on her face. He hesitated.

So he isn't ready yet, Ella thought. But he would be. She had nothing but time, all the time there was in the world. She would wait. She and Louis Sabine would wait.

"You go play," she said.

Larue retreated to the shade of the hackberry where he tried to fix the cab. Mr. Hudson stood holding the umbrella and talking with

Miss Ella. The men had gathered together by the side of the building again. Soon she and Hudson stopped talking.

The next time Larue looked up from his play Mr. Hudson was walking down the hill and Miss Ella was holding the umbrella. Larue hoped Hudson had not agreed to take him in. The big man talked to the men again, waving his arms about. Then he went into the office.

Most of the men drifted out to their cars and drove up the hill, leaving only five who sat with their backs against the side of the shed. Larue supposed they'd wait there all afternoon until their wives or girlfriends appeared to pick them up. He watched the blinds carefully as the parade of cars and trucks went up to the street. The blinds remained closed. Mr. Hudson was probably sitting in front of the air-conditioner trying to decide how he could get Miss Ella to lift the hex from the garbage trucks. Larue thought of Biloxi and going out with his father on the shrimp boat. He saw himself scooping those pink shrimp out of the net, the sea breeze in his face, his father's hands with those long fingers getting mixed up with his as they grabbed double handfuls of shrimp.

Hudson stood in front of the air conditioner, the wind rippling his damp shirt. He felt his heart beating rapidly and thought he should sit down, which he did. Tom Guess kept walking back and forth by the window. Finally he went out the door. Hudson dialed Wendell's number at the office. Wendell was not there, the secretary told him. He thought of trying at home but didn't feel like talking to his mother. Soon customers would start calling, wondering why their garbage was not being picked up. Pretty soon Maurice was going to be calling again.

He opened the blinds and turned his chair around so he could see the old woman and the boy. She was rocking back and forth while he held the umbrella over her head. It was the same as a strike except there was no strike. All he had to do was take in the boy. But that was Wendell's responsibility. Dammit, he thought, he wasn't going to let Wendell put his mess off on him.

Hudson went out of the office and found Tom Guess talking with the men in the shop. He told Guess to get a pickup. Guess hesitated.

"Well, she don't have a pickup in her lap," Hudson said. "That makes it all right."

Scott Ely

"Yes, sir," Guess said.

Hudson unlocked the room in the rear of the shop where he had stored the plastic bags.

"You call me when you get a full load of bags," he said. "You distribute them. Same places as we did in '82."

It had worked in '82, the people behind the city and not the workers. They'd brought their garbage in bags provided by the city to pickup points. Then Hudson had done the job with five garbage trucks and some trash trailers. But now he thought it unlikely he would find someone willing to drive a garbage truck.

"Who's gonna drive?" Guess asked.

"I'll get drivers," Hudson said. "I'm one and you're two. Peavy is three. All we need is about five more."

Let Wendell and Maurice drive, he thought. He laughed to himself at the thought of that. Let her sit out there in the hot sun. He would find drivers; he would outlast her.

As he walked back to the office he glanced at Miss Ella rocking back and forth. She didn't have him yet, he thought.

He sat down at his desk and dialed the number of the state unemployment office.

Chapter 11

Larue stood in the bathroom and looked down at the new toilet bowl, the white porcelain gleaming under the single bulb hanging from a cord over his head. Earlier in the day the TV people had taken pictures while he and Miss Ella stood in front of it. It was too hot to sleep. Larue left the bathroom, his feet making little pats against the boards, the rhythmic sound of Miss Ella's rocking chair coming from her room.

The house smelled of food: cakes and pies and bread, all stacked on the kitchen table. The refrigerator was full of ribs and chicken and cold drinks brought by their neighbors. People had begun to show up at supper, Larue and Miss Ella both sitting down to more hamburgers. Larue had switched right away to barbecued ribs.

As he walked slowly into his mother's room, he wondered if her ghost was still about. He closed his eyes and listened hard for her, but there was nothing, just the sound of a bug banging against the screen, drawn in by the light. Her smell was gone too, that mixture of sweat and the cream she rubbed on her face and neck every night. Not until after the funeral tomorrow would things be settled for her and Tiffany, their souls rising up together to Jesus. The mattress was gone from the bed, and through the springs he saw a cardboard wardrobe and a shoebox where she kept old photographs of her grandparents' farm. From the window sill he took the curved seashell his father had given her and held it to his ear, the sound of the sea sighing there. He opened the closet and took out the air mattress.

Out on the porch he sat on the steps and blew up the mattress. By the time he was finished he felt dizzy. There was a steady hiss because one of the tubes had a hole in it, but he always forgot and blew it up anyway. And he was hot again, the sweat clinging to his skin, a prickly feeling.

Larue walked across the street beneath the streetlights, which had swarms of bugs circling about them, and under the hackberry tree and down the slope toward the garbage department parking lot.

The TV people had asked him if he wanted to live with Mr. Hudson Loom. He told them he didn't want to live with no white man. He told them he was going to live with his father on a shrimp boat. They'd laughed at that.

"He won't be there long," his mother had said. "That man can't keep no job."

Larue reached the parking lot. The gate was usually wide open, but even though it was closed and locked he found it easy to throw the mattress over and climb, though he had to be careful going over the single strand of barbed wire at the top. The trucks were parked in rows, and he walked between them, their open bins smelling of garbage. The hiss from the leaky tube had stopped.

At the end of the lot was the river, behind a low levee faced with rock. Mr. Guess had caught him playing there one day and told him the rocks were full of rattlesnakes, that all you had to do was get close and they would start rattling. But Larue wasn't afraid of snakes. He went along the path up one side of the levee and then down to the river. A series of splashes came from the river as frogs hopped into the water and snakes dropped off the limbs of the willows.

Then he was by the water, Hudson Loom's flat-bottom fishing boat a dark shape where it was pulled up on the sandbar and chained to a tree. Often Larue would see him going fishing after all the garbage trucks were parked in the lot and the workers gone home. Mr. Hudson would drive to the river in his pickup and carry the little outboard motor and the red gas can over the levee. Larue walked over to the boat and tugged on the chain. One day he'd spent hours trying to pick the lock but had failed. If he had that boat, he could go all the way down the river to the Gulf, find his father and become a shrimp

A Song For Alice Loom   85

fisherman.

Larue took off his basketball shoes and waded out into the sluggish river, the water warm against his legs, and launched himself on the air mattress. He paddled with his hands, the mattress shooting out into the river where, caught by the stronger mid-stream current, it was pulled downstream. Larue might have saved himself the trouble because at this point he could have waded across. He crossed over into the slack water by the bank, the mattrress giving a little quiver as the current tugged at it.

Above his head the bank rose dark and smooth, the river making little sucking sounds as it slipped by in the dark. He thought about his father working on a shrimp boat out in the Gulf and wondered if he was looking at the same stars. Larue knew he could be useful on the boat if he could just get there. One night he'd steal a pair of bolt cutters from the shop and cut the chain on Mr. Hudson's boat. In a few days, just running at night and sleeping during the day, he would be at the coast.

Larue paddled about on the air mattress for a while and then decided this was the night he'd steal Mr. Hudson's boat. He didn't want to live with the white man or go live with the social services lady. Larue crossed the river again, leaving the air mattress by the boat. Then he made his way to the shop. He planned on breaking one of the little windows around back and climbing through it. His only problem was that the window was too high.

Larue had rolled an empty steel drum up to the window when he heard a car come into the yard on the other side of the building, its tires crunching on the gravel. It stopped. People got out. Two doors slammed. He went along the side of the building until he reached a corner. When he peeked around it, he saw Mr. Wendell and Anse Carter standing by the car. But it wasn't Mr. Wendell's car. It was an old beat-up car with the front hubcap missing. Anse Carter held a pair of bolt cutters in his hand, his arm hanging loose by his side.

They disappeared around the corner. Then Larue heard the sound of a chain being cut. He hoped Anse Carter would leave the bolt cutters when they were finished stealing whatever it was they were going to steal out of the shop. Mr. Wendell reappeared and got in the car. He started it without turning the lights on and then drove down

Scott Ely

the dirt track which led to where they kept the broken-down garbage trucks, some no more than wheelless chassis.

What happened next Larue couldn't quite believe. Anse Carter was pulling a machine, both his arms wrapped around a long trailer hitch. Under the mercury vapor lights, which made everything look purple, Larue saw the picture of an alligator eating a tire and the words TIRE GATOR printed underneath. Anse Carter stopped and went back behind the shop. He returned with the bolt cutters. Then he walked off pulling the machine.

Larue checked the door to the shop. The chain was still in place around it. They'd just cut the chain to the machine. He followed along behind Anse Carter, hoping to get his hands on those bolt cutters. But not too close because he remembered how well Anse could see in the dark. He heard the man breathing hard ahead of him in the darkness, heard the trailer wheels bouncing on the gravel. Those bolt cutters could bounce off and Anse would never miss them. Larue thought of himself lying in the bottom of the boat drifting down the river and watching the stars. And the sea. He would drift right out into the Gulf, the boat riding those gentle swells, the lights of Biloxi and Gulfport twinkling in the distance.

The road bent next to the levee. Larue went up the bank, knowing the road opened up into the lot. It was unlighted, but Anse Carter would see him for sure in the open darkness. Larue walked at a crouch along the top of the levee. He saw Mr. Wendell had parked the car at the end of the lot next to a thick stand of cane. Anse Carter, who had stopped in the middle of the lot, was sitting on the trailer hitch. Larue halted too until Anse was up and moving again.

Then Larue had to stop. The angle of the levee was wrong. From where they were, Anse Carter sitting on the hitch again and Mr. Wendell standing beside him, they would be sure to spot him. Larue went down on the river side of the levee. He planned to work his way up close to them through the cane.

It was easy to move silently through the canebrake, the ground carpeted with dead leaves. He had momentarily given up on getting the bolt cutters, was simply curious about what they were doing with the machine. They had it backed up to the end of a pickup body set on concrete blocks, its wheels stripped away.

A Song For Alice Loom

"Start it," Mr. Wendell said.

"It's my heart," Anse Carter said. "I feel pains in it."

"There's nothing wrong with your damn heart," Mr. Wendell said. "You should have gotten a car with a trailer hitch."

"Ain't right for me to tote it," Anse said. "Didn't make me tote at Parchman."

"Well, it's done. Get her out of the trunk," Mr. Wendell said.

"She tried to bite me," Anse said.

"She can't bite nobody now," Mr. Wendell said. "Remember, no names. And put that stocking over your head."

"That old woman can't see past her nose."

"Just do it."

Larue heard the trunk swing open. Someone was pulling a starter on a motor. The motor caught. He heard no more voices. He crawled forward through the leaves. When he put his head up again, he saw the long trailer hitch was only a few yards away, the bolt cutters still hanging on it. Mr. Wendell and Anse Carter were behind the machine. Larue crawled on his belly across the open ground. He was scared but made himself go. He thought about drifting down the river towards his father. As he crawled he smelled the exhaust from the machine's motor, felt its vibration through his body. And then he had the bolt cutters, pulling them up and off the tongue with one hand.

As he turned to go back into the cane, his body in a half crouch, he looked up and saw Anse Carter standing in the pickup bed, his back to him, holding Miss Ella in his arms, her dress fallen away from her legs. Mr. Wendell had a tire in his hands. He tossed it into the machine. So that was it, Larue thought. The machine ate tires. Mr. Wendell said something to Anse Carter or Miss Ella. Anse Carter put his hand up to her mouth and pulled at something. Miss Ella raised her head and looked like she was trying to give Anse Carter a kiss. Then Anse Carter suddenly dropped her into the machine—her body making a heavy sound like a snake slipping off a limb into the river—but not so much dropped Miss Ella as recoiled from her, Anse Carter falling backwards into the truck bed.

At first Larue didn't think he could move. He expected her to rise up out of the machine. The machine shuddered a little. Anse Carter peered down into it. Rise up, Larue thought, Rise up. But nothing happened. They'd killed her. He wanted to shout, to scream. The machine stopped.

Anse Carter turned and looked directly at him. Anse Carter had no face, he thought. Even in the darkness he could see that he had no face, as if all his features had been smoothed over with something, leaving a head like the head of a worm. Larue ran.

"Goddamn, stop him!" Mr. Wendell yelled.

Larue ran along the top of the levee, someone close behind him. The person was already breathing hard as if they had run a long race. He thought he would be able to outrun him easily. Over his shoulder he saw another figure running across the gravel lot. They were trying to cut him off from the road that ran up to the street. But whoever was on the levee was already losing ground. Larue could hear him panting far behind.

He reached the place where Mr. Hudson had his fishing boat moored. The person on the levee was two hundred yards away. Larue guessed it was Anse Carter. Larue took the bolt cutters and cut the chain on the johnboat, the chain rattling against the metal as he pulled it free. Anse Carter was sure to hear that. Larue pushed the boat out into the current and then dived into a stand of willows. Water snakes dropped off the branches, making little splats in the river, but he didn't care. Anse Carter was worse than a thousand snakes.

Larue stood very still, trying to control his breathing. Miss Ella would rise up, he thought. She would rise up. Please, he said softly. Let her rise up.

"Larue," the voice said.

Larue thought about diving into the river but was too scared to move.

"Larue," the voice said again.

Larue held his breath and tried to remain motionless.

You look out for that boy, Miss Ella says. And I talk to him, hoping that he'll answer. I'm crying over Miss Ella. My field sparkles. Saki and Ernie tell me to calm down. I tell her that I'll help him stay clear of Wendell Loom and Anse Carter. But first I've got to persuade him to answer me. I continue to cry, so hard I can hardly talk. Little streaks of light go round and round the field.

Anse arrived breathing hard. Larue felt safe behind the thick growth of willows. He heard the rattle of the chain. Then there was the pop of his pistol and the thwack as a bullet hit something. Mr. Wendell arrived.

"Larue," the voice said again.

Larue hoped that Anse Carter and Mr. Wendell couldn't hear it.

The pistol went pop again.

"Stop!" Mr. Wendell said. "Do you want the police down on us?"

"Won't nobody pay it any mind," Anse Carter said.

"He'll have to go under the railroad bridge," Mr. Wendell said. "We'll go down there and make sure of him. You sure it was that Sabine woman's boy?"

"Yes, sir," Anse said. "I seen him good."

They left, going up over the levee.

"Larue," the voice said. "Miss Ella wants me to talk to you."

"Where you at?" Larue asked.

"It doesn't matter where I am. You tell me where you are. Tell me what's happening."

"You'll tell them."

"No, I'm a Sabine. Like you. I won't tell them."

"I want to talk with Miss Ella. She went up in the air. Done it with her magic."

I decide to let Larue go on believing that Miss Ella is alive, saved by her voodoo. Larue tells me where he is and where he thinks Anse Carter and Wendell Loom have gone.

"You find Alice Loom," the voice said. "She'll know what to do."

"She kin to Mr. Wendell," Larue said.

He waited for the voice to speak again, but nothing happened. Larue considered Miss Ella flying up in the air and this voice, of someone who claimed he was kin, talking to him out of the air. He resolved to be careful following the advice of spirits. Miss Ella knew how to talk to them but he didn't. She'd told him stories of folks being tricked by spirits.

I continue to talk to Larue, but I don't hear him reply. Another living person I can talk with. I wonder where all this will lead.

Larue, I say. Larue.

But he doesn't answer.

Find Alice Loom, I say. Find Alice.

Scott Ely

Larue stayed in the willows a long time after they were gone. He imagined snakes climbing up on him, thinking he was an old cypress stump. Then he made his way back over the levee and through the garbage department grounds, keeping to the shadows.

He was standing in the shadows by the hackberry, waiting to dart across the street, when a car pulled up, the headlights catching him.

"Larue," a woman's voice said. "You get in."

It was the woman with the tape recorder.

He poked his head around the tree.

Miss Rosalind smiled at him, beckoning with her hand.

"Larue, quick!" she said.

She had turned her shoulder and opened the door. Larue thought of the house. They would look for him there. Going home had been a bad idea. He ran for the car. She tried to make him sit in the front with her, but he climbed into the back seat and lay down on the floorboards.

"Larue?" she said.

Larue said nothing. The car started to move. He was frightened, so afraid that he could hardly breathe. At least, he told himself, he knew the source of this voice and that Rosalind wasn't a spirit. He wished he was lying in the bottom of the boat, drifting down the river toward the sea and his father.

Chapter 12

Rosalind parked the car in the driveway of her house. The cicadas hummed from the trees; the house loomed big and dark. Someone had been chasing the boy. She'd seen him looking back over his shoulder. The boy lay on the floorboards, not moving or making a sound. She could hear him breathing.

It had been pure chance that she'd spotted him. She was on her way to an interview with a woman she'd been trying to persuade to talk with her for months. Rosalind almost hadn't stopped, thinking Larue was playing some child's game. It was the fear she saw on his face, a face illuminated for only an instant by the headlights, that had made her stop.

"You're safe," she said.

The boy remained on the floorboards.

"Larue, you're safe," she said.

She wished Miss Ella would consent to come stay at the house. Whoever was chasing Larue would not dare follow him there.

"Larue?" she said.

The boy sat up on the seat. The security light over the garage illuminated the his calm face.

"Yes ma'am," he said.

"Who was after you?" she asked.

"They done threw Miss Ella in the Tire Gator."

The boy was crying now, his face still rigid. A single tear caught up the light as it rolled down his cheek.

"What?" she asked.

"In the Tire Gator," Larue said.

"Tire Gator?"

"It chews up tires."

She put her arm around him. The boy smelled of sweat and mud.

"Who?" she asked.

The boy looked up at her, his eyes going beyond her to the house. She turned to see what he was looking at, but there was nothing, only the facade of the house.

"Tell me," she said.

"Mr. Wendell and Anse Carter," Larue said. "There ain't no place I can hide."

Rosalind wanted to cry; she wanted to scream. But she said nothing, only put her arms around the boy and pulled him close.

"Are you sure?" she asked.

"I seen 'em good," he said.

"You lie back down," she said. "Don't you move."

"Whose house is this?"

"My mother's."

"Alice Loom?"

Larue started to get out of the car.

"No, you stay here," she said.

"Alice Loom will take care of me," he said.

The spirit had said her name clearly. He was sure of it. And he knew that Rosalind was Alice's daughter. Possibly the spirit had sent Rosalind for him.

"He sent you for me?" Larue asked.

"What?" Rosalind asked.

"He sent you."

"Who?"

"He said that Alice Loom would take care of me."

"Who?"

"It was just a voice."

Rosalind believed what the boy had told her about Miss Ella. Now he was babbling about voices in the night. And it was no wonder, after seeing what happened to Miss Ella.

"Wendell Loom owns this house," Rosalind said. "He comes here often. My mother can't do anything for you."

"He said Alice Loom," Larue insisted.

"I'm Rosalind. That is close enough. You stay on the floor. Wendell could drive up here anytime. Anse Carter lives in a cabin out back."

Larue promised he would. He didn't want to stay any place that was close to Anse Cater. And he thought that maybe the daughter would do as well as the mother. Right now the spirit wasn't complaining. So it must be all right. He'd stay with Rosalind and do what she asked.

Rosalind went into the house through the kitchen. Her mother was sitting in the dark watching a movie on TV, the neon glow from the screen flicking into the hallway from the den. Her mother didn't hear her come in or was ignoring her. Alice was like that when she was interested in a movie. Rosalind went to her room. She threw clothes into a suitcase. She put a small Beretta automatic pistol in last and a box of ammunition. It had been a long time since she'd practiced with it on the range. Then she wrote Alice a note.

I'm going to visit Peyton for a few days. I didn't want to interrupt the movie.

Love, Rosalind

Rosalind went out to the car. There was a part of her that wondered if Larue was going to be there, if all this was some kind of dream. The boy still lay on the seat breathing calmly. She usually visited Peyton, a lover from her Vietnam days, every month or so. No one would think it unusual that she'd suddenly driven over to Alabama on a whim.

She drove north towards Vicksburg. No one would think of looking for the boy at Hudson's cabin. There she could have time to think. Then she thought of Miss Ella. Tears rolled down her face. Her body felt hot and prickly all over. She tried to control herself. It would do Larue no good to watch her falling apart.

"I'm going to take you to a safe place," she said. "To a cabin on a lake."

Larue climbed out of the back seat and sat beside her. Outside there were rolling hills dotted with lights from farmhouses. The air-conditioner brought the smell of fertilizer and herbicide into the car, a summer smell she was comfortable with. They were smells that took

Scott Ely

her to Eagle Lake. First this smell and then the smell of the Delta and the water.

"Those men won't find us where we're going," she said.

The boy didn't reply; her voice sounded small and unsteady to her.

Larue thought of the dress pushed up around Miss Ella's legs; he thought of Miss Ella dropping out of Anse Carter's arms. But no, he thought, she couldn't have dropped. She went up, not down. And he saw her clearly rising into the sky, and the feeling of terror within him subsided, grew calm. He'd told the spirit she went up, and he hadn't denied it was so.

Miss Ella accounted for, Larue coolly looked at the white woman. He remembered the men chasing him and the sound Anse Carter's pistol made as he shot at the drifting johnboat.

"Miss Ella got powerful charms," Larue said. "She all right someplace."

Rosalind decided that was it. Miss Ella had filled the boy's head with voodoo. No wonder he was talking about voices that told him to go seek out her mother.

"Larue, you said they put her in the machine."

The boy looked like he hadn't understood.

"She's dead," Rosalind said. "In the machine. Dead. Like your mother and your sister. You saw it. Those men want to hurt you. But now you're safe from them."

She looked at the boy, for some sign that he understood, but he just sat there.

"She's dead?" Rosalind said.

"Yes, ma'am," Larue said.

She wondered what he was thinking, wished he would cry or scream, the only appropriate response she could think of to the sight he had witnessed. He might be in shock. But she didn't want to pull over and hold him. She was afraid he might dart out of the car. She had lost a cat once that way. At a filling station she had stopped for gas and the cat, maddened by the unfamiliarity of the car, dashed out and was gone, never to be found.

"I'm going to take care of you," she said.

"Where's she gone?" Larue asked.

He had seen her go up, he thought. She was safe.

"To heaven," Rosalind said.

"Flying up through the air?"

"I don't know. But she's there."

She had gone up, alive not dead. She'd said she'd be up there with the brightest star. He wanted to jump out of the car, but it was going too fast. He thought of Tiffany and his mother. They were going to put them in the ground. Miss Ella had told him they were with Jesus. Miss Ella said he was going to live with Mr. Hudson. Larue wished he'd gone with the boat, taken his chances out on the river. Maybe out there the spirit would've talked to him again. But then he thought of Anse Carter and shuddered.

But maybe, Larue thought, it had not been Miss Ella at all. He wanted to go to sleep smelling that rose soap smell next to him.

"She's at home," Larue said.

"No, Larue, she's not at home," Rosalind said. "Not if they did what you told me. They killed her. You saw it."

She was becoming exasperated with the boy and had to remind herself that he was a child, that she must be patient and gentle. She wished she'd had more experience with children. Larue said nothing. She could hear him breathing.

"She gone," Larue said.

Larue tried to understand about Miss Ella and the machine. Anse Carter had dropped Miss Ella inside it. It chewed up tires but not her. It didn't get her.

"She can make herself alive," Larue said, thinking of the herbs and the owl bones and especially of the skull of the mad dog. "She got the power."

Rosalind wondered what went on in the house with the old voodoo woman and the child's mother who was a prostitute and those men coming and going.

"Magic can't keep you from dying," Rosalind said.

Larue saw Miss Ella rising up out of the machine. That was what had happened, but he had been distracted by the bolt cutters and had missed it. That was the way it had to have happened. Maybe if he went down to Biloxi he might find her there too. She'd said more than once she wanted to get back down by the water again, where she could use the magic of the Virgin. There weren't many teeth left in the skull. Where was she going to get another one? Getting there would be easy for her. She could just sail right down the Pearl River. Not even touch the water.

"She ain't dead," Larue said. "She gone down to the ocean."

It felt good to know that Miss Ella had been stronger than Mr. Wendell or Anse Carter. He thought of her in Anse Carter's arms on top of the machine and then she was gone. She had disappeared from them too. He wondered if Miss Ella would visit his father. She might and then his father would drive up to Pine and take him to the ocean.

"Move over here, Larue," Rosalind said. "You put your head in my lap."

She realized he was going to deny what he saw, at least for the time being.

Larue stretched out on the seat. She had on a summer dress which was pulled up on her legs a little. The material was cool and smooth; she was hard beneath it. His mother had been a thin woman, and Miss Ella too was all hard angles.

"You try to sleep," she said.

"What do they call that lake?" he asked.

"Eagle Lake," she said. "We'll stay in a cabin."

"Can I go fishing?"

"Yes."

Larue thought of fishing on Eagle Lake, which he had never seen, the shape of it: trees, water, sky, clouds, deep water, shallow water sliding about in his mind but taking no definite form.

"I ain't got a pole," he said.

"Hudson has fishing things," she said.

"And bait."

"Bait too. Hush, go to sleep."

Larue listened to the click of the tires going over the grooves in the concrete. He closed his eyes.

Rosalind was relieved the boy was asleep, his breath slow and regular. But he would wake and remember. He was beginning to seem like a malfunctioning tape recorder which refused to play back what she had recorded. She thought of how it might have been if she'd married Peyton, had children. Then she thought of that rocket—that memory always with her—its fuel spent, pausing at the top of its arc before gravity drew it to earth and through the tin roof of the barracks, exploding in the next room. Then the roof, rafters and tin, had fallen in on her and the sergeant. She'd hurt her head. Peyton was not there. She'd met him later at the hospital in Japan where the doctors were treating a bullet wound in his elbow that refused to heal.

She thought of the sergeant and shuddered. When she and the girls had gone to Vietnam: Kelly Will, the Australian bass player, and Sally Ryan Smith, her drummer from Alabama, they'd discovered that since they were on their own, without the protection of official entertainers with the USO, the senior NCOs at the base camps demanded sexual favors in return for gigs. The first time it happened they were broke and discouraged and Kelly had volunteered. From then on, when they decided they had no other choice, they drew straws. This time, at the 4th Infantry base camp on Dragon Mountain near Pleiku, the lot had fallen to Kelly. It had fallen that way once before but Rosalind had liked the looks of the sergeant, and noticing Kelly's hesitation, had volunteered. All this was her first experience at prostitution. She felt sick at the thought of it. But she was not going to call home and beg for money, not after she'd left New York without even bothering to inform her mother.

The walls of the sergeant's room were pine paneled. He saw her staring at it and laughed.

"They shipped that all the way from the states for the 103rd Engineer mess hall," he said. "I traded some plywood for it. Don't know how those troopers stole it without the cook catching them."

Rosalind remembered feeling she should be in someone's den back in Pine. And this man should be a friend's father. She'd never made love to a man that age. The sergeant was almost old enough to be her father.

"I want to hear those big guns go off," the sergeant said.

Rosalind remembered that for a moment she had stared at him. He laughed.

"Take your clothes off and do it for me, sweet thing," he said. "I know hippie girls like to do it."

He had looked old, although now she knew that at the outside he

Scott Ely

was forty. He was from Alabama, his hair cut so close it looked like his head had been shaved. He was not tall, but his body was like a gymnast's, perfectly proportioned. A sculptor could have used him as a model. At another time and place and under different circumstances she might have been happy to go to bed with him.

He sat down on the cot.

"You take off your pants first," she said.

He laughed and did as she asked.

The sergeant took a long time to come. By the time it was over she felt exhausted and was covered with sweat, as if she had run a long race, the salty taste of him in her mouth.

"Now you do yourself," he said.

"We made a bargain," she said. "I kept my end of it."

"Just like the girls in Pleiku," he said and laughed.

He pulled out a white tube from beneath the bed.

"You're right," he said. "We made a bargain and now you're going to keep your end of it."

Rosalind shook her head and started to pick up her clothes. Then there was a big pistol in his hand.

"I could say I thought you was a VC sapper," he said. "Shot you before I discovered my mistake."

He had her sit down on the bed. He explained to her about the white tube.

"A parachute flare," he said. "It's got a charge inside that sends up a magnesium flare. The package that's got the flare has little razor wings that pop open in case you got to fire it up through the branches. Cuts right through 'em. You send it up by hitting the bottom with the palm of your hand. So you be careful Miss Hippie."

Rosalind used the flare on herself as he directed. It was cold and hard. It hurt. He sat and watched her.

"You come and our bargain's complete," he said. "No fake stuff. I want to see that pussy turn all rosy."

Then as she moved the flare gently in and out of her, knowing she would never be able to come, the rocket fell on them. Rosalind woke up in the hospital. She could remember nothing but her experience with the flare: not her name or what country she was in or what had put her in the hospital. And that memory never left her.

A Song For Alice Loom

The next day she woke up from a restless sleep and found a tube wrapped in brown paper on her bed beside her. The nurse told her the sergeant had brought it. She carefully unwrapped it, cutting the tape with a pair of scissors the nurse gave her. Then there was the flare, smooth and heavy in her hands. She didn't know whether to laugh or cry. But she quickly wrapped it up in the paper again and put it in her suitcase. At the time she'd had some vague idea of directing it at his head and popping the flare. She fantasized she'd run into him some day. She imagined aiming the flare at his head and slapping the butt with her palm. The flare would cover that perfect body of his with fire. She suspected there were more complex reasons for her keeping it, but this simple version satisfied her. A few days after the sergeant's visit the army flew her to Japan for tests. Gradually her memory returned.

Larue turned in his sleep, his head heavy and warm against her legs, the skin of his cheek very smooth.

Suddenly memories of her and Peyton came to her in a rush. She kept her hands very still on the steering wheel, afraid to move while she waited to see how far the memory would carry her. Yes, she thought, she and Peyton had fallen in love in Japan. That first night at the hotel in Tokyo had been wonderful. And the second too. But on the third night they spent hours in foreplay, leaving both of them exhausted. That was the beginning of his impotence. Peyton left the bed and stared out the window for a long time. She got out of bed and put her arms around him. He was trembling; he said he was cold. He put on a University of Alabama sweatshirt and she the silk kimono he'd bought her. Someone had cut a peace symbol into a corner of the glass. She ran her fingertip over the symbol, feeling the sharp edges of the cut. She thought of some soldier in the room with a girl who perhaps lay on the bed while he stood naked by the window and incised the symbol with a diamond ring. After Peyton calmed down he joked that it was like the bullet had hit something besides his elbow. She'd told him not to worry, that it would be all right.

But the next time they returned to Tokyo it happened again: one good night and the others failures. After they returned home, it was she who had tracked him down in Alabama. Now for years they had circled warily around each other. Occasionally it was good in bed

Scott Ely

with him but mostly it was not. For both of them there had been other lovers. She thought of the ways in which she'd made sure that nothing came of any of them. Some had been good men. She was sure Peyton had spent time with some good women. But neither of them ever committed to anyone and they always came back to each other. Then the memory of Peyton and Tokyo was gone, dissolving to bits and pieces: the feel of the silk against her skin, the way she traced the outline of the peace symbol with her finger, Peyton's body trembling in her arms as if he were a frightened animal.

Now Peyton laughed about it and said that it was the rocket. No lover could ever hope to equal that finale. But he didn't mean it.

And the sergeant. She remembered his name at the hospital in Japan. She'd come home and returned to school. She'd written letters to the Army and made phone calls and finally, three years later she had his name and an address in Alabama.

She had learned to shoot a handgun on the local range, thinking as she fired at the human silhouettes that the sergeant, Cale Nathan, would be nothing more to her than one of those pieces of paper.

In July she found him. It was outside the town of Snead in northern Alabama. She'd become lost on a maze of gravel roads that wound through the hills. She asked directions from children playing on a bridge. The bridge was cypress planks laid over steel girders. A small river ran below, its water dark and swift.

"Mr. Nathan's place is just over there," a boy said.

She hadn't considered what she was going to do after she killed him. If there were others there, she'd let them decide. If he were alone, she'd drive away.

She found the farm: a chicken house, a silo, a field planted with soybeans slanting down towards the river—the fruits of twenty years in the army. She knocked on the door, her purse heavy with the weight of the revolver. A woman opened it. She was old. A grandmother.

"I need to see Mr. Nathan," she said.

The woman stared at her.

"Cale is dead," the woman said. "It was a nice funeral."

"How?" Rosalind asked.

"Shot himself. Down at the river. Done it in a real pretty place."

"That's good."

A Song For Alice Loom

The woman looked carefully at Rosalind.

"Prettiness was what he couldn't stand, you see," the woman said. "To Cale it was like poison. Lost himself over there in them Vietnam swamps."

The woman looked out over the fields toward the river.

"Guess Cale never could understand why the Lord make this the prettiest place," the woman said.

Rosalind was suddenly struck by how blue the woman's eyes were.

"All this grieved him," the woman said. "His mind was filled with swamps. No place for the Lord."

Rosalind turned her back on the woman, who called after her, asking if she knew Cale. At the bridge the children were gone. She took the flare out of the car. She thought of Cale Nathan shooting himself and wondered how he'd done it. The head? The heart? The flare felt heavy, as if the tube was filled with lead. She'd allowed it to become a part of her life and that had been a mistake. She knelt and brought the butt of the tube down sharply against the boards. There was a whoosh, the package containing the flare and the parachute shooting up into the trees. The parachute opened with a pop, and the flare began to burn with a hard white light. But the parachute became entangled momentarily in the limbs of a big poplar. Then it pulled free and floated down to land in the pool, the magnesium fire hissing in the water and the white silk falling over it like the petals of some huge burning flower.

She wondered if killing the sergeant might have meant some kind of release. It was almost as if he'd deliberately injured her again, cheated her out of killing him.

Yet something had happened when she'd popped the flare. She remembered the smell of the mud and the light on the water and long-legged insects running on the surface. Setting off the flare made an end but no new beginning for her. She'd put the gun in her dresser drawer, underneath her bras and panties.

She'd hide Larue where they would never find him. She considered what had happened to Cale Nathan who put a bullet in his head because he lived in a place that was too beautiful for him to stand. The woman might have been right about that.

Scott Ely

The land was beginning to rise, the hills larger as they approached the series of bluffs on which Vicksburg was built. She left the interstate and drove through the hills, cutting across a corner of the military park, its monuments to the dead standing white in the moonlight. Then she dropped down out of the hills onto the tabletop flat Delta, the black earth smelling different from the loam of the hills, the headlights parting an immense flat emptiness.

Larue stirred in his sleep when they met the first big truck. He smelled perfume, and for a moment thought he had his head on Miss Ella's lap. Then he remembered where he was and thought of Miss Ella, rising up out of the machine over the river and over the trees, her black dress flapping, her black hat with the green ribbon pulled on tight. And for a moment he imagined he saw through her eyes: river and trees and the night sky as she turned in the wind to follow the river toward the sea.

Chapter 13

"You help Larue," Miss Ella says.

"I talked to him," I say. "Alice will take care of him. I told him to go to Alice."

"A rainbow," she says.

She's probably looking at whatever has happened to her body and is terrified of those flashing lights her unstable field is making.

Ernie is trying to talk with me.

"Wait," I say. "I'm talking."

"Lou's talking to the volcano," Ernie says.

Saki laughs.

"No," I say. "Not that."

"Lou's talking to a dead person," Saki says.

"Yes," I say. "Be quiet."

"He just a little boy," she says.

Then she gives out a cry, and I know that her field is collapsing.

So I tell her how talking makes the field unstable. I tell her the signs it gives off when it starts to collapse. A smell like cinnamon.

"Alice will take care of him," I say.

I think of how Saki calls us the strengthless dead. I can do nothing for Larue except talk.

"He could be dead," she says.

"No, I talked with him. He's alive."

Ella Sabine is now afraid of what will happen to her. She wants to go to heaven. I tell her how long I've been lying in my field and that I know nothing of heaven or hell.

"You could kill Wendell Loom," she says. "You could kill Anse Carter."

Sometimes the newly dead are like that, caught up in the desire for revenge.

"Love," I say. "Love."

And I explain to her again that all any of us can do is lie in our fields and talk. She should know that. I talked to her and she acted. She was forcing Hudson Loom to take responsibility.

"I could work a charm," she says.

"Too late for voodoo," I say.

I tell her that I never believed in any of that. And I haven't talked with anyone who does. No spooks or evil spirits, just unburied dead lying in their fields and trying to stay that way because no one knows what comes after a field is destroyed.

"It's got to stop," I say.

"No, she says. "Looms have to pay."

"Pay how?"

"Blood."

"I'm both Loom and Sabine. Should I destroy one part of myself to revenge the other?"

Ella Sabine is crying now. That's usual. No tears shedding, but I imagine her field pulsing with a circle of light. That's what happens to mine when I feel sad. I wish I had my sax. I'd play something for her that'd make her feel better.

"I'm afraid," she says.

I tell about Ernie lying out in the water. That makes her laugh.

"Sharks?" she asks.

"Swim right through him," I say.

She laughs.

"You tell me how to save Larue," she says.

"I can't," I say. "The living will have to save him."

I tell her about my talking with Alice Loom all these years. How sometimes I can't get through.

"You're closer," I say. "You try to talk with Alice. I've tried but I don't know if she's heard."

"What should I say?" she asks.

"Tell her to love," I say. "Tell her to save both Looms and Sabines."

I hear Ella Sabine sigh. She's trying to figure it all out. And it's hard. But it's too late for voodoo charms or knives or guns. All she has is words.

"Love Wendell Loom?" she asks. "Love Anse Carter?"

"Yes," I say.

"I want to break their bones."

"No, it just goes on and on. Think, Ella. Think."

Then she tells me that the sparks are flying about her field.

"I smell jasmine," she says.

I tell her that I don't know what that means. I tell her to watch the shape of her field and be careful. Then she tells me that there are sparks flying about the field and lots of blue light.

"You quit trying to talk," I say. "We'll talk again. Soon."

"Louis, I—"

And then her voice is gone. I lie still and wonder what's going on back in Mississippi and if there will ever be an end to it.

I concentrate hard and talk to Alice. My field pops and crackles. Then I smell cinnamon.

"Careful, Lou," Ernie says.

"I will be," I say.

So I lie back and talk quietly with my friends. I tell them about Ella Sabine and they feel bad about her. We talk and I feel better. My friends' voices wrap about me as we talk on and on into what is neither day nor night.

Scott Ely

Chapter 14

Wendell stood on the railroad bridge with Anse Carter. It was cooler out over the water but not much, the night air thick and heavy. Wendell smelled cinders and creosote and Anse. There was always an unwashed smell about him, that effluvium compounded of cigarette smoke and boiled peanuts, which Anse ate in great quantities, and tonight of sweat. That scent of sweat on Anse was unusual. Sometimes he wondered if Anse was like a dog, sweating through his tongue. Anse still had his blue, grease-stained suit coat on, while Wendell was in shirt sleeves. Wendell had installed the shower in the cabin specifically for the purpose of allaying the scent of the man, but Anse seldom used it. He supposed they would have to jump in the river if a train caught them on the tracks. Then they'd both smell of fish and the run-off from the slaughter house. Hudson was always threatening to shut them down for dumping in the river. Off to the northwest were the lights of Pine, a curved glow above the trees.

"He should be here," Wendell said.

Anse nodded and peered over the edge of the trestle. Wendell wondered how he could see so well in the dark. He carried a flashlight but didn't plan on having to use it. Once he had seen Anse shoot a hummingbird out of the air with the pistol, the bird exploding into a shower of tiny green feathers. It was like magic, Wendell thought. The boy would be simple for Anse.

But Wendell didn't like being exposed on the tracks. He reflected that he should have given Anse the job and then walked back to town. He could have gone to have a drink someplace, be seen by people.

"Is it coming out again?" Anse asked.

He rubbed his neck and then looked at his hand as if he could see blood in the darkness. The old woman had started to struggle to breathe. Wendell had been worried she might die on them so he ordered Anse to pull the tape off her mouth. Anse hadn't wanted to take the tape off. She'd already tried to bite him once.

It had been done to frighten her. He reflected on how it had gone wrong. But he hoped some good would come out of that. The next person who started a strike would think twice. But it was still an accident. She had bitten Anse on the neck, and he, recoiling in disgust, had dropped her in the Tire Gator. Wendell had never seen a person killed like that. It was the only time Anse had ever failed him. Well, Wendell thought, you put your faith in white trash and sooner or later they let you down. He'd made Anse wipe off the trailer hitch and the side of the truck when Anse wanted to run, leaving behind the evidence that could send them both to Parchman. He'd made him find the bolt cutters. He would see that Anse finished the job, made everything right. Twenty years ago her death wouldn't have been a problem. No one would have cared. Now there was going to be trouble.

"We missed him," Wendell said.

Anse shook his head.

"He ain't had time to get this far."

"He'll drift down here after a while."

It was Hudson's fault, Wendell thought. He could have had Ella Sabine hauled off by the police that very first day. Maurice could be hurt by all this. Maurice needed to remain mayor. Things needed to stay the same.

A breeze stirred the leaves of the riverbank trees; the river gurgled against the trestle pilings. Somewhere upstream the boat was creeping along in the slow-moving current. He wanted to be with a woman, not here on the trestle. After this was over he was going to the Leather & Lace Club and take some dancer into the back room.

His father Marion would be proud of him. That was why he'd left

Scott Ely

the house and property to him and not to Alice. Alice had been high and mighty up there in New York until she got arthritis. She could've gone to Ole Miss and gotten a teaching certificate and taught music in the public schools. Instead she preferred to give lessons at home, those students filling the house with their out-of-tune scraping. That was one reason he'd built the apartment at his office. And her daughter Rosalind was crazy. It wasn't that rocket in Vietnam. She'd been crazy before she'd gone over with that garage band of hers. It was Alice's fault, letting that girl have her way from the moment she was born until Rosalind got used to doing whatever she wanted. Rosalind was what came of having babies without getting married.

Anse nudged his shoulder and pointed into the darkness. He was still rubbing his neck.

"There," Anse said.

Anse squatted down and Wendell with him. Wendell could see nothing in the darkness. The moon was not up yet. He stared hard at the lighter darkness of the river but could still see nothing. Anse had said it was there. He believed him.

"Ain't nobody in it," Anse said.

Wendell turned the flashlight on the river below. There was nothing.

"Over there," Anse said.

Wendell turned the beam where Anse's arm pointed, the boat almost directly below them and to the left. Like Anse had said, it was empty.

"You get down there and look in it," Wendell said. "See if he left anything. You wipe clean what you touch. You get done, meet me at the car."

Anse moved away from him in the darkness.

Before Wendell was off the trestle Anse was already in the water and swimming toward the boat.

Wendell sat in the car and smoked a cigarette. He should have sent Anse alone but had been afraid Anse would kill her. Now he was an accessory to murder. He hoped Anse would find the boy's body floating in the river. He wondered how far he could push John Stone, the chief of police. He'd helped get John his job. He'd hate to miscalculate about John and do time at Parchman because of it. If you knew people well enough, if they owed you favors, something could always be worked out. He noticed his hands were shaking as he lit a fresh cigarette. Again he thought of the girls at the Leather & Lace club. A session with one of them would calm him, put him in a state where he could think clearly.

But Wendell didn't like slipping off into the state where he thought only of death and sex. He hadn't been there since the war and remembered how then too the two had interlocked, getting mixed up in his mind and making him feel uneasy. For a moment he was back in a Normandy hedgerow and there were Germans about, he trying to concentrate on the Germans while at the same time thinking of a French girl in a hayloft, how she had hair on her legs and under her arms. He took a series of slow deep breaths to calm himself.

He heard footsteps on the gravel; Anse opened the driver's door. The smell of Anse, heightened by the water, filled the car. Wendell would have preferred the river smell. Anse's hair was wet, and the man was running his fingers through it.

"Ain't nothing there," Anse said. "Just a bullet hole in the seat."

"Make sure you get rid of that pistol," Wendell said.

"You'll get me a new one?" Anse asked.

"We don't find that boy it won't matter much," Wendell said savagely. "We'll both be spending the rest of our lives in Parchman. That's if we're lucky. Remember you didn't like it much last time you was there."

"You think he's out in the woods?"

"I don't know where he is. You drop me at the office and put this car back where you found it. You watch that Sabine woman's place. I'll look around town for him. It's one o'clock now. You meet me at the Leather & Lace at three. Don't you be late."

Wendell thought, as he opened the office door, that no one would find it unusual he was working late. He took a .45 military issue automatic out of his desk drawer, one he'd worn all the way from Normandy to Berlin, and stuck it in the waistband of his pants. As he went out the door, he was trying to decide what kind of story he would make up about why he had shot a ten year old boy. It would be easier if the boy were four or five years older. Everyone knew they became dangerous then. That was the age when they began to blow policemen's heads off with shotguns.

He got in the car and drove through French Town. No one would think that was unusual either. He owned much of the property there. He had a right to inspect what belonged to him anytime he wanted. The best method, he decided, would be just to shoot the boy the moment he found him. No, he thought, he'd find him and then let Anse do it. He turned off Longstreet, the light of the town behind him, and drove up River Street past the old woman's house. There was no sign of Anse. Maybe he had already found the boy. Shoot him and get rid of the pistol, he thought. He hoped Anse remembered to get rid of the pistol.

After two hours of driving Wendell was frantic. He'd taken the big pistol out and laid it on the seat beside him. During that time he'd seen only a few people coming home late from the bars or an after hours club and a drunk asleep beneath a streetlight. He'd stopped and laughed at that. The whole street was dark for a block and the drunk was asleep under a streetlight.

He gave up and went to the Leather & Lace Club. He didn't waste time, just uttered one word to the woman who ran it.

"Mona."

"Yes, sir, Mr. Loom," Mrs. Mabis said. "You just go right back and make yourself comfortable."

He left the big room where a few men were watching a girl wrap herself around a brass fireman's pole to the accompaniment of rock music. Mrs. Mabis was proud of that pole, which Wendell had arranged for her to get when they tore down the old firehouse.

Wendell poured himself a glass of whiskey and gulped a couple of swallows. Then he sat on the couch. Mrs. Mabis had decorated the room, he supposed. The room reminded him of the cheap living rooms in the subdivisions on the western side of town. There was a painting on black velvet of a bullfighter and two pictures of cowboys fighting Indians. On the wall above his head were two framed and autographed pictures of men in leisure suits. Wendell didn't know either one of them.

Mona came in dressed in a black leotard and warm-up socks around her ankles. She didn't say a word, just started going through a

A Song For Alice Loom

stretching routine.

"I didn't pay to see a ballet," Wendell said.

Mona handed him a condom.

"Do I look like I'm queer?" Wendell said.

Mona shrugged and pulled off the leotard.

Wendell leaned back on the couch while Mona knelt before him. One thing about Mona, she knew how to give a blowjob.

He'd been married for a time years ago when he was just out of college. She was a good woman, but he just couldn't stay out of the bars or leave other women alone. Now a woman had ruined everything for him. Ella Sabine, who probably couldn't even remember the last time she'd been with a man. He chuckled at his own joke and Mona looked up at him. He closed his eyes and ignored her.

Maybe, he thought, it wasn't too late. If he could just get himself out of this fix, then he might marry and have a son to carry on the business. It wouldn't be a young woman. You couldn't trust them. He might call up an old girl friend or two from college, see if they were available. He still knew how to court women: bring them flowers and take them out to dinner. He was a good dancer. They could adopt a child. No, he thought, it would have to be a child with his blood. The woman would have to be young, and if she was going to be young, she might as well be as young as Mona. The pleasant thoughts of firm breasts and smooth, unwrinkled skin ran through his mind. But then the image of the boy appeared again and ruined everything.

Mona put her hand on him.

"I ain't paying for that," he said. "I can do that myself."

Mona sighed and resigned herself to her job.

He pushed the boy out of his mind. It wouldn't look good when the police talked to Mona if she told them he paid and got nothing for it.

Wendell gave Mona a big tip for her trouble. She was still mad about not getting to go through her routine and didn't say much.

Out in the bar Anse was sitting on a stool watching a girl swing on the brass pole.

"Let's go," Wendell said.

"I got to finish my beer," Anse said.

"Bring it. We're leaving."

Scott Ely

They went out of the club. The half moon was up, just over the trees.

"The boy?" Wendell asked.

Anse shook his head.

"What are we gonna do?" Anse asked.

"Nothing," Wendell said. "He may have fallen out of that boat and drowned. It was dark. He might not recognize us. Can't do nothing but wait."

"I got some cousins in California," Anse said.

Wendell reached out and took him by the arm.

"You're not going to do anything like that," he said. "You will suck it up and stay put."

"Yes, sir," Anse said.

Anse reached in his pocket.

Wendell flinched. For a moment he thought Anse was going to draw the gun he had promised to get rid of. But instead Anse pulled out the skull of a dog, most of its teeth missing.

"Mad dog skull," Anse said. "I remember when they shot it. She came out of the house with a butcher knife and cut off its head."

"Where'd you get it?" Wendell asked.

"Out of the house. She's got all sorts of things there. They say she was a voodoo woman. I can sell this to some nigger."

"Goddamit! You idiot! What else did you take?"

"Nothing."

"And the gun?"

"Where nobody'll ever find it."

"Get rid of that thing."

Anse dropped the skull in the gravel lot.

He stamped on it with the heel of his shoe, the dried bones shattering with a crunch, and ground the fragments into the gravel.

"It's gone," Anse said and laughed.

They got in the car, Anse at the wheel.

"Take me home," Wendell said. "I want you out looking for that boy."

He didn't know if he would be able to sleep but he was going to try. Anse could sleep anywhere. He had seen him curl up on a hardwood floor like a dog and go sound asleep in five minutes.

A Song For Alice Loom

They drove through the deserted streets. Wendell comforted himself with the picture of the rescue squad pulling the body of the boy from that brown water.

Scott Ely

Chapter 15

Larue sat at the table across from Rosalind drinking a Coke. He'd been very quiet. Rosalind guessed that he was thinking about what happened to Ella. Rosalind wanted to comfort him but didn't know how.

"You're safe here," Rosalind said.

She imagined that she'd said it to him ten times since they entered the cabin.

"She flew up over the river," Larue said. "Gone down to the ocean to be with my Daddy. He works on a shrimp boat. He was an airborne ranger."

Larue drained the last of his Coke. He was satisfied with that account of what had happened. He could close his eyes and see Miss Ella clearly anytime he wanted. The voice of the spirit hadn't returned. Now the image of Miss Ella ascending was much more real to him than that of the bodiless voice.

"Who?" Rosalind asked.

Over Larue's shoulder a cloud of moths flew round and round the light at the end of the boat dock.

"Miss Ella," Larue said. "She up and gone."

Rosalind decided to ignore him.

"You get yourself another Coke-a-cola," she said.

Larue went to the refrigerator and opened the door. The light shined in his face, and a cloud of fog rolled out of the freezer. He returned with the drink. The air conditioner had come on briefly, coughed and rumbled a few times and then quit. So they'd opened the windows, and now the last of the stale air was being blown out by a breeze off the lake.

He imagined Miss Ella following the gentle loops of the Pearl to the Gulf. He imagined the wind ruffling that black dress, she holding onto her hat with one hand, that green ribbon blowing out behind her.

"Up in the air," Larue said.

Rosalind listened to the hum of the refrigerator. A moth banged against the screen, drawn by the light over the table.

"She's dead," Rosalind said.

Larue grinned at her and took a drink from the bottle.

Rosalind wished he'd break down and cry so she could hold him in her arms. They were kin, the same blood flowing in their veins. Only Lou Sabine, if he had been real and her mother had not made him up, must have been very light, for Rosalind saw nothing Negroid when she looked in the mirror. Her nose was thin, her brown hair straight.

"She a voodoo woman," Larue said.

It was the same discussion they'd had in the car. Now Rosalind wanted to take the boy by the shoulders and shake him. She wished she'd hidden him in town and gone to take a look at the Tire Gator herself.

"It doesn't matter," Rosalind said. "Even voodoo women die."

The bluntness of her statement made Rosalind feel uncomfortable.

"She fell but she rose up," Larue said.

Larue saw her dress billowing in the wind as Miss Ella ascended into the night sky.

"Larue—" Rosalind began.

"Fell but rose," Larue said.

Larue thought of Michael Jordan going up for a dunk in one of those tennis shoe commercials. It had been like that, just as if Michael Jordan had dunked the ball and then kept going up and up, over the backboard and the heads of the crowd.

"Just like on the TV," Larue said.

Scott Ely

"What?" Rosalind said.

Perhaps the boy was hyperactive, she thought. Drinking all that Coke had done this to him.

"Rose up like Michael Jordan," Larue said.

"You saw him drop her in the machine?" Rosalind asked.

"Yes, ma'am."

"You know what the machine does?"

"Chews up tires."

Rosalind felt sick. She reached over and took the Coke bottle and pressed it against her cheek. It was awful thinking about Ella falling on those blades. She'd take Larue to Steven, her therapist. He was supposed to be good with children. He could tell her what to do.

"You want some Coke?" Larue asked.

He shoved the bottle across the table to her.

"No, thanks," she said, pushing it back to him.

Larue drained the rest of the bottle in one long swallow.

"I'm going fishing in the morning," Larue said.

Larue thought of his chances of catching a glimpse of Miss Ella at sunrise. But he would have to go to the river to do that. She'd be over moving water, going down to the sea.

"You can catch bream off the dock," she said. "Do you know how to swim?"

"Yes, ma'am," he said.

The moth bumped against the screen again. The cicadas were shrill from the trees.

"He wants to come in," Larue said.

Rosalind remembered, the image startling to her in its clarity, of catching those moths as a child, how the surface of their wings came off on her hands like talcum powder.

"It's the light," she said.

"Mr. Wendell turned off our lights," he said.

"You're safe here."

"I sleep with Miss Ella."

"You can sleep with me."

Larue thought of lying next to this woman's unwrinkled body.

"We can leave a light on," Rosalind said.

"Don't need no light," Larue said. "I ain't scared of the dark."

A Song For Alice Loom

Larue thought of Anse Carter. How he could come up through the darkness to the cabin, walking through it just like it was daylight.

"Anse Carter can see in the dark," Larue said.

"Nonsense," she said. "That's just a story people made up. Cats can see in the dark. Anse Carter can't."

She'd have to take the boy firmly in hand, she thought. Ella Sabine had filled his head with nonsense about voodoo. That and the shock of seeing the murder had produced all this fantasy about Ella flying off.

"Anse Carter kin to y'all?"

Rosalind laughed.

"No, he just works for Wendell."

"You think Mr. Hudson would let me keep one of his fishing poles?" Larue asked.

"You can have one," she said.

"Now?"

"You pick one out. But then you're going to bed."

The rods were on a rack on the wall beside the fireplace. Rosalind always marveled at how very neat the cabin was, too neat for a bachelor.

Larue returned with a rod and reel.

She put him to bed. He wanted to take the rod and reel to bed with him, but she persuaded him to lean it against the wall. Larue went to sleep almost immediately. He slept in his airborne T-shirt and a pair of underwear in need of washing. After he was sleeping soundly, she undressed him and put his clothes in the washer. He groaned in his sleep but did not wake.

"Are you with Alice?" the voice said.

Larue sat up in bed. Rosalind was moving about in the kitchen, but she wasn't talking to him. He searched for a speaker, but it was as it had been on the river. Just darkness all around him. The doorway was a rectangle of light. Rosalind was running water in the kitchen.

"Rosalind," he said.

"That's good," the voice said.

Saki and Ernie are mad at me. They're mad and frightened at the same time. My field is pulsing, and as if in sympathy theirs are too. The same thing happened when I tried to talk with those dead Americans in Cambodia.

Stop, Saki says.

You'll destroy us, Ernie says.

Ernie starts telling me about how the bottom of the ocean looks when there's a storm. But I ignore him and concentrate on the boy.

"Miss Ella is down at the beach," Larue whispered. "She's with my father. That's where I'm going."

"You stay with Rosalind," the voice said.

"No, I'm going to the ocean."

I start to protest. But then my field goes crazy. Sparks fly everywhere. And Miss Ella breaks in.

"You ain't going nowhere," she says. "You stay like he done told you."

"Larue," I say.

"You set that boy right," she says. "You cut up Wendell Loom and Anse Carter. Feed 'em to the turtles."

"Love," I say. "Love."

"The ocean," Larue says.

"Kill them," she says.

"No," I say.

But then the field explodes in a blaze of colors. I lie very still, drawing my legs up and put my arms over my head, like a fetus in a womb. Saki and Ernie are screaming for me to stop.

"Larue!" Miss Ella says. "Larue!"

Rosalind made a pot of coffee. In the morning she'd take Larue to the FBI. That would be the end of Wendell and Anse. She took the notebook entitled LOU SABINE out of her briefcase.

> When I heard him blow the saxophone, I knew he was
> the one.

Her mother had told her that. Rosalind read on, her mother's words covering the page.

> I was living in Greenwich Village. At first I thought
> he was a white man, but then I knew. I asked a friend to
> introduce me. You can imagine my shock when I heard
> that name Sabine. He was a beautiful man. He kept his
> fingernails so nice. He was a better musician than I. When

he ate a fish at a restaurant, he'd leave a perfect skeleton on his plate, not a bone out of place. I remember seeing his face when he heard the name Loom. He said, "There've been some Looms in my past." He thought it was funny. He didn't care. And his not caring made me not care either. So it was easy to fall in love with him.

One day we were walking in Central Park. It was the Sunday of Pearl Harbor. By then he'd told me his family history, how his grandfather Leonidas had been Henry Loom's body servant and had deserted to the Yankee side.

Times were flush for Lou then. He had plenty of work and we ate in the best restaurants. We heard someone running across the park shouting to a friend on a bench that the Japanese had bombed Pearl Harbor. Then he volunteered. In 1944 he came home on leave. That's when I got pregnant with Rosalind. I wrote him about her. It made him happy. He was proud to be a father. I never saw him again.

The washer stopped. Rosalind took the clothes out and put them in the dryer. She heard Larue moan in his sleep. She went into the room. He'd gotten up and put the fishing pole into the bed with him. She removed it and propped it against the wall again. She read more of the notebook. None of it was really important, just a recording of places they went to dinner and people they met and the places where Lou got to play his music.

She drank more coffee.

The dryer stopped. She took his clothes out and after folding them, put them on the table. Then she took a flashlight and a fresh cup of coffee and went out of the cabin. She shined the light on the ground before her, on the lookout for snakes, and walked to the dock. There at the end was a screened-in enclosure.

She sat in a canvas chair and watched the moths circle around the light. Occasionally one would hit it and fall, momentarily stunned into the water, where fish would strike at it, the splash sounding huge in the night. She looked out on the lake and the lights of other people's boat docks. Most of the cabins were now dark. The lake was the shape of a crescent, bellied out away from the river, Hudson's cabin near the tip of the northernmost horn. At the south end was a dam used to control the level of the water where the lake joined the Mississippi.

She knew she was not going to sleep as she watched the moths circle the light. Occasionally one was taken by bullbats, which swooped among them. She would sit in the chair and wait for daybreak and the FBI office to open in Vicksburg.

Instead of thinking of the murder or Larue, she thought of Peyton. Peyton's blue eyes and the feel of his body against hers. How he made her laugh. She thought of Vietnam. It wasn't fair that things were so uncertain between them. It was like when the cabin flooded and for months and months there was the smell of mud, a faint fish-like scent. With time that went away, but the memory of what Cale Nathan had done to her had not. The memory was like a needle stuck in the groove of a record. She played it over and over in her mind; she had let it destroy her life. Now she'd wished that she'd faced him, even killed him, a way of purging him from her memory forever. The crime of taking his life was something she didn't think would haunt her. But then she thought of how he'd killed himself amid those green hills. She resolved that she'd think no more of the sergeant. She lay back in the chair and looked across the smooth, seamless blackness of the lake and thought of Peyton holding her.

Chapter 16

The birds woke Rosalind at dawn. Patches of mist covered the lake. Off toward the river the sun was beginning to rise over a stand of cypresses, a dark green wall against the brown water. The smooth surface of the lake was dimpled with rising fish. A gar rolled, gulping air. She got up, feeling stiff. She went to wake Larue and let him make some casts while she fixed breakfast. Then they'd drive in to Vicksburg and talk to the FBI, who could keep Larue safe until the trial.

She walked into the bedroom and found the bed empty. Then she checked the bathroom. Empty too. In the three-room cabin she was out of places to look. She went outside and walked around the cabin calling his name. Then she went back inside. The fishing rod was gone too. That might mean he'd simply gotten up early to go fishing. Her purse was open. She sat down on the bed and went through it. He'd taken one hundred dollars and left her a hundred. She sat on the bed for a while with the purse in her lap. The boy's smell was still in the bed, a sour locker room scent of sweat and unwashed clothes. It was funny, she thought, but it occurred to her that she would always remember that smell and connect it with him.

She drove the car slowly along the road, hoping she might overtake him. In the cabins people were still asleep. She saw bass boats, a pirogue upside down in a yard, canoes, a sailboat. She checked the docks of the deserted cabins. A flock of mallard ducks was on one and a sleeping dog on another. A fawn the people in a neighboring cabin had made a pet of browsed in a yard. But no little boy. She drove out to the highway, hoping she'd find him walking along the road. But there was nothing. She tried the other side of the lake where she asked two men cutting up a tree if they had seen a little black boy. They told her they had been there all morning and had seen only adults going fishing.

Rosalind wondered if Anse Carter had somehow found the boy. If that was true, then Larue was dead. They'd find his body in the lake in a few days. The image of him floating, arms and legs spread, the body not ready to rise yet, slowly filling with gas, was a startling one she hadn't expected. It upset her so much she had to pull the car over. She decided she'd return to the cabin and have a cup of coffee.

She went into the cabin, hoping Larue would be there, maybe with a string of fish. He'd want her to cook them for his breakfast. The cabin was empty. Hudson's rods were neatly in the rack, the fireplace had wood laid across the andirons although it would be months before a fire was needed, the hunting and fishing prints were all in place where Hudson had hung them too high, the windows curtainless but all the panes recently cleaned. She sat at the table and waited for the water to boil, thinking not of Larue but curtains for the windows. She made coffee and drank it slowly in small sips.

Larue was gone. Probably to look for Ella, whose death he'd simply refused to accept. She could imagine his despair and how out of that anger and fear he'd simply chosen to believe she was alive. Anse hadn't come in the night for the boy. Larue had taken the money and gone to find the old woman.

She shut up the cabin and drove the road around the lake one last time. The vista unreeled on either side of her: cabins, trees, ducks now in the lake, swallows swooping low to drink, the men with the chain saw. She had no idea where he'd gone. At least Anse had no better chance of finding him than she. She thought of the small boy out on the highway with a hundred dollars.

Rosalind drove out of the Delta on Highway 61 toward Vicksburg, the bluffs rising up out of the flat land. All the time she hoped she'd see Larue with his thumb out on the side of the road. She passed a group of people, men and women fishing at a bridge where the highway ran over a creek. The women wore long gingham dresses with wide-brimmed straw hats, the men in overalls. They were all old. She stopped and asked them if they'd seen a little boy with a fishing rod. They hadn't.

It was late morning by the time she arrived at the courthouse. The town was spread out over the bluffs, sloping down toward the river.

At a newsstand she bought a *Pine Sentinel*. She hadn't expected to see anything about Ella Sabine, but there it was. WOMAN DIES IN TIRE GATOR. A picture below of the Tire Gator surrounded by yellow barrier tape and police cars. The woman, and they knew it was a woman only because of her clothing, had been found by a bum who had spent the night asleep on the seat of one of the garbage trucks. He'd been roused from sleep by delirium tremens. Catfish walking on his chest, he'd claimed. At first the police hadn't believed him about what he had found in the Tire Gator. But just in case, someone went to look. There was not much else, except that the police had leads and were investigating.

She imagined Larue buying the paper off a rack and reading about Ella. What would the boy think? She wondered if he'd still cling to that image of her flying off above the treetops. But he might not be able to read. That would not be unusual.

Rosalind folded up the paper. Then she went in search of the FBI office. She found two agents drinking coffee out of white styrofoam cups and eating doughnuts. They were in their shirtsleeves and wore their pistols in holsters attached to their belts. Here, she thought, was the solution to all of it. They could worry about finding Larue and, once found, protecting him from Wendell and Anse Carter. Then for the first time she thought about protecting herself.

"My name is Rosalind Loom and I know who killed Miss Ella Sabine," she said.

She showed them the front page of the paper.

The men put on their jackets.

"You should report it to the police in Jackson," the blond one said.

His hair was curly and cut short. The other was not as good looking. It was his nose, Rosalind thought. His nose was too big and his ears stuck out.

Scott Ely

"I'm Agent Anderton and this is Agent Wright," the curly-haired man said.

They all shook hands. Agent Wright got her a cup of coffee.

"We just have jurisdiction over federal crimes," Agent Anderton explained. "But we'll call the Pine police for you."

"Civil rights," Rosalind said. "Ella Sabine's civil rights were violated. That's a federal crime." She'd thought about that before, the answer all ready for them.

She explained to them about Ella picketing the garbage department.

"Maybe," Agent Wright said. "We'll have to check with the federal district attorney. You tell us about it first. Then we can decide."

He then asked her a series of questions.

"You've always worked part time?" Agent Wright asked.

"Just as soon as I finish my dissertation, I'm going to get a permanent job," she said.

The agents looked at each other.

"And you didn't actually see the murder," Agent Anderton said. "But you know who did."

She told them about Larue.

"You find him," she said. "They saw him. Wendell will have him killed."

All the coffee had made her nervous, and she realized that she was trembling.

"Are you ok?" Agent Wright asked.

He put his hand on her shoulder. She began to cry. Somehow she was glad it was him instead of Agent Anderton. He was like an older brother. He handed her a handkerchief, which had JBW embroidered on the corner. It was neatly folded and smelled of the laundry.

They had her tell her story to the federal district attorney, a little man with glasses, dressed in a pinstriped suit. Mr. Caldwell kept blowing his nose with tissue from a box he kept on his desk. He complained someone had let a cat in the office. He was allergic to cats.

She waited in a room alone where she read the newspaper story again. She read the rest of the paper, including some of the classifieds, before they returned to get her.

A Song For Alice Loom   125

They met in Mr. Caldwell's office.

"We want you to go to Alabama just like you told your mother," Mr. Caldwell said.

"Aren't you going to put Anse Carter and Wendell in jail?" she asked.

"We'll talk to the Pine police," Mr. Caldwell said.

He took a tissue and blew his nose again. She noticed she still had Agent Wright's handkerchief and handed it to him.

"Don't do that," she said. "Wendell helped the chief get his job."

The agents and the district attorney looked at one another.

"Jesus," Agent Anderton said.

Mr. Caldwell looked hard at him. Agent Anderton adjusted his tie.

"We can't go to court without the boy," Mr. Caldwell said.

"He'll have a fishing rod with him," she said.

Agent Wright wrote it down.

"If you don't put them in jail and they find Larue, you won't have a witness," she said.

Agent Wright escorted her out of the office. She went downstairs to the lobby and then outside. On a bench under a tree she sat until she felt calm enough to drive. She wondered how much she'd tell Peyton. Probably everything. She just hoped that the agents believed her and didn't tell it all to the Pine Police Force. Once the agents found Larue, Wendell and Anse Carter would be finished.

Then she drove out of town on the interstate. She'd call Peyton later and tell him she was coming. Right now he was in class. At every interchange she looked for Larue, who might be standing there on the on ramp trying to hitch a ride.

By now the police had probably found Larue. He would be easy to find. A small boy like that. She recalled his fixation on the idea of Miss Ella flying up out of the machine. To the ocean, Larue had said. He believed she was flying to the ocean. She'd forgotten to tell the agents that. She stopped to call them but then changed her mind. She suspected they didn't believe her account. They might take days to make up their minds. She'd find Larue. He'd told her his father worked on a shrimp boat. That would be a place to begin. She would find him herself.

At the first opportunity she turned south toward the Gulf. And if Anse Carter was on the boy's trail, she'd deal with him herself. She'd find Larue. Wendell and Anse Carter would be spending their time growing cotton at Parchman.

Chapter 17

Alice watched Wendell and Anse Carter talking beneath the pecan tree as she put the breakfast dishes in the dishwasher. Anse sat on an iron bench. Wendell stood. Anse had a bandage on his neck. She thought of Wendell as a child playing beneath that same tree with his friends. They were building a tree house in it, and her father had interrupted her practice to send her out to make them stop driving ten penny nails into the tree.

"They do that, it won't bear," he'd said. "It won't bear."

So she'd gone out in the yard and taken the hammer and nails away from him until he promised to build the tree house in a big oak behind the garage. That tree was gone now, toppled by the remnants of a hurricane which blew up from the Gulf. Both men had that overly serious look of small boys at play. She wished Wendell would sell his rental property and get rid of Anse Carter.

Wendell saw Alice watching them from the kitchen window.

"Where is he?" Wendell asked.

Anse lolled on the bench, wearing a pair of dark glasses against the glare, which penetrated even beneath the tree.

"He ain't in this town," Anse said.

Wendell almost got mad but checked himself. Anse knew something and wanted to enjoy the power of withholding the information until the last possible moment.

Scott Ely

"I knew you'd be the one to find out," Wendell said.

Anse grinned.

"His daddy got work on a shrimp boat out of Biloxi," Anse said. "I expect we'll find him there."

"Who told you?"

Anse grinned again.

"That's the good part. I didn't even have to ask. I went around early this morning to get me some breakfast at the Sportsman's. One of them nigger garbage truck drivers was in there talking with another nigger. He was laughing about how that nigger woman upset the whole garbage department. Said he'd expect the boy'd go to his daddy in Biloxi. Didn't even have to risk asking."

"We can't go running off to Biloxi on that kind of information," Wendell said.

Anse Carter's face fell.

"He ain't in this town," he said. "I looked. I know the places a boy like that would go."

Wendell considered how Anse had never failed him before. No one knew French Town better than Anse.

"OK," Wendell said. "You go down there and tie up the loose ends."

Anse seemed sure of himself, and they had no better alternative.

"You let me take the car," Anse said. "All that water and sand. It's bright."

"Get yourself an extra pair of dark glasses," Wendell said. "I'll rent you a car. Too many people know my car."

"It wouldn't have the dark glass."

"You can stand it this one time. I'm going to drop in on Chief Stone today, find out how much he knows. Don't you get yourself caught doing it. Work fast but don't get caught."

"He won't never know what happened."

Anse made a sucking sound. Wendell was sure he'd wait until dark, all that light shining off the sand and sea more than he could stand.

Wendell took out his billfold and gave Anse money for the trip.

"I ain't got a pistol," Anse complained.

"You don't need to be buying another pistol right now," Wendell said. "He's just a boy."

A Song For Alice Loom   129

"But he's lively. Got away from us once already."

"You can't buy a pistol. You have to wait three days on it."

Anse grinned.

"I'll have one in an hour. Won't nobody be able to trace it."

Anse went into the cabin. Wendell walked across the yard to his car. Wendell thought maybe Alice was right about Anse. He was the kind of person you kept out of the house, and even the guest cabin might be too close. The best thing that could happen would be for Anse to kill the boy and then be killed by someone else. Wendell thought of trying to make that happen, but it was all too complicated, and if anything went wrong he'd come out the loser. He'd go see Chief Stone. Wendell didn't like to operate in the dark.

Alice watched Anse come out of the cabin carrying a black vinyl bag, the kind soldiers carried when they went on leave. The bag didn't look like much was in it because it didn't pull his shoulder down. She went to the kitchen door and watched them get in Wendell's car and leave, Anse at the wheel.

She finished the dishes and sat at the table and drank a cup of coffee. Today Lou had been trying to speak with her. His voice was a gentle murmur in her ears, like the sound of the sea. Sometimes it was like that for weeks and then suddenly his words would appear as clear as a bell.

I don't know why I can't talk with Alice. But I've got to be careful. Our fields are stable now. As Saki tells us a story about his grandfather and a jade vase, I carefully try to make her hear me.

Alice began to get ready for the funeral of Ruth Sabine and her daughter at eleven. She hadn't been to a funeral in a long time. When she returned to Pine, after the arthritis struck her hands, they were burying soldiers from the Korean War. She felt comfortable at the soldiers' funerals, Lou's brothers-in-arms; it was as if she were watching Lou buried over and over.

Sometimes she and Lou talked of love at those funerals. At other times all she could hear was the murmur. But he was always there. She could count on it. She'd always stood a little off to one side of the party so she could whisper to him. People would think she was saying a prayer for the dead.

That first graveside visit took place on a cold November day. The

Scott Ely

honor squad had fired their volleys, the sound of the last shots trailing off into a grove of cedars on the hill above the grave. They'd folded the flag, and an officer wearing white gloves had given it to a woman who in turn gave it to a young boy. The boy, standing stiffly by his mother, her hand resting on his shoulder, held the flag in two hands before him as they began to fill the grave.

"I'll never marry," she'd told him.

And Lou had laughed, that beautiful laugh of his.

"I'm dead," he'd said.

"You'll stop talking to me."

"No. You've got to live. Love is what is important."

"I can't."

"Try."

Their conversations had been like that. She couldn't imagine loving another man, even if Lou had said it was all right to do that. As that man caressed her, she'd be waiting for the sound of Lou's voice in her ears, its insubstantiality better than being held in any lover's arms.

Pine had three cemeteries. The old one was called Hunt Gardens. If they'd shipped Lou's body home, he would have been buried there. It had an iron fence around it and after the Korean War was pretty much full. There were already plenty of soldiers in it from World Wars I&II. So now the keeper, Mr. Lawson, who lived in the center of it in a white frame house beside a pond where he kept a flock of mallards with clipped wings, had little to do but keep the grass mowed and chase kids. The kids came to drink or smoke marijuana and make love among the tombstones. Love and death, Alice thought, it was all the same thing. Young bodies that felt the cool marble against them on a summer's night would soon rest under it.

She'd gotten to know Mr. Lawson well during the Korean War. He liked to grow flowers in the open spaces between the big oaks and poplars. Although there were some who criticized this practice—she suspected it was the florists—she approved.

The second was over to the west, established as the town, during World War I, had begun to spread out away from the river onto the high ground. It had the uninspired name of Memorial Gardens. Here there was no Mr. Lawson. Instead a succession of keepers had lived in the little white house in the center. One had murdered his wife and another had been caught digging up corpses for the wedding rings or the gold in their teeth. Finally during the Vietnam War they'd installed Mr. Fox. She remembered him as a man of thirty or so who, dressed in an Ole Miss sweatshirt, drove a lawnmower. Once Mr. Fox had played football, but all his muscle had gone to fat. Now he barely fit on the seat of the mower. She wondered if she would find him there. There was the third, a black cemetery known as Cedar Hill. She'd been there too. It had groves of cedars and a grave keeper's house, but she had never made friends with the man, who was old and hard of hearing. She tried to remember when they'd started burying whites and blacks together. She supposed it was during the Korean War.

Upstairs she laid out a simple black dress. Then she took a long bath in the huge bird-footed tub. She looked at her body under the water, her legs long and straight, but her breasts sagging, wrinkles everywhere. This was the bathtub where she had lain in scented soap bubbles while young men sat downstairs and were forced to make conversation with her father. But she thought it was a good body for a woman almost seventy. She had been mistaken for much less when she got dressed up. Her legs were still very good; she was proud of the way she looked.

They wouldn't get to the cemetery until one o'clock, she thought, as she ran more water into the tub. It was going to be very hot, and she told herself to remember to take a parasol. Still there was the murmur in her ears but no distinct words. She let her legs float free and waited for the voice to come, the light falling through the stained glass window turning the water red and yellow and green. On the window was the image of a peacock, displaying its tail. She looked up at the window, wishing she'd see Lou there, like an angel shining above her head, the glass all turned to crystal white. Sometimes it would be months between those visits from Lou Sabine.

Lou had landed in the first wave. She thought of his graceful hands on his rifle as he went through the manual of arms, under the gaze of some sergeant who had no idea how beautifully he could play. She kept a map of the island which was included in a pamphlet published by the Defense Department. She knew the waterless island well: the single volcano on the western end, the airfield, Meatgrinder Hill where so many men had died. She knew the account of the invasion

Scott Ely

almost by heart.

The two officers who had come to the house were confused when she'd told them her last name was Loom and not Sabine. Then they were embarrassed when she told them there was no marriage certificate, despite what Lou Sabine had written on the document they'd brought with them. She'd wondered at the time what they would say if she told them Lou was talking.

At ten o'clock she got out of her bath and dressed. She regarded herself in the mirror, thinking the hat with a bit of black lace on the front gave her a 1940s look. She could be going out on a date with Lou. By ten thirty she was in the car driving to the church on Market Street. She was not surprised to see the TV truck outside and the street jammed with cars, the police directing traffic. Both Maurice and Sydney Cable had expressed outrage over the deaths. It was too close to the election for either one of them to let the opportunity to attend the funeral slip by. She double parked, and leaving the car running so she could use the air conditioner, put a tape on, the strains of a Bach piano concerto filling the car. A policeman stared at her for a moment but let her stay. Alice never attended the services. She hated churches. She took off her hat and leaned her head back against the seat, careful not to ruin her hair, and closed her eyes, letting the music fill her.

Alice heard a tap, tap, tap on the window beside her. She opened her eyes and there, his face close to the window, was a seedy little man. He stepped back when she looked at him and smiled as if to apologize for disturbing her. As she looked at him more closely, she realized he was not drunk as she had first supposed and was dressed better than she'd thought. His shoes were shined, the suit new but cheap. The tie was a paisley pattern. She turned off the music and rolled down the window.

"Morning, Miss Loom," the man said.

He had a south Mississippi accent but not an educated one. Probably came from a line of farmers and small tradesmen. His voice and manner were respectable.

"Do I know you?" Alice asked.

"I'm Tom Guess," the man said. "I work for Mr. Hudson Loom. You knew my Daddy."

A Song For Alice Loom

Alice knew Grafton Guess well. He was a visitor of graveyards too. This, she thought, must be the boy he sometimes had with him when she attended those graveside ceremonies during the Vietnam War. Tom didn't look much like his father. Grafton had worked for the city too, a supervisor in the water department, who spent most of his time investigating cases of his meter readers being bitten by dogs. Grafton had talked in the same mumbling way.

"Daddy spoke of you often," Tom said.

"He was a fine man," she said.

Grafton had dressed in the same sorts of cheap suits. But there would have been no way for either of them to be elegant, even in a thousand-dollar suit. The redneck would show through. The children, if Tom had any, would have to go to college and get far away from Pine for any progress to be made. But there had been a courtly side of Grafton. Once or twice they'd had coffee together after the service, at the cafe (one of those places that specialized in home cooking and announced it on the window in big letters) across the street from the cemetery, where she was always uncomfortable, but she could tell he felt at home. He liked to joke with the waitresses and call them sweetheart.

Usually after a burial he went to visit Mr. Fox in his house. She had wondered what they talked about. Once, at the cafe, he'd started to explain about Mr. Fox's grave-digging machine, but she'd silenced him with a stare. The boy had been there, she remembered. He had started demanding that his father tell him, and the older Mr. Guess had silenced the younger with a cuff on the ear.

"We got Daddy a good spot," Mr. Guess said. "Up on that little rise under a big oak. It was a nice service."

Alice nodded in agreement. She knew the spot well.

She wondered whether Mr. Fox had pulled strings to help Mr. Guess land that choice spot. She'd felt guilty about not going to his funeral when she had read about his death in the paper. But that was long after they had stood together and watched them bury young victims of the Vietnam War, both of them always discreet enough to stand a little away from the gathering at the graveside. She'd long since stopped going to funerals.

"You going in the church?" he asked. "We're late. The mayor's there and the TV folks."

"I'm just going to the grave," she said.

"If they hadn't been in such a hurry to get 'em in the ground, they could have buried 'em all together. All except the boy. They're dragging the river for him."

"What?" she asked.

"Ella Sabine," he said. "Ain't you heard? She got missed by the neighbors. And then a woman got tossed into the tire shredder. Tire Gator they call it. It was a mess. I seen it. Old woman got missed by Mrs. Adams. She went down there and identified pieces of her dress and that tooth of a mad dog she wore around her waist on a gold chain under her clothes. They're putting her face back together so they can make sure. Got someone to come from Ole Miss to do it. But it's her all right. Suppose that lifts the spell. They'll find the boy in the river. Excuse me, ma'am, but I'm gonna miss the service."

Alice watched Tom Guess cross the street and go up the steps of the church. It was too much, too much. She could feel her eyes filling with tears, as she thought of dead Ella Sabine and the boy in the river. She got out her purse and dried her eyes with a tissue. Then she repaired the damage done to her makeup.

She turned the music back on, then turned it off. There was no murmur in her ears. She missed the sound of Lou's voice, wished she could hear it anytime, like putting her ear to a seashell. She wished he could talk for days to her, explain it all, for the dead would know of the dead. She thought of all those years she'd been drawn to the graves of the soldiers who, rendered speechless, had that kinship with Lou, a brotherhood of silence out of which she'd foolishly expected to learn something.

Ella Sabine was dead and Larue gone. Tom Guess had said the magic was lifted. She tried to find some connection between Lou's voice and her memories of the dead soldiers, the echo of rifle volleys still in her ears, and Tom Guess, and Anse Carter going out of the cabin with his little black bag, a soldier's bag, the sunlight shining off it. But she could make nothing of it. She took solace in the fact that the burial would be familiar, everything happening in a predictable order.

They came out of the church with the coffin, a TV camera trained

A Song For Alice Loom

on it from the top of a truck. Maurice came out, then Sydney Cable and a gaggle of reporters with cameras and tape recorders in their hands. Maurice was talking fast into one camera and Sydney Cable into another. They exchanged places, nodding at each other in embarrassment when they did it.

The procession was organized. She switched on the lights of the Lincoln and fell in line behind one of the limousines. The police thought she was someone important and waved her through. They drove down Market Street and turned right, policemen at the intersection blocking traffic, and onto Fortification which later changed into the old Vicksburg highway. They drove past storefronts and gas stations and then through a housing project and past a neighborhood of tree-lined streets which in her youth had been open pasture. Ahead she saw the clump of trees that marked Memorial Gardens.

At the entrance was a guard box which, as long as she could remember, never had anyone in it. Now there were policemen at the gates, waving the procession through. The gates themselves were of iron and set into a brick wall fronting the street. But it was only a kind of facade. The rest of the cemetery was encircled by chain-link fence.

As was her custom, she stood off at a little distance from the burial service. The Sabines had not received good ground. It was on the somewhat swampy lower end of the cemetery. The area had sometimes been flooded, although now she could see a low levee had been built along the bank of the creek. The ground she stood on felt slightly spongy under her feet. She saw the top of Maurice's head but not Sydney Cable's curly hair. He was much shorter. Tom Guess stood beside her.

"They're picking up garbage, right now," Tom Guess said. "I saw two trucks. With full crews."

So the strike she had read about in the papers, which was not really a strike, but a reaction to fear, was over. Again she wished Lou would talk to her, not murmur but talk. She wanted him to sing to her from the treetops. The preacher droned on and on. Off on a hilltop someone was driving a mower. She wondered if it could be Mr. Fox, but her eyes were not very good anymore even with glasses, and she couldn't see the figure on the mower clearly. It was very hot, even under the shade of her umbrella. She was sweating up her dress, could feel the sweat making furrows in her lilac-scented bath powder. She felt lightheaded but steadied herself with the thought of the indignity of fainting into the arms of Mr. Guess.

"They'll be burying her before the week's out," Mr. Guess said. "Then the boy, if they find him. Nothing but Sabine funerals for a few days."

She looked at the group around the grave, the light flashing off a camera lens, the locusts shrill in the trees, the scent of freshly cut grass drifting down on them from the mower.

"Do you think the dead can talk?" Alice asked.

"I don't know, Miss Loom," he said. "I don't hold with ghosts. Why, I'd driven a garbage truck right past Ella Sabine if Mr. Hudson had asked me."

Alice thought of Hudson and Rosalind childless. When they died, there would be no Looms to live in the house.

"Goodbye, Mr. Guess," she said.

They were lowering the coffins into the ground.

"Goodbye, Miss Loom," he said. "Someday I'll show you where Daddy is buried."

Alice hurried off toward the car, afraid she was going to be in for a lecture on waterproof caskets and the best method for keeping the side of a freshly dug grave from caving in, marginalia dear to the heart of Grafton Guess and undoubtedly passed on to his son.

Alice was relieved that she'd beaten the swarm of traffic away from the grave. At the top of a ridge she came upon a bald-headed man wearing an Ole Miss sweatshirt driving a mower across the road. But he was thin, at least as thin as a man built on the model of a fireplug could be. He must have taken up jogging. They glanced at each other. He nodded to her.

Then he was saying something to her, but she couldn't understand what because of the sound of the mower engine.

"Save them," Lou said.

The words were like perfect notes dropping out of his saxophone.

"Save them."

"Who?" she asked.

Mr. Fox was saying something to her. She ignored him.

"Save them."

Alice held her hands over her ears and listened to the beating of her heart, to her breath going in and out.

"Save who?"

"Looms and Sabines."

"How?" she asked. "How?"

Mr. Fox was shouting something at her now. She held up her hand for him to wait and concentrated hard on listening for Lou's voice. The only Sabine in need of saving she knew of was Larue.

"Save them."

"What do you mean?" she asked. "Lou?"

"Save them. Save you."

"How?"

"Love."

Then there was silence as if a switch had been thrown somewhere.

"Lou, talk to me," she said.

She wanted him to speak brilliantly to her.

"Talk to me," she demanded.

There was nothing. She was talking to the air.

"Miss Loom?"

It was Mr. Fox. He'd cut the motor. He was standing in front of her. She could smell the scent of gasoline and cut grass on him.

"Are you all right?" he asked.

"Thank you, Mr. Fox," she said. "I'm fine. I felt a little faint. The heat, I suppose."

Mr. Fox glanced up at the sky.

"Yes, ma'am," he said. "It's a hot one."

He started the mower again and drove off among the tombstones, leaving her standing motionless, waiting for Lou to speak.

"Lou?" she asked. "Dammit, speak to me."

The only reply was the songs of the birds from the trees.

"That's all?" she said. "Love?"

She considered that day on the subway when she'd first heard Lou speak. And felt love for him for the first time. That voice had changed her life. It had kept her from marrying someone in New York. It was beautiful, just the murmur of it, even when she couldn't understand the words, like a piece of music continually playing inside her.

"I can't save anyone," she said.

She was angry again.

"Lou, I can't," she shouted.

A mockingbird, disturbed by her voice, screamed at her from a tree. Other birds took up the call. It was as if she were a snake, or a hawk.

"It won't be love," she said. "It will have to be something else that saves us."

She walked back to her car. She drove through the gates where two policeman waited. They both saluted the big car. She reflected that they were confused just like she was. For them it was too many dignitaries; for her it was too many dead people.

Chapter 18

Alice drove home. That couldn't have been all he'd had to say. Love wasn't going to stop Wendell from doing as he wished. And love hadn't stopped Henry from dying or Lou from dying or Rosalind coming home from Vietnam a cripple. No, Lou was going to speak to her again and what he had to say was going to be something other than the saving of the Looms and the Sabines through love.

She thought of Ella Sabine and the boy, the one dead, the other lost. Then, as if it were an image superimposed over the woman and the child, she saw her father standing on the green lawn with the pistol at his side, the ladies gathered in little knots, their faces averted, the man lying sprawled on the grass. Her father had kicked the poles out from under an awning, and with the help of the white-coated servants, had thrown it over him. So what had been a man was transformed into a lump of gaily striped canvas.

"Love can't do everything," she said. "You could love my father and it wouldn't have changed him. Just made it easier for him to kill you."

She waited but there was no reply.

"Lou, do you hear what I'm saying?" she cried.

Again there was nothing, not even a murmur in her ears.

She was crying again and dabbed at her eyes with her handkerchief. At all those burials she had attended she'd never cried. She retraced the route back into town, the store fronts unreeling before her eyes, then the housing project with clothes hanging on lines, then the tree-lined streets of the old neighborhood, the trees disappearing as the downtown skyline sprang into view. Now she felt like driving by Hunt Gardens and having coffee with Mr. Lawson. Afterwards they would feed the ducks; he'd show her his flowers. That was peaceful and calming after a burial. But she decided she didn't want to start reliving those days. So instead she turned in the opposite direction and drove out of the concrete and brick onto the tree-lined street which would take her home.

Back at the house she sat in the car for a long time, waiting for the tape to finish. She didn't think about Ella Sabine or Larue. She didn't think about Lou's words. She just tried to let the music fill her and push everything else out of her mind.

The tape played itself out and the car was in silence. In the interim between switching off the player and stepping out of the car into the afternoon heat, she thought of Anse Carter and his traveling bag. He'd never gone anywhere before. Probably the only places he'd been in his life were Pine and Parchman. Maybe the bag meant Anse had moved out and taken a room at a boarding house. She could imagine how easily he could get all his possessions into a small bag.

Instead of going into the house, she went around back to the cabin. She hadn't been inside the cabin since she was a girl, when Mary the cook lived there. After her mother died, Mrs. Peabody, the housekeeper, let her spend the night in Mary's cabin when her father was away on business.

She pushed open the door. There was the smell of cigarettes, boiled peanuts, and the cloying scent of men's cologne. The cabin was just as she remembered it. On one wall was faded blue wallpaper, but all the others were bare, the holes in the mud chink between the logs filled in with concrete. Wendell had added running water and electricity and air-conditioning. It was cold in the cabin. There was a toilet and a shower behind a blue plastic curtain.

The metal camp cot Anse slept on was made up, and against the wall was a cheap plywood dresser with a broken mirror. A cardboard wardrobe stood against the opposite wall, one end of it sagging. The fourth wall was taken up with the fireplace, the mud-chinked chimney no longer safe to use.

A Song For Alice Loom

Alice looked around the room again: bed, dresser, wardrobe, toilet-shower. On the top of the dresser was a collection of fine black hairs. She imagined Anse Carter standing before it trimming his hair. When she opened the top drawer of the dresser, the scent of men's cologne filled the room. The empty bottle lay in pieces in the corner of the drawer next to a pair of scissors. She wondered if Anse had done it deliberately because he liked the smell or to try to cover up some other kind of smell. The second drawer was filled with sunglasses, the cheap kind they sold at Wal-mart. Some had a lens broken out of them. They had been tossed into the drawer carelessly, their frames entangled with each other. There were even two pairs of ski goggles. She looked up and saw her face in the cracked mirror, a large piece missing in the lower left hand corner. There was a pattern of dried glue on the empty space where Anse had tried to stick the glass back but failed.

She opened the next drawer. Inside was a single black sock and nothing else. Opening the fourth drawer, she found a wool sweater and some long underwear. The bottom drawer had nothing but the piece of glass from the mirror, a few peanut hulls, and a used tube of glue. Inside the wardrobe she found an old winter jacket of Hudson's. She remembered when he had received it for Christmas in the seventh grade. On a coathanger were two striped ties, one blue and the other red. The red one had a hole burned in it. Wendell had done it with a cigarette a couple of years ago when he fell asleep watching a football game on TV. On a shelf were the straw cowboy hats Anse liked to wear. She was beginning to think he intended to return, for he was never without a hat.

So he hadn't moved out. She knew she should leave, but now curiosity about the man took over. She looked behind the blue plastic curtain at the shower and toilet. There was a piece of sticky soap in the soap rack and a bottle of dandruff shampoo. The sink had a washcloth laid on it with a disposable razor on top. The trash can under it was empty. From the toilet came the faint odor of feces. There was no toilet brush or can of cleanser behind it. But the place was in better order than she'd thought possible for Anse.

The metal desk, its surface stained with what looked like spaghetti sauce, had once been in Wendell's office. Now its drawers were missing. She opened the tiny refrigerator and found a six pack of Pabst Blue Ribbon Beer, a package of processed cheese, a bowl of boiled peanuts, a dried-out onion, and the freezer full of TV dinners. Love, she thought. Love wasn't going to change Anse Carter. On the top was a frying pan, two saucepans, and a collection of silverware. Now she found herself in a kind of frenzy of discovery. She imagined a truck backed up to the porch and a couple of men throwing Anse's junk in the back to be hauled off somewhere and burned. That would leave the cabin bare and clean. She'd have it restored, the chimney repaired; it could be turned into a guest house.

She noticed a duffel bag jammed between the cot and the wall. She'd seen him carrying it back and forth to the laundry. Alice pulled it onto the bed and unsnapped the clasp, hooked through the metal eyelets at the top, and opened the bag, the sour smell of soiled clothes spilling out. She took the bag by the bottom and dumped the clothes out on the bed. It was underwear and socks and towels, thrown into the bag partly wet and now mildewed. There was also a straw hat with a green visor built into the brim. She wondered why he was planning to wash a straw hat.

Alice went to the wardrobe and returned with one of the cowboy hats. She read the hat size. It was a six, the hat shaped to accommodate Anse Carter's long, thin skull, the hat band dark with sweat. The gardening hat didn't have a size. But it had been worn on a round head. She turned on the lamp by the bed and put on her reading glasses. When she held the hat under the light she saw a collection of curly white hairs caught up in the straw above the hatband.

Then it came to her. She remembered seeing on TV Ella Sabine with a similar hat on her head as she sat in the rocking chair. So it was Anse who'd thrown Ella in the tire shredder and had stolen her hat. Wendell had been kind to him, but Anse had turned on that kindness and killed again. For some reason she thought of herself and Wendell sitting by Mary's fire and she reading a story to Mary and Wendell. Then they'd gone back to the house. It had been a very cold night. Wendell had slipped on the ice-covered steps. She'd led him wailing to the house. She sat down on the bed, ignoring the dirty clothes and the smell of mildew. She wondered if Anse was planning to wash and then wear the dead woman's hat. She could imagine him trying it on after he killed her. It must not have fit perfectly, but he could expect it in a few wearings to assume the shape of his head.

Alice took several deep breaths to calm herself. She looked at the hat. There were no marks of ownership on it. It could have been anyone's hat, anyone who had kinky white hair. Any old black woman.

"Look what they've done, Lou," she said. "How is love going to help that? What do you think Anse Carter would have to say about love?"

She stuffed the dirty clothes back into the bag, a job that filled her with disgust but nevertheless had to be done, and went out of the cabin, taking the hat with her. She crossed the yard and, seeing that only her car was in the garage, went into the house through the kitchen door. She went upstairs to her room. From her closet she took out a hat box and, removing her own hat, put the straw hat in it, tying up the string again. Then she put the box in a Macy's sack. Everyone who saw her would think she'd been shopping.

She sat on the bed and looked at the sack with its bright red lettering, listening to the hum of the air conditioning. She thought of Lou. He'd written her letters. She hadn't received any letters from Hudson's father Henry nor did she want to. Lou hadn't talked about the war or even music in his letters. Instead he told her how much he loved her and after she was pregnant how much he was going to love their child.

"Lou," she said. "Should I love Anse Carter for killing Miss Ella?"

She didn't expect him to answer. Talking to her right now was obviously difficult for him. That had happened before. But she'd have liked to hear the murmur in her ears. Love wasn't going to save Larue Sabine if he were still alive. But if Anse was in jail that might save Larue. Action, not love, was what was needed.

Alice drove to City Hall, the sack on the seat beside her. She was glad, as she walked up the stairs, that she hadn't run into Maurice or one of the other councilmen. She went into Jack Tisdale's office. He was seated behind his secretary's desk, leafing through some files. Wendell would protect Anse this time just like he'd managed to get him that light sentence at Parchman when Anse killed those men. Anse hadn't served half of it before he was paroled into Wendell's custody and came to live in the cabin.

Scott Ely

Wendell disliked Jack. That was why she had chosen him as her attorney, to make sure Wendell wouldn't meddle in her affairs. Jack would not be one to discuss her with Wendell over drinks.

"Hello, Miss Loom," he said. "Did Hudson get that fire put out?"

"What?" Alice asked.

Then she remembered Hudson complaining about a landfill fire. There was something about tires too. That was why he had that tire shredding machine. Something about a fire and tires.

"In the landfill," Jack said. "Moses has named it Charlene."

Alice thought Jack looked harried and upset. He didn't have a tie on and had rolled his shirtsleeves up. He wore such nice clothes. That was another reason she trusted him to handle her affairs. She believed he'd be as careful and methodical with them as with his clothes.

"I don't know," she said.

"Now Hudson has got his hands full with that old woman and that boy," Jack said. "They'll find that boy in the river before long."

"I need to discuss a matter with you," Alice said.

"A legal matter?"

"Yes."

Jack ushered her into his office and closed the door. There was a Bible open on his desk, a red ribbon marking the place. The floor to ceiling bookshelves were filled with books. Jack had a wife, whose name Alice could never remember. Because they didn't get along, he spent as much time at his office as possible. Alice noticed that since she'd been there last many of the law books and sets of the state code of Mississippi were gone. In their place were new books, some of them paperbacks. Others had call numbers along their spines.

"I got to be fifty years old," Jack said, motioning to the books. "And I realized I didn't know anything."

Alice took the hat box out of the package, deciding that if she didn't get down to business, Jack would talk at her all afternoon.

Jack shut up and watched her untie the string. She wondered if he thought she'd brought him stocks and bonds in a hat box. Her father had left her a little money which she'd invested.

Alice took out the hat and put it on his desk.

"I found that in Mr. Anse Carter's dirty clothes," she said. "And I think it belonged to Ella Sabine."

"That landfill fire," he said. "I knew it was a sign."

Alice had heard about Jack's Bible reading.

"God may have known about it," she said. "But Anse Carter did it. After Wendell has done so much for him."

Jack turned the hat over in his hands.

"This could be anybody's hat," he said.

She explained about the white hair.

"There's plenty of it left," she said. "Can they tell if it's hers?"

"They can tell a lot," he said.

Jack picked out one of the white hairs and held it up to the light

"I'm going to talk to Wendell," she said. "This time I don't want him calling in favors some judge owes him."

Jack sighed.

"Alice, Anse don't do a thing unless Wendell tells him."

She laughed.

"Wendell is greedy, and he is responsible for what happened to that family. But he has good impulses. Just look what he's done for Anse Carter."

"Now listen to me, Alice," Jack said. "He's your brother and it's hard for you to see . . ."

He paused, opened and closed the Bible. She was afraid he was going to read to her.

"I don't know if he was there," Jack said. "But I'd guess he ordered it."

She started to protest. He stopped her with a wave of his hand.

"I can't prove it, but it's what I think," he said. "That old woman was causing trouble for Hudson which meant trouble for Maurice and in the end trouble for Wendell. Wendell just can't afford to let Sydney Cable become mayor. And it's not because he's black. Sydney is a crusader. I believe he's honest. Not a good person to do business with from Wendell's point of view."

"Look at you," she said. "Shouting Bible verses behind closed doors. You don't know Wendell."

Jack laughed.

"Remember, Alice, you came to me," he said. "And you came to me in the first place because Wendell and I aren't friends."

Alice thought of running down the steps with Wendell's hand in

Scott Ely

hers and him tripping, sprawling across the frozen grass. His tears had been warm against her face when she picked him up.

"Wendell couldn't," she said. "He's greedy but he's a good man. He's taken care of Rosalind. He didn't have to do that. He—"

It was the sad look on Jack's face that told her it was probably true.

"What should we do?" she asked.

"Chief Stone owes Wendell for his job," Jack said. "But even Stone can't ignore murder. That would make him an accessory. But he could suppress evidence, not look in the right places. You leave this hat with me."

She stood up.

"Wait," he said. "Anse Carter will be missing it. Then he'll know."

She explained it looked like Anse had gone off on a trip.

"You leave it with me," he said. "You go on home. I'll find out about this hair."

"It's hers," Alice said.

"I know, but I just want to make sure. And, Alice, don't you decide to talk this over with Wendell. You know, have him turn himself in. A man with a murder charge hanging over him will do most anything. You be careful what you say. Anse Carter comes back, you get in the car and come straight to my office or my house. You understand?"

"Yes," Alice said.

It was difficult for her to say it, the single word sounding ludicrous. She found it strange that she wasn't frightened. She thought she would be frightened if Anse Carter returned.

Alice went out of the building with the empty hatbox in the Macy's sack and through the lobby smelling of cigarette butts in the sand-filled urns by the door. She found it disturbing to take advice from a man who believed landfill fires were signs from God. She wondered what Jack would say if she told him about her conversations with Lou Sabine. Maybe Jack would be the only one in town who wouldn't laugh at her and think she was mad.

But what Jack had said made sense to her. She still found it hard to believe Wendell had anything to do with Ella Sabine's death. She wanted it to be all Anse. She turned on another tape, the strains of Mozart's 3rd Symphony filling the car. There were beautiful things in

A Song For Alice Loom

the world. Love was one of them. She thought of Wendell destroying his own blood. She wanted Wendell and Anse in prison. There they could love or not love, but at least the rest of the world would be safe from them.

Chapter 19

Alice saw Hudson's car in the driveway. She found him sitting at the kitchen table. He held a soldering iron and was working on a toy truck. The truck had numbers drawn on it in red paint and a series of wavy lines. The kitchen was filled with the acrid scent of solder. It was as if he were a child again, putting model airplanes together on the table. He'd always been very good at such things, those big and clumsy-looking hands of his able to perform delicate work.

Hudson had heard about Miss Ella.

"Don't you imagine Wendell knows something about that?" Hudson said. "This family has a history of killing Sabines."

Alice wondered if she should tell him about the hat.

"I don't think Wendell would," she said.

Hudson smiled.

"Oh, he would, Mama," Hudson said. "She dies in my machine. It's just like those bribes to legislators. Next thing you know he'll be asking me to serve his sentence again."

Hudson thought that surely Wendell was involved but was probably too smart to get caught.

"I couldn't live with him if I thought he'd done that," she said.

"Then you better find another place to live," Hudson said. "You come stay with me."

"And Rosalind?"

"Why not."

Alice thought how Wendell might try to find a way to place it all on Hudson. Once she was certain about the hat then she'd tell Hudson.

"We don't know Wendell had anything to do with it," she said.

"And like I said," Hudson said. "We'll never know for sure. I suppose I could ask him one morning at breakfast."

"Stop it."

"I'm sorry. He's going to get away with it and there's nothing anyone can do. Maybe that boy will turn up alive. I'd like that. For the boy's sake. Maybe that boy knows some things that'll make Wendell uncomfortable."

Alice thought of Lou's words. What could love do in the face of such rapacity?

"I hope he's alive," she said.

"So do I," Hudson said. "But I've got a garbage department to run. I can't do anything for Miss Ella now. I don't know if the boy is alive or dead. If I knew where to go look for him, I'd go look. I can't touch Wendell. And it could've been voodoo people who did it." Hudson ran his fingers over the truck. "John Stone didn't want to let me have this truck. I had to get Maurice to give him a call. John said it was evidence. Well, whoever killed her didn't use the truck. They didn't use magic."

"What are you doing?" Alice asked.

She considered again how Jack had cautioned her not to tell anyone, not even Hudson. Jack had said Hudson was a suspect.

Hudson explained that he was repairing the latch so the cab-over would stay closed and then he was going to repaint the truck.

"Miss Ella put a hex on my trucks," Hudson said. "Used this model. Put that damn red paint all over it. You know that. I've only got half my crews working. Once this goes back on the shelf, all fixed up fine, the others will go out. There won't be any strike. Maurice will get elected mayor again."

"Sydney Cable will make a political issue out of Ella," Alice said.

Wendell was surprised Alice concerned herself about political issues.

"How's that?" Hudson asked although he already knew the

answer.

"Maurice will take the blame if the police don't find out who killed Ella," she said. "Everyone knows he and Wendell are in business together."

"I'm a suspect," Hudson said. "John Stone sent a detective around. I don't even have an alibi. I was home in bed asleep."

"Were they serious?" she asked.

Hudson laughed.

"Not really," he said. "Miss Ella was all mixed up with that voodoo stuff. I think they're looking hard in that direction."

Alice was relieved that Hudson didn't seem concerned.

Hudson tried the latch again, putting the cab-over up and down. On the fifth try the piece of solder broke off. Hudson cursed. He wanted the truck back on the shelf as good as new. Someone would slip into his office to make sure it was in perfect working order. He'd already tried glue and that hadn't worked.

Alice made coffee while Hudson continued to work on the truck. He had always been exact and serious, even as a child. Henry hadn't been like him at all.

"I went to the funeral," Alice said.

Hudson looked up from his work.

"I'm gonna have to take this to a machine shop, have someone make a new latch," he said. "I suppose Tom Guess was there."

"I met him," Alice said. "I knew his father."

"I should fire him," Hudson said. "The garbage department is falling apart and he spends half the day at a funeral. But I can't. Those damn Guesses control too many votes."

She held her coffee cup with both hands and sipped at it. Then the murmur started. It was Lou again. She closed her eyes and tried to see the place on the island where he lay as if she were in an airplane flying over that desolate moonscape of black ash.

"Mama?" she heard Hudson say.

She looked up at him, the soldering iron in his hands, the tip smoldering, a little curl of bluish smoke rising off it.

"You've got to stop," Hudson said.

"Stop what?" she asked.

"Whatever it is you're doing. Who are you talking to?"

"No one. Just myself. I'm thinking about what to have for supper."

She paused and continued, "You know, Hudson, sometimes I think that you are Lou's child and not Henry's. Isn't that funny."

Hudson looked up from his work. He'd heard that before.

"I don't know, Mama," he said. "It seems like you should know."

Then he wished he had the words back. That was like something Wendell might say. A few times when his uncle had had too many whiskeys he'd heard him say it. But she didn't even seem to notice. She was concentrating on something else. But that was not unusual either. She'd been that way for years. Usually when they asked, she said she was thinking about music, moving her lips as she hummed a complex passage, the better to examine it.

"Lou Sabine was a handsome man," she said. "He always brought me flowers."

Hudson thought of Wendell's account of his birth and Rosalind's, his mother's meetings with dozens of men in her apartment, their apartments, or hotel rooms. Probably men who played in the orchestra.

He tried the latch again. This time it held. After giving it a new paint job, he decided he would risk putting it back on the shelf. He thought of the possibly fictional Lou Sabine. She kept a Japanese flag and a sword in her closet, brought to her by the man she claimed was Rosalind's father. When he was a boy he'd often gone into her room and taken the sword out of its scabbard. Then he'd stand before the full length mirror, holding the sword by two hands as he cut and thrust with it.

"Lou Sabine," he said. "I think you made him up."

Right away he was sorry he said it. It was a subject they'd talked about before. Sometimes she got angry at his questions. And he wondered why over the years he kept asking them.

"No," she said firmly. "He was real. He was a good man. He would have made you a good stepfather."

"Was my father really a piano player?"

"Yes. I know exactly who he was."

"Did you love him?"

"No."

"But you loved Rosalind's father?"

"Yes, I found out how much I loved him too late."

Love, Alice thought. Wendell was immune to it. Love could make nothing happen.

"I think I'll go stay with Drusilla for a few days," Alice said. "I don't think I'll come back here."

"You go to my house," he said.

"No, I'll go to Drusilla's."

"You keep out of Wendell's way."

Hudson turned his attention to the truck. He was going to concentrate on garbage. There was no garbage left on the street in their neighborhood but out in the suburbs to the west of town and in French Town it was piling up to rot in the August sun. Even if he got all his crews back it would take weeks to catch up. And they were picking up none of the pine straw, lawn clippings, branches, refrigerators, and mattresses. People weren't bringing their garbage to the pickup points. They assumed that Miss Ella's death meant the end of the strike.

"Did you throw out my model airplane stuff?" Hudson asked.

"No, all that is still up in your room," she said.

Hudson ran his fingers over the markings, wondering what the old woman had intended by the numbers, sevens and fives, and the wavy lines.

"I've got to paint this," he said. "It's got to be like new."

His mother went to pack a few things. He climbed the stairs to his room. The model planes he'd built still hung on wires from the ceiling. He'd imagined his father as a pilot, not as a piano player who was drowned at sea. Overhead a P-38 did battle with a Messerschmitt. Now he had put those romantic fantasies to rest. His mother had decided not to marry and had picked out men to father the children she wanted. Now she was claiming she loved one of them. It had been convenient for her to have them die. No child could feel rejected by a dead father. Still from time to time he wondered. Most likely the piano player story was closer to being true. He wondered if it had been someone in the orchestra, a fellow viola player or someone from the woodwinds.

Hudson found the bottle of airplane dope which he'd used to paint the white numerals on the planes.

A Song For Alice Loom

In the kitchen he wet a cloth with nail polish remover and rubbed at the red markings, managing to fade them a little. The red paint came off on the cloth. Two or three coats would be better, but he had time for only one.

The paint was not covering well so he gave it another coat. Then he set the oven on low and put the truck on the rack. He set the timer for ten minutes and poured himself a cup of coffee. When the timer rang, he turned off the oven and allowed it to cool. But when he took the truck out, the markings were still faintly visible, the metal still warm in his hands. He sat and drank coffee and waited for the metal to cool off enough to paint. Then he gave it a third coat and returned it to the oven, the timer ticking as he drank coffee.

They'd impounded the Tire Gator. McWill had already called from Texas and complained he and the Spence boy were going to lose opportunities. He'd hinted about suing. Everyone was expressing official concern; but privately, because of the bizarre nature of the murder, they were making jokes about it. Hudson was sick of listening to them.

The timer went off. Hudson turned off the oven. After the truck cooled, he planned to use the Macy's bag to carry it to the department. That would explain his absence and why no one could get him on the radio in his car. He opened the bag and found the old hatbox. He untied the strings. The box was empty.

This time the markings on the truck had disappeared. He held it under a lamp to be sure there were no ghosts of them showing through, but there was nothing, the surface gleaming white again. He left it on the table to finish cooling.

Hudson touched the truck lightly with a fingertip to see if the paint had hardened. It had, the surface dry and slick to his touch. He wrapped it in a dish towel and put it in the Macy's sack.

When he drove by Miss Ella's house, there was a police car outside and an officer standing on the porch. Off in the junked truck lot yellow barrier tape was strung around the place where the Tire Gator had been. There were two police cars. Officers were walking along the edge of the lot by the levee.

Hudson got out of the car. Tom Guess was looking through the window at him. Then Guess's face disappeared from the doorway.

Scott Ely

By the time he reached the building Tom was at work at his desk. Hudson closed his office door behind him, and sitting at his desk, took the truck out of the sack. He unwrapped the towel, pleased that the paint hadn't stuck to it. The truck was good and dry.

He put the truck back on the shelf. Once he looked up to see Tom Guess staring at him through the window. Hudson ignored him. Late in the afternoon, he opened the blinds so he could see the trucks come in. Tom Guess went out to greet them with his clipboard. After the men had changed out of their uniforms and washed themselves in the showers Hudson had to fight with City Hall to install, they one by one and in small groups slipped into the office. He worked at his desk, his head lowered, but heard the door open and close as they came to look at the truck on the shelf above his head.

Chapter 20

Hudson sat at his desk and looked at the truck. Tomorrow he hoped there'd be drivers for all the trucks, the spell removed by Miss Ella's death and the return of the gleaming white better-than-new truck to its place on the shelf. He was proud of the job he'd done on it. Something that looked that good, was that white and clean, couldn't have a spell on it. He looked at the map on the wall and imagined the whole fleet back in service, fanning out over the city early in the morning. If they worked hard, they might be able to get the garbage before it piled up and rotted and began to stink. That was what happened the last time in some sections of the city. You could drive into a neighborhood and instead of the sharp scent of pine trees there was the stink of rotting garbage.

"Worse than a hog farm," Maurice had said. "And that's the worst smell I know. Least that's the smell of money. What I'm smelling is lost votes."

Hudson decided to ask Maurice if he could pay overtime to allow them to catch up.

The pump and plastic pipe had arrived so he could draw water from the river. If the fire had not burned itself out in another day, he'd start putting water on it.

He went out of the office and drove up the hill. On his way home he planned to swing by the landfill and take a look at Charlene. Tomorrow they were going to bury Miss Ella. He imagined that Tom

Guess would be useless for most of the day because of it, the man a frustrated undertaker just like his father. Alice would probably go too, along with Maurice and Sydney Cable. He wished he could go. The old woman had caused him trouble, but he admired her for it. She'd done exactly what she'd set out to do, had confounded them all just by sitting out there in a rocking chair and playing off the superstitions of the workers. And she'd taken good care of the boy. Now she was dead and it was sad. You could tell just by watching her walk that she had character. She was the kind of person he'd like to pay his respects to. But instead he was going to work. It wouldn't look good to the men if he seemed too concerned over the burial of the old woman, he the remover of magic spells. And Miss Ella the tough negotiator would understand about that.

He chuckled to himself as he thought of the parade of men who had found an excuse to come to the office to view the truck.

They hadn't found the boy yet. Probably the body would be discovered in a few days by some fisherman tending his lines. Unless those voodoo people had it. He'd heard they did strange things with dead bodies. If he had to do it over again he'd have taken Larue home with him. He was going to feel bad about Larue for a long time and in a different way than he did about Miss Ella.

But I can't be responsible for all of them, he thought. No one expects me to be responsible.

Wendell and Anse might be looking hard for the boy. He wondered if Wendell had anything to do with Miss Ella's death. It wouldn't have surprised him if Wendell had ordered Anse to do it. But murder. That was a thing Wendell would find hard to cover up with a few bribes. Sidney Cable would be screaming for justice and Maurice would probably be screaming louder.

It was as much social services' fault as his. Ultimately Wendell was to blame, no matter whether he'd actually ordered Miss Ella killed. Hudson recognized the convoluted logic he was using to avoid any responsibility. There was no escaping his part in it, although he still couldn't decide who was right and who was wrong. But he'd bear his part of the blame, be ready to face whatever accounting would come of it.

Up ahead he saw the crows sailing over the trees. He stopped to talk with Moses.

"How is she?" Hudson asked.

"Swishing around, dancing in that methane," Moses said. "Green eyed, sucking up that gas. Moved the tape. She's growing."

"I think it's tires."

Moses glanced at the mountain of tires.

"Ain't no tires," he said. "Nobody gets tires past me."

"Soon as the police release it we'll get that Gator on 'em," Hudson said.

"Chopped up that old lady."

"You think it was voodoo folks that did it?"

"I don't hold with none of that. I'm a Methodist. My daddy believed but not me. Mr. Guess came out and asked me if I'd be scared to have that Tire Gator out here. I told him I didn't care."

"Soon as the police release it we'll put it on those tires."

"When we gonna put water on Charlene?"

"We'll wait one more day, then start pumping."

Hudson put the car in gear.

"Mr. Tisdale is out by Charlene waiting for you," Moses said.

Hudson was surprised. The landfill had too many flies and too much blowing dust to suit Jack, not to mention the stink of the garbage.

He drove onto the landfill, and there was Jack's car parked just outside the barrier tape. What was strange was that Jack stood well inside the tape near Charlene's vent. Hudson pushed on the gas pedal, the car bouncing in the tracks left by the bulldozer. The soles of the man's shoes must be beginning to burn, he thought.

Jack stepped even closer to the vent and tossed something into it. He seemed to totter on the edge for a moment and then stepped back. By the time Hudson reached him he was standing outside the tape, wiping his sweat-covered face with a handkerchief. He swatted at a swarm of flies trying to land on his face.

Hudson opened the door, the combination of Charlene and the afternoon sun almost more than he could bear.

"Didn't Moses tell you to stay clear?" Hudson asked.

"He told me," Jack said.

He'd taken off his suit coat. He was wearing red suspenders.

Scott Ely

"She's hot," Jack said.

"Dammit, Jack, don't you know it could cave in. What'd you toss in there?"

"What belongs to her," Jack said.

"You're not making sense."

Jack smiled at him.

"You going to start being like Joe Wallace with his cup?" Jack asked. "Listening at doors. You think I'm crazy."

"No, but if you don't stay away from that fire, you're gonna be dead. What'd you toss in there?"

"Just an old hat. This is a dump isn't it? A place where you throw away things you don't want. Once Moses found a baby here. Somebody didn't want that."

Some flies had settled on Jack's face, but he paid no attention to them. Hudson was reminded of pictures of people in Africa, their faces covered with flies. A few flies tried to settle on his face, but he brushed them away.

"We're going to put this out day after tomorrow," Hudson said.

Jack laughed.

"I don't want you to put it out," he said. "I'm the councilman in charge of dumps, of garbage, of things that are thrown away."

This was August, Hudson thought. When dogs went mad. And now it seemed as if he was having more than his share of conversations with people on the edge. He brushed a fly out of his ear.

"Jack, let's get in your car," he said. "Turn on the air conditioning. Get away from these flies."

Hudson's chest hurt. He found it difficult to breathe. He thought this would be a strange place to have a heart attack. But then the feeling passed, his concern shifting from the heat to the flies. The phrase "spontaneous generation" passed through his mind. It was as if they were being born out of the very dust, there were so many.

"Listen, Hudson," Jack said. "It's in Malachi. 'For behold, the day cometh, that shall burn as an oven; and all the proud, yea, and all that do wickedly, shall be stubble.'"

Hudson had heard it all before. You could go hear that anytime you wanted at a dozen churches on a Sunday morning. Jack wasn't even crazy in an interesting sort of way.

A Song For Alice Loom

"This is it," Jack said.

He knelt down and patted the ground inside the tape.

"Hot," he said. "Like an oven."

Hudson wondered why Jack had come all the way out to the landfill to throw a hat in the vent. If that had been what it was. He could have burned it at home or just thrown it away.

"Let's get in the car," Hudson said.

"Who do you suppose killed that old woman?" Jack asked.

"The police are looking."

"That's why HE's going to burn us all. You too, Hudson. You have the beginning of the oven right here in your dump."

"Jack, get in your car," Hudson said. "You can follow me home."

"And that boy," Jack said. "Where do you suppose he is?"

"In the goddamn river."

Hudson was losing patience with Jack.

"No more water," Jack said. "Only fire."

Hudson thought of the boy floating in the river. It made him sick to think of that.

"Let's go now," Hudson said.

"You've got to promise not to put water on this," Jack said. "I shouldn't have signed that requisition. I didn't know. Then your mother came, and I realized we were beyond redemption."

"My mother?"

"Brought me the hat."

Hudson remembered the empty hat box he'd taken out of the Macy's sack. He could not imagine his mother bringing Jack a hat. He wasn't going to play Jack's game, ask him questions so Jack could give him ambiguous answers.

"We need to go," Hudson said.

"You should've taken that boy in," Jack said. "Then he wouldn't be floating in the river."

Hudson felt an uncomfortable twinge of guilt.

"It was voodoo folks who killed him," Hudson said.

Immediately he regretted mentioning voodoo in front of Jack.

Jack laughed.

"You were responsible for that boy. That's why the oven is here. No one wants to be responsible. Now Sydney and Maurice are fighting over who's responsible. But it's too late. Don't count after."

Jack swept his open hand across the barren landscape. The crows had swooped down to feed on fresh garbage. Despite the cover of dirt John had placed over it there were still good pickings for them.

"This is what we do," Jack said. "Cover it all up."

Hudson noticed he'd left his car door open. Now it would be full of flies.

"Can you feel the heat of it under us?" Jack asked.

Hudson wanted to leave him, but he'd be responsible if Jack walked into the vent.

"It's a fire feeding off methane from the garbage," Hudson said. "That's *all* it is."

The crows rose up and sailed over the trees.

"When this was just a' dump we shot crows here," Jack said. "I know it surprises you that I'd be doing that. But I was a good shot. We'd put up an owl decoy in a dead cypress and I started blowing the call. Nothing draws crows like the prospect of swooping down on an owl.

"We'd give the birds we shot to those scavengers. There'd always be some that'd take them. Black folks, white folks. It was a dump that was integrated before its time. I knocked down a crow. Broke its wing. Usually I'd just wring its neck, but this time I kept it and took it home. Built a cage in the back yard.

"Its wing healed and I let it go. It flew up to the top of a big oak and just sat there for a while. Then the jays began to scream at it and it flew off. Do you suppose that'd count, Hudson? I think of my whole life and I feel closer to that crow than my wife or my children. Katie spends all her time playing golf. She lies to me about the money she spends. Those two boys are already waiting for me to die. They don't want to get up in the morning and go to work at the law firm I built for them. I guess I caused all that. It must be my fault. But that crow should count for something. You haven't done much better, Hudson. We both better do something before it's too late."

They watched the crows sail back down to feed on the garbage.

"You should be home having dinner," Jack said. "So should I. Just remember. Leave this fire be. It'll burn itself out."

Jack brushed the flies off his face and clothes, got in his car, and drove off.

Hudson opened all the windows of his car to give some of the flies a chance to escape. Then he walked the circuit of the barrier tape, stopping every so often to feel the ground. Moses was right, the fire had grown. He changed his mind and decided to start pumping water into the vent the next day.

Jack was ready for the state hospital, but what he had said had made Hudson think. He thought of Larue and Miss Ella looking at him as he drove the car down the hill. Jack was right, had confirmed what Hudson had been thinking. He wanted to be absolved of it, but he didn't think the priest at the Episcopal church, which he had not attended in years, could absolve him of anything. It was all very simple. If he had taken in Larue, the boy would now be safe. Now it was too late. Hudson found himself breathing hard as if he'd just finished running a race. He told himself that he needed to calm down.

Hudson drove out of the landfill with all the windows down, the wind whistling through the car. But the flies were still everywhere, still clung to the upholstery and buzzed in his hair. He hit the paved road and drove fast, the wind cleaning the car of them.

Scott Ely

Chapter 21

Larue woke in the cabin thinking of Miss Ella flying out above the river. Then he thought she might be in the cabin. Maybe she'd removed his clothes. She'd done that many times before. He got out of bed and went into the kitchen where he found the clothes neatly folded on the table, Miss Rosalind's purse beside it. Miss Ella was not there so it had been Miss Rosalind.

He stood for a moment in the silent house, waiting for the voice to speak to him again.

"Ain't you there no more?" he asked.

But there was only the sound of the birds singing their morning songs.

"Miss Ella is alive," Larue said.

A car went by on the road.

"Go ahead," he said. "Tell me it ain't so."

His only reply was silence.

"You don't know everything," Larue said. "Miss Ella knows about the voodoo. She got the power."

Satisfied that the voice had nothing to say to him, he laid a Mississippi road map he'd found in a desk drawer out on the table and located Vicksburg and then Eagle Lake. He traced the red lines down to Biloxi. He decided he would take a bus from Vicksburg. Highway 49 ran all the way from Pine to Gulfport. He opened the purse. There was two hundred dollars in it. He took a hundred and left the rest. He felt bad about taking the hundred dollars. Once he found his father in Biloxi, Larue planned to work on the shrimp boat to earn money to pay Miss Rosalind back. Miss Ella had taught him to pay his debts. She'd also talked about stealing, and there was no way to give any other name to what he was doing. But when he paid it back it would make it some better. It was going to be hard to face Miss Ella and explain about how he was going to pay it back. He could already see her face turning hard against him. He dressed and, taking the fishing rod and the single lure, a topwater plug with three treble hooks, he went out of the cabin.

Now he'd left the lake behind, walking in the light from the rising sun along the road which intersected with Highway 61 at a tiny dot on the map marked Redwood. The sun wasn't hot yet, but it looked like a long way to Redwood. His legs were tired. A truck approached on the road behind him. Larue turned and stuck out his thumb. The pickup with a black man at the wheel passed, but then the brake lights went on. Larue ran.

"Where you going, boy?" the man asked.

"Redwood," Larue said.

"What you doing out here?"

"My grandmother lives in Redwood."

"You live out at the lake?"

"Yes, sir."

"You must be one of them Landrum boys."

"Yes, sir."

Larue was surprised at how easy it was to create this fiction about himself. But all those lies were going to add up, a heavy weight on him when there was the reckoning with Miss Ella.

The man didn't have time to ask many more questions because they were soon in Redwood, the town consisting of a store and a gas station. Larue thanked the man for the ride and walked over to the store, trying to pretend it was all familiar territory.

In front of the store a truck was parked, the back open. Inside were cardboard boxes. The storefront was covered with rusted Coke a cola signs, an old cold drink box lying on its side by the door, a cat curled up in it. Next to the door was a big outdoor thermometer advertising Dr. Pepper. It read twenty degrees. At the end of the porch was a Greyhound bus sign, but there were no people standing around waiting for the bus. He went inside.

A bald-headed white man and a black man with a baseball cap were bent over some papers on the linoleum-topped counter by the cash register. There was a stack of cardboard boxes on the floor. The white man signed the papers and handed them to the black man.

"Tony, are you sure nobody's been in them cartons?"

Tony laughed.

"I loaded that truck myself," he said. "Ain't a single can of tuna missing."

They shook hands. Larue slipped up to the counter.

"When's the bus come?" he asked.

"Gone twenty minutes ago," the bald-headed man said. "Won't be another til this evening."

"Where you going, boy?" Tony asked.

Larue decided to try the truth.

"To stay with my papa in Biloxi," he said.

"You got your ticket money?" the bald-headed man asked.

"Yes, sir," Larue said.

He pulled out three twenty-dollar bills.

"He sent it to me," Larue said. "He works on a shrimp boat. He'll be waiting at the station this evening."

"I'll take you with me," Tony said. "You can catch a bus at Columbia."

The bald-headed man took out a small book with a picture of a Greyhound Bus on the front. He put on a pair of glasses and studied the book, running his finger up and down on a page.

"You can do it if you're in Columbia by 3:36," he said.

"We can do it easy," Tony said.

Larue thought that as soon as he got a chance he'd take out his map and find out where Columbia was.

He got in the truck with Tony. When Tony put his fishing rod behind the seat, Larue saw there were two fishing rods and a tackle box already there. They drove off down Highway 61 towards Vicksburg. For a time they rode in silence, Larue looking off across the flat fields. The sun was well up now, the hot air blowing through the cab.

A Song For Alice Loom   165

"Your mama didn't pack you no suitcase?" Tony asked.

Larue realized that was going to be difficult to explain.

"My mama got her this new man," Larue said. "He don't like me. Woke me up this morning while Mama was asleep. Told me I needed to be up and gone."

Tony clucked his tongue.

"Didn't even let you say goodbye to your mama. My stepfather didn't like me at all. When he took off his belt, I knew I was in for it. He took it off 'bout every day."

Tony paused and looked hard at him.

"You sure you got a father in Biloxi?"

"He works on a shrimp boat," Larue said. "I've been on it."

"What's its name?"

"Sally Jean."

"You gonna catch a fish out of the Gulf with that rod?"

"My papa will show me how."

"I expect he will. We've got deliveries to make all down in south Mississippi. You'll be my man. Help me with the light stuff."

Tony told Larue how he drove the truck for a wholesale grocery company based in Jackson. His route covered little stores in southwest Mississippi. Larue took out his map as Tony explained his route.

"We'll go down through Port Gibson. Then at Fayette we take state 33 to Roxie. Then we go across on Highway 98 through Meadville, then over to Summit and McComb. We'll have lunch at the river. The ole Bogue Chitto. I know a place where you can catch a big bass."

They went through Vicksburg and on down Highway 61 to Port Gipson where they made a delivery to a restaurant. Larue helped to carry in the lighter cartons. In the kitchen women were snapping beans and chopping okra. Tony joked with a pretty black woman who wore a green dress and high heels. Everyone complained about the heat. Larue smelled turnip greens cooking. He was hungry.

"This your boy?" the woman asked. "All these times you telling me you was single."

Tony laughed.

"I'm just giving this boy a ride," he said. "He ain't no kin of mine. When you gonna let me show you that sandbar down on the Bayou Pierre in the moonlight?"

Scott Ely

All the women in the kitchen laughed.

"You get the rest of that lard unloaded," she said. "I don't have time for your foolishness. You can go down there by yourself and play with those cottonmouths any time you want."

The women laughed again. They were all big women, the kitchen knives looking small in their hands. He looked up and the woman was standing over him.

"Child, has this man given you any breakfast?" she asked.

Larue shook his head.

After she finished telling Tony what she thought of that, she gave Larue a carton of milk and a sausage and biscuit left over from breakfast.

Back in the truck Tony talked about the woman.

"I keep asking Rachel out, but she keeps saying no. Maybe I need to walk in the front door in a coat and tie and ask. I ain't tried that yet. One Saturday I'll drive down from Pine and do it."

They delivered canned vegetables to a Headstart School in Lorman. And cattle feed to a little store in Fayette. The feed came in fifty pound sacks which Tony carried from the truck two at a time. Then Tony and the store owner counted them.

Then they were on a smaller highway, state 33. Larue had found the Bogue Chitto River on the map. It was near McComb and far away to the east was Columbia.

"You sure your daddy'll be at the station?" Tony asked.

"He'll be waiting there," Larue said. "I called him on the phone."

Larue thought this was one more lie he'd have to reckon with. In one morning he had already told more lies than he had in his whole life. Miss Ella would make him count them. He'd have to tell her every one. But she'd be glad to see him. Even if she was mad. He looked on the map and traced the path of the Pearl River to the Gulf. She would have followed that, flying down the river to the ocean. He thought of his mother and Tiffany. They'd be going into the ground, no chance for them to escape as Miss Ella had. He began to cry, his head lowered.

He felt Tony's hand on his shoulder.

"Larue, there ain't no need to cry," Tony said. "You miss your mama. But you'll be with your daddy tonight. You catch him a big fish out of the Bouge Chitto. Won't he be surprised when you show up with that."

So Larue concentrated on fishing. Somewhere beneath the dark water of the river a fish was waiting for him. He hadn't thought about Anse Carter all day. And when the thought of him sprang up again, he was not frightened at all. He was with Tony who could put two fifty pound cattle feed sacks on one shoulder and walk off with them. It'd be different if he were back in Pine in the narrow streets and alleys of French Town with Anse Carter who could see in the dark on his trail. Then not even Tony could help him. Once in Biloxi his father would protect him. He'd been in the airborne. He wouldn't be afraid of Anse Carter day or night.

After they made a delivery outside of McComb the truck was nearly empty. Tony was complaining about the long route he had to drive, but Larue could tell he was proud that he always got it done on time. He loaded the truck himself at the warehouse and delivered undamaged, unpilfered goods.

"Except when they make me take ice cream," Tony said. "Don't matter if it's January. It melts some and the customers complain. Don't never buy ice cream in a little store in Mississippi. Mr. Heatherhill is too cheap to buy some extra refrigerated trucks."

They left the highway and drove on a gravel road. Then on a dirt road, the branches whipping against the side of the truck. Tony had him roll up the window. The truck stopped, and they got out on the banks of the river. They were on a low bluff; the river, black and slow-flowing, meandered by below.

They made their way down the side of the bluff on a narrow trail, the air getting cooler by the water. Larue carried the fishing rods, and Tony their lunch and a minnow bucket. Tony had been worried about the minnows because it was so hot, but only a couple had died. Tony rigged his rod for him. Larue had never fished with anything but a cane pole. But he knew how to put a minnow on the hook by threading the point of the hook through its lips. They stayed alive longer that way. Tony threw out his line for him. He said that if Larue did it he'd get a backlash they'd spend the rest of the day picking out. Their lines set, they propped the rods up on forked sticks. Then they ate their lunch of sardines, cheese, and crackers. Tony drank a beer. Larue a strawberry drink.

Scott Ely

Larue looked at the dark water, the color of coffee. The Pearl was probably like that this far south, he thought.

He couldn't help thinking of Miss Ella. As long as she followed the Pearl she'd be all right. It would take her straight to the sea, to safety amid all that light and open space. He'd look hard for her when he got to Biloxi.

"Boy," Tony said.

Larue looked up and saw his red and white float bob twice and then go under. He grabbed the rod, feeling the weight of the fish, the line ripping back and forth across the water. The rod jerked. Tony was yelling at him to keep the line tight. He cranked the reel frantically. The fish jumped, bigger than he could have imagined, coming out of the black water, the light shining off its green sides. Then it was gone, the line ripping through the water again. The tug on it was less powerful, and he gained line. He could see it now in the water, shaking its head against the pull of the line. Tony was telling him to reel. He cranked, the rod tip dipping. Then it was before him and Tony was saying that he should keep a tight line. Tony went into the water. With a smooth motion he pulled the fish out by placing his thumb on the edge of its lower jaw. What had been frantically in motion was now completely still, water dripping off it.

"Big fish for a little boy," Tony said and laughed.

Tony cleaned the fish. Larue liked watching him slit the fish's belly and pull the entrails out, tossing them into the river. They took it back to the truck and put it in a small ice chest.

"It'll make a meal for you and your daddy," Tony said. "You can take it on the bus with you. Surprise him when you get there."

As they drove toward Columbia, Larue sat in the seat and had another strawberry drink and a fruit pie. Every time he took a bite of the pie he smelled the fish on his hands. He understood about the fish. It was alive when it came out of the water. Dead after Tony had cut off its head even though it still wiggled a few times. Tony had said it was dead even though it wiggled. But Miss Ella was still alive. He smelled the sweet scent of the rose soap even though the stink of the fish was such that he thought he could even taste the smell of it. The two smells mixed together. One he could explain. Anytime he wanted he could open the ice chest and put his nose to the fish. But the other

A Song For Alice Loom 169

he couldn't explain any other way than that she was still alive. The fish had come up out of the water and was dead. Miss Ella had come up out of the machine and had flown above the water. She was not dead. She'd never be dead.

Scott Ely

Chapter 22

Tony bought Larue a ticket to Biloxi and left him waiting on a bench outside the station in Columbia. The ice chest was at his feet. Tony had bought a bag of ice. Now the fish lay stiff between layers of crushed ice along with two strawberry drinks. Every so often Larue would open the lid and push his hand down through the ice to touch the side of the fish. He unwrapped the hamburger he'd bought and ate it, the smell of the fish on his hands mixing with that of onions and mustard.

The bus arrived, the running dog long and grey painted on its side. Larue went up the steps and gave the driver his ticket. He took a seat by the window near the front. He put the cooler on the floor and rested his feet on it. The seat smelled of cigarette smoke, the green fabric worn through in places.

Once the bus started the seat beside him was still empty so he put the cooler up on it and checked the fish. Then he opened a strawberry drink and watched the woods and fields pass by. The bus stopped at Kokomo at a little crossroads store and picked up a woman and two small children, the oldest, a boy, not more than five. They sat in the seat behind Larue. The boy ran up and down the aisle until the mother swatted him and made him sit down. Larue thought of Tiffany and his mother. They were in the ground, as dead as the fish in the ice chest. Stiff and cold. No chance for them to fly up like Miss

Ella had. He thought he was going to start crying but was afraid if he did it would attract attention to himself. He took a big drink of the strawberry soda and felt better.

They went through Hattiesburg and picked up more people at a big station. This one had a picture of the dog done in red neon. Larue wished it was dark so he could see what it looked like lighted up. He turned his head and saw the little boy looking at him.

His mother said, "You get back in your seat, Jimmy."

Larue realized the boy was interested in the ice chest. He opened the lid so the boy could see the fish. The boy looked inside at the bottle of strawberry soda. Larue pushed the ice away with his hands and revealed the fish.

"You can touch it," Larue said.

The boy put his hand on the fish. Larue cleared more ice away. The fish's eye bulged out at them, its shiny surface catching the light.

"It's dead," Larue said.

He was glad Tony hadn't cut the head off. The head was most of the fish. Larue could put his fist in its mouth. Then Jimmy touched the eye very softly with his finger. Larue pushed the ice back over the fish and took out the strawberry drink, opened it, and gave it to Jimmy.

"What you boys doing?" the woman asked.

She had poked her head up over the seat. The little girl whimpered and the woman hushed her up.

"He got a big fish," Jimmy said.

"You thank him for that drink," the woman said.

"Thank you," Jimmy said.

"Where you traveling to?" the woman asked.

"Biloxi," Larue said. "My papa lives in Biloxi."

The woman's questions made Larue nervous. She was like Mrs. Adams. It wouldn't stop with just one question. She'd have to know everything. Larue was tired but told himself he would have to be alert or she'd trip him up. He never thought that lying would be such hard work. He told her the same story he had told Tony. She seemed to believe it, clucking her tongue when he described how his stepfather sent him off without letting him say goodbye to his mother.

"And your mama didn't even pack you a suitcase," the woman said.

Scott Ely

"Does she take a drink?"

"Yes, ma'am," Larue said. "They both do."

"Least it's not crack," the woman said. "We even got crack at Kokomo. We're going to Gulfport. Your father's not waiting for you at the station, you call me."

She wrote her number and name on a slip of paper and handed it over the seat to Larue. She was Mrs. Wiggins. She began to talk about her husband who'd left her with the two children. She was going to live with her sister in Gulfport.

The girl started to cry and distracted Mrs. Wiggins, who put her in her lap and began to rock her, murmuring some song to her as she did.

Larue felt very tired. He put his head back against the seat, listening to Mrs. Wiggins. He slept. Larue dreamed he was flying up in the air with Miss Ella, the green ribbon flapping in the wind, and he saw his mother and Tiffany. Tiffany was flying loops around them and laughing. Then he had the rod in his hands, and there was the fish on the end of it going round and round in circles in the air and shaking its head and water was falling off it, although there was no water up in the clear blue sky.

Larue woke up. The empty drink bottle was in his lap. Jimmy had the ice chest open and was sucking on a piece of ice, the front of his shirt damp from it. Out of Larue's side of the bus he saw pine trees that went on and on as the bus passed. The shoulder of the road was sand instead of dirt. In a field full of cattle there were white birds moving among them, some of them sitting on the backs of the cows. Then it was pines again and Larue saw a flock of the white cattle egrets sailing over the tops of the trees.

They came into Gulfport. Mrs. Wiggins and her children got off at the station. She reminded him to call her. Larue gave Jimmy the two empty drink bottles. Larue saw a woman dressed in a pair of jeans and a green shirt greet Mrs. Wiggins, both women throwing their arms about each other.

The bus pulled out of the station. Ahead of them through the windshield, Larue could see the sea. It went out stretching on and on. Gulls sailed over the water. They turned onto Highway 90 and passed a collection of boats, some with nets hanging from the masts. The beach was dotted with people. He thought of Miss Ella flying out over that great expanse of light and space. On the map there was marked a chain of islands just offshore: Cat Island, Ship Island, Horn Island, and one whose name he couldn't pronounce. He spelled it out P-e-t-i-t B-o-i-s. He sounded it out like he had been taught in school but the vowels and constants were in unfamiliar places. It came out Pet-it Boys.

He got off at the bus station and walked over to Bayview Street where he guessed the shrimp boats would be moored. Larue realized he wasn't quite sure what a shrimp boat would look like. Down at the dock where there were rows and rows of boats moored and other boats out in the water moving up and down Biloxi Bay, he bought a drink at a machine. He had to settle for a Coke because they didn't have strawberry. At the store they sold fresh shrimp, and he thought about asking for his father but decided he'd look around on his own a little. He sat down on the ice chest and watched a pelican fold its wings and drop into the water, disappearing beneath the surface. It came flapping out of the water, the drops falling shining off it, and flew in circles over the bay.

Then Larue began to walk along the dock, looking at the boats. He came upon a line of squat boats with nets hanging from their masts. An Asian boy about his age was working on a piece of machinery, a silver wrench in his hand. A yellow-skinned man came out of a doorway on the boat and said something in a strange language to the boy. Larue wondered if they were Chinese. The man looked at him and smiled.

"Screaming Eagles," the man said.

Larue looked down at his "airborne" shirt. Perhaps these people knew his father.

"Airborne!" Larue said.

The man grinned and said something to him that Larue couldn't understand.

"He says come aboard," the boy said.

Larue walked up the gangplank onto the boat. Miss Janis, the lettering on the bow read.

The boy did most of the talking with the father putting in a word now and then, a mixture of English and Vietnamese and some other language. The boy's name was Tran Lien. His father had been a colonel in the Vietnamese Airborne. They came from a family who owned a fleet of fishing boats in Vietnam.

"Sometimes Dad gets excited and speaks French too," the boy said. "His English is not very good. He likes the 101st Airborne. He trained at Fort Bragg."

Larue told Tran about his search for his father and Tran translated for Mr. Lien. Tran's father shook his head and spoke in Vietnamese to Tran.

"He says he will help you look. You can stay with us until you find him," Tran said.

Larue spent the rest of the afternoon watching Tran work on the winch. Tran was the youngest of three brothers. The other brothers made up the crew of the shrimp boat. Tran did very well in school, and his father wanted him to become an engineer. He helped on the boat in the summer. Tran explained how the nets and the trawl worked and how they could make a lot of money if they had good fishing, but sometimes they came home with barely enough to pay for diesel fuel. His mother worked at Sears.

Larue rode home in the pickup, the ice chest on the floor in front of him. Neither father nor son had asked him what he had in it. They lived in a house with crushed oyster shells for a driveway and a palm tree in the front yard. To Larue it seemed like a very large house. The screen doors did not have holes in them plugged with pieces of cotton. The smells were different, a sort of sweet smell through the whole house as he walked through the room with a TV set. In a corner of the room on a table was a plaster statue of the Virgin Mary with baby Jesus in her arms. Larue recognized them because of their golden halos. This was the baby Jesus who later became a man and was killed and rose up just like Miss Ella did. He was the one who was supposed to save Larue's mother and Tiffany. But they were buried now, sealed in coffins with dirt on top of them. He thought of Miss Ella's Virgin and how she could do business with it down here where people believed in the power of the Virgin.

The table was covered with candles and on the wall above were row after row of photographs in identical gold frames. They were men and women and children. Most of the men were in uniform.

A Song For Alice Loom   175

Mrs. Lien was cooking at the stove. Larue smelled rice. He hoped they weren't going to eat with chopsticks. She was tiny like Miss Ella and wore a dress with flower designs on it. She and Mr. Lien talked in Vietnamese. Larue supposed he was telling her the story. Larue almost wished that it could be true. That he had a mother at Eagle Lake and a stepfather who didn't like him. At least that was better than having his mother in the ground and Miss Ella gone off into the sky, flying in big circles like a pelican over the sea.

"Are your clothes in that ice chest?" Mrs. Lien asked.

Larue opened the chest and showed them the fish. They all began to laugh. She picked the fish up by hooking her fingers in its gill slit. It came out of the chest stiff and shiny. Then she washed it in the sink and scaled it, the scales popping off in a shining shower beneath her knife. She filleted it and dropped the pieces in a pot on the stove.

At supper they said the blessing like Miss Ella always insisted they do. These people made the sign of the cross after they said it. The brothers had come home. Tien and Co. They talked just like Tran and were a head taller than their father. Mr. Lien spoke to them in Vietnamese. Tran explained that he was asking them if they knew Larue's father. The brothers shook their heads.

Larue went to sleep that night in a room with Tran. Tran had a stereo and rock music posters on the walls. He was twelve. Larue could smell the sea through the open window, hear the breeze rustle the palm fronds. He couldn't sleep and got up to go into the kitchen and get a drink of water.

When he passed by the room with the TV, he saw that all the candles were lit. Mrs. Lien was kneeling before them. She turned and, motioning for him to come in, stood up.

"These are members of my family," she said, motioning toward the photographs with a wave of her hand. "They are dead in the war."

Larue looked at the pictures and wondered if any of them had been able to rise up like Miss Ella or were they in the ground like his mother and Tiffany. And he thought of the voice of the spirit, who hadn't spoken to him again. He wanted to ask Mrs. Lien if those dead ancestors ever spoke to her but he decided against it.

"Are they with Jesus?" Larue asked.

"Yes, I'm praying for their souls," Mrs. Lien said.

Scott Ely

Larue thought of Jesus with his white man's face watching all those dead people rising up to him. He almost told her that his mother was dead and his sister was dead and he wanted to pray for them but stopped himself just in time. It was probably too late for those people dead in the war. He thought with excitement how Miss Ella had risen up, thought of Jesus on the cross on the wall of Tran's room and of the baby Jesus in the arms of the serene Virgin, their halos catching the light from the candles. They were plaster, not real. But Miss Ella was real. He had seen her go up and if everyone could go up like her, right out of that machine and out of the hands of Mr. Wendell and Anse Carter, then there'd be no need for candles and prayers.

"Did you run away from home, Larue?" Mrs. Lien asked.

"No, ma'am," he said.

If the Virgin had heard the lie, and she could hardly have avoided it, he thought, she gave no sign. The flames of the candles burned straight and steady. The baby Jesus looked up at her, the golden halo about his head.

"Mr. Lien will help you look for your father tomorrow," she said. "Don't you have him look for a person who's not there."

"He works on a shrimp boat in Biloxi," he said.

"Crewmen come and go," she said. "We will look hard. You go back to sleep."

He got his drink of water, inclining his head under the faucet to drink instead of using a glass. The water tasted strange. He opened the refrigerator as he went out of the kitchen. It was there just as it had been there when he had opened the door earlier, food for weeks and weeks stacked in it, the cold drifting out over him and the light shining in his eyes.

Larue closed the door and went out of the kitchen, passing Mrs. Lien again who was still on her knees at the Virgin's shrine, communing with her ancestors. If they let him stay and if he had a picture of Miss Ella, he'd never allow them to put it on the wall. He closed his eyes and thought of her rising up, hoped he'd have dreams of flight above the blue sea.

Chapter 23

Rosalind drove on the highway. The blue Gulf was on one side, and houses with live-oak covered lawns were on the other. She'd had no luck finding any hint of where Larue might be. It seemed to her that she'd been to every dock in Gulfport and Biloxi. No one had seen a little black boy hanging around the boats. No one knew of a black man with the last name of Sabine working on a shrimp boat. She was thinking of driving over to Mobile and trying there.

She looked at the beach again, the glare of the sun off water and sand hurting her eyes. Off by the water a group of black children were playing on the sand. One held a bat. Another was throwing a ball. Others waited in the outfield behind the pitcher. She turned the car around and drove back and parked under a palm tree.

As she stood beside the car, she watched a boy running the bases. Any of the children could be Larue. They were too far away for her to see their faces. She walked out on the beach. Her shoes filled up with sand. She took them off. There was a palmetto-thatched cabana not far from where the children were playing. Several adult figures sat at a table underneath the shade of the palmetto fronds. She decided that she'd walk to the cabana. She'd sit there in the shade and watch the children, see if one was Larue. Maybe even ask the people if they'd seen a solitary black boy on the beach.

She reached the cabana. The people there didn't know who the boys were who were playing baseball. As they made their introductions, she learned they were from Mendenhall. They were eating boiled shrimp and drinking beer.

"What do you want with that boy?" Cheryl asked.

She was a big red-headed woman. A school teacher.

"I'm responsible for him," Rosalind said.

"Are you a social worker?" her husband Bobby asked.

The other couple, Darrell and Louise, were rubbing suntan oil on each other.

"No," Rosalind said. "His cousin works for my family. He ran away to find his father."

"Poor thing," Cheryl said.

"Like Joe Barber's boy," Louise said, her back shiny with suntan oil. "Kept running away to Birmingham. That's where his father lives. What's that boy's name?"

"Donnie," Darrell said.

He was rubbing oil on the backs of her legs.

"That's right, Donnie," she said.

"He's a grown man now," Bobby said.

"A good-looking boy," Cheryl said. "Don't drink."

There was a silence. Rosalind watched them try to think of more details about the boy Donnie who ran away to Birmingham but didn't drink.

"He turned out fine," Cheryl finally said.

They all agreed.

Then Cheryl began to ask Rosalind questions about her family.

"I know those Looms," Bobby said. "My great granddaddy worked in old man Looms' factory during the war. Moved to Mendenhall. Was on his way to New Orleans but Mendenhall was as far as he got."

They all laughed.

"What's that boy's name?" Cheryl asked.

"Larue Sabine," Rosalind said.

"No Sabines in Mendenhall," Louise said. "We're Harts. Our people came over from Alabama. We got some Choctaw blood in us. But I still burn. I have to watch my skin."

"That's just a story your father tells," Bobby said.

"It's true," Louise said. "I can tell. All I've got to do is look in a mirror. Look how straight my hair is."

It might be true, Rosalind thought. Louise's hair was dark and glossy, like a blackbird's wing. Rosalind considered the web of blood, how it bound her to Larue. She wondered what these people would say if she told them the truth, that Larue was kin. She gave them her room number at the hotel. They promised they'd be on the lookout for Larue.

"He'll end up on this beach," Louise said. "You should go talk to those boys."

Louise pointed to the baseball players. Rosalind looked at the boys playing on the beach. And then she saw a figure walking slowly across the sand. It was a man carrying an umbrella. He wore a straw hat and a coat and long pants.

"Look at that," Cheryl said.

"He's got him a parasol," Louise said.

Rosalind watched Anse Carter approach the boys. He skirted the edge of the game and then stood and watched them for a while. Rosalind felt the weight of the Beretta in her purse. She was no longer sure that none of the boys playing on the sand was Larue.

A boy hit the ball. It went over an outfielder's head and landed at Anse Carter's feet. A boy ran across the sand after it. A seagull sailed over Anse Carter's head. He didn't look up. Instead he was watching the boy. The boy hesitated a moment, as if he expected Anse to toss him the ball. The other player yelled at him. Rosalind heard their shouts, fragmented and scattered by the wind. Then the boy darted forward. Rosalind involuntarily put her hand into her purse. But Anse Carter didn't move. The boy picked up the ball and threw it to another player. He ran back to the game.

Anse Carter started to walk towards the cabana.

"Look at that," Bobby said.

"At least he's not going to get sunburned," Louise said.

They all laughed.

"He's looking for Larue," Rosalind said. "Don't ask why. But don't you tell him that I was here."

"Why sure, honey," Cheryl said.

"What's he to you?" Darrell asked.

Scott Ely

"Hush," Louise said.

Rosalind understood that the women were responding to her fear.

"We'll play dumb," Louise said.

Rosalind turned her back on the group at the cabana and walked across the sand. It was hard not looking back, but she was afraid Anse Carter might recognize her. She reached the highway and the car before she felt it was safe to look back.

Anse Carter stood beneath the cabana talking with the people. She hoped they would do as she'd asked. She got in the car and turned on the air conditioning. Anse Carter stayed at the cabana for a long time. Then he slowly walked across the sand toward the highway.

She started her car. She'd stick close to Anse Carter. If he found the boy, she'd stop him from harming Larue. She thought of the sergeant, how she'd been spared by luck from killing him. It was not likely that the same thing would happen with Anse.

Anse spent the rest of the afternoon at the docks, talking to boat owners. He stood around and watched them unload catches of shrimp and fish. Then he talked for a long time to one particular man. After that conversation ended, he got back in his car.

He checked into a motel. Rosalind sat in her car across the street at a public beach parking lot and waited for him to come out of his room.

Inside his room Anse stripped off his clothes and lay down on the bed. He set the air conditioner on high. He'd learned that the boy had taken up with some Vietnamese fisherman. He knew where they lived. Anse tried not to sleep. Usually if he went out in the heat when it was this hot he got a headache. He could feel one coming on. And he'd have strange dreams if he slept. Last time he'd wakened screaming because he was back at Parchman working in an immense cotton field.

"Larue Sabine," the voice said.

Anse sat up straight in bed with his pistol in his hand.

"Who's there?" he demanded.

"Where's Larue?" the voice asked.

Anse assumed that he'd fallen asleep, that he was still in a dream. His head was throbbing right behind his eyes. At the window a few pieces of brightness seeped through the drapes.

"With them Chinamen," Anse said. "I'll put a hole in that little nigger's head. That'll be the end of it."

"Who are you?"

Anse hesitated. He didn't like to give out his name for no reason at all, not even in a dream.

I lie in my field and hear his words come in. They are terrible words, so full of hate. I wonder how I made contact with him. I wonder why my field doesn't collapse. Even the most bitter of the dead are not filled with such hate. His hate is almost something I can taste, a sense that I only dimly remember.

"Who are you?" the voice asked.

"Anse Carter. Come out where I can see you."

I'm speaking to one of the killers of Miss Ella. I wonder what he would do if she spoke to him. But I know she won't. She's probably having difficulty maintaining her field if she's still lying all shredded to pieces in that machine. He is connected with her death so I'm not surprised that I've ended up talking with him. That's happened before. But it's always been the dead I talked with. I suppose I'm going to have to get used to speaking with the living.

"Let that boy be," the voice said.

Anse lay back down on the bed and put his hands over his face. He'd never had a dream like this before.

I start to warn him again, but my field quivers some. I decide to talk with Larue instead, not waste any more time with Anse.

"Love that boy," the voice said.

"I will, after he's dead."

When he returned home, he planned to go to the doctor about his headaches. He didn't want to have hallucinations like these again. And Wendell could pay. Wendell had known that if he sent him down to the Gulf he'd have trouble with all the light and heat.

The voice had stopped. Anse lay back on the bed and slept. When he woke, it was dark outside. He looked out through a crack in the drapes. The motel parking lot was empty. Across the street in the parking lot was a single car. He sat in the room and watched the TV until all the stations signed off. When he looked out the drapes again, the car was still in the parking lot.

Scott Ely

On the chance that someone was watching him, he went out the door and into a courtyard where there was a swimming pool. Then he walked across the courtyard and through the other wing of the motel. He crossed a set of railroad tracks. The Chinaman's house was not far away. They could watch the car all night, and it'd never move.

Rosalind was asleep on the front seat of the car and never saw Anse go out of the room. She'd planned to wake in the morning long before she imagined he might get up. He'd never been an early riser. Usually he'd didn't come out of his cabin until noon. Most of what Wendell used him for Anse did at night.

Anse went up the railroad embankment and paused on the tracks. He turned his head, like a hound catching a scent on the wind, toward the rows of streetlights marking a group of tract houses. He headed down the other side toward the house where the boy lay sleeping.

Chapter 24

Larue lay in bed with Tran and tried to sleep. He was tired, but he couldn't sleep. He'd cut his hand on a fish's fin and it ached. He closed his eyes and thought of the day on the boat.

In the early morning darkness, before even the birds began to sing, Larue had gone to the boat with Tran and Mr. Lien. Larue watched the sun rise over the Biloxi Bay, the water calm and smooth like a polished piece of metal. A flight of ducks flew overhead, white patches on their wings catching the light. He wouldn't have been surprised if he had seen Miss Ella flying at the head of the V, the green ribbons on her hat flapping in the wind. Larue hoped they'd soon find his father. He'd tell him everything, and his father would take him far away from Mississippi to some place of safety.

But Larue's musings had been interrupted when Tran began to tell him about the boat. It was a coastal boat of sixty feet with a four foot draft.

"Dad salvaged it," Tran said. "It got tossed up on top of some trailers during Hurricane Camille. It'd been sitting out behind that trailer park for years, set up on blocks. Her timbers were sound, and part of the hull. We all worked on her. Mother would work all day. Me and my brothers would come help when we got out of school. After Dad got off his job at the grocery store he'd join us. We worked at night by lights. Dad is saving up to buy a steel-hulled boat so we can go out beyond the barrier islands for deep-sea shrimping."

They'd loaded ice into the bin that would hold the shrimp. It came in blocks, and Larue enjoyed running his finger over it, the ice shot through with star-shaped lines. Larue and Tran broke it up with ice picks. Larue liked the feel of the pick entering the ice, the cold chips falling in a shower on his face and hair.

Just before they left the dock Tran and Larue finished working on the winch. The brothers had returned and as Mr. Lien backed the boat out of the slip and steered it into the channel, they told Larue what they had found out about his father. He'd worked for Captain Barnett but had left in May. No one knew where. He'd just not reported for work.

Mr. Lien spoke in Vietnamese to Tran.

"He says we will try Gulfport when we get back," Tran said.

They went out of the bay, Big Island on their left, and then rounded the point and out past Deer Island into the Gulf. Mr. Lien had put on a tape, the music coming out of two speakers set on either side of the pilot house. A woman sang with a kind of frantic energy.

"Janis Joplin," Tran said. "He loves Janis Joplin. Later, if we start catching shrimp, he lets us play some of our music."

The sea was much smoother than Larue had expected. He was glad because Tran had told him about getting seasick during rough weather. Larue and Tran stood on the bow and watched a porpoise play in the bow wake. They were going to fish off Horn Island, a thin bluish line on the horizon.

By the time they reached the water off Horn Island the sun was well up and it was hot. Now they were close enough to see a grove of pines on one end. They cruised back and forth, Tien at the wheel. Suddenly Mr. Lien began giving instructions to the brothers in rapid Vietnamese. They left the pilot house and went out on the stern, standing by the winches that controlled the twin booms.

Tran explained they were going to fish for brown shrimp. They'd pull a light chain called a "tickler" to stir them up off the bottom so they could be scooped up by the net coming along behind it.

Mr. Lien eased the throttle back almost to idle and Tien and Co each lowered a boom. As the booms came down, carrying the nets with them, Larue was struck how like they were to wings. It was a sign, he thought, that Miss Ella was nearby, maybe on Horn Island. The brothers lowered the nets, with the floats on top to hold them on the surface and chains on the other end to keep them on the bottom, into the water. They both nodded to their father when they were ready. The boat began to move. They started to work the nets, the boat's engines straining against the resistance.

"Come on," Tran said. "We'll pick out the fish."

Larue and Tran put on gloves and went out on the stern where the brothers were working the nets from the booms. Gulls hovered about the boat. They waited and waited. Larue felt the boat shudder as Mr. Lien applied more power. They continued to work the nets, Tien raising the angle of his boom. Then finally the boat slowed, rocking back and forth in the shallow trough of a wave.

First Co brought his in, the cable piled high on his winch again, and the net broke the surface, water spilling out of it. It was full of fish. Larue saw them wiggling, their silver sides flashing in the light. Co brought the boom over the deck. Tran grabbed the rope tie at the opening of the net and with a pull opened the "money hole." Fish and crabs but not many shrimp spilled out onto the deck.

Once Co had cleared his boom, Tien brought his in. This time the net was bulging with shrimp. Tran pulled the tie, the shrimp cascading onto the deck. Co began to shovel the shrimp into the open hole while Tien went below to pack them between layers of ice. The boys picked out the trash fish and crabs and threw them overboard. They packed good fish like lemon fish, flounder, and grouper in the ice chests.

Tran held up a fat red fish.

"This is a red snapper," he said. "They're about fished out. We throw them back."

"Watch yourself if you run across a shark or a cuda," Tran said.

He described them for Larue. Larue knew what a shark looked like but had never heard of a barracuda. He planned to leave any fish with big teeth alone.

Once they'd picked out the trash fish Larue and Tran went below and picked up any shrimp that had missed the bin. Then the boat began to move, and the brothers swung their booms out over the water again.

Scott Ely

They did it again and again. In one load there were two small sharks not much bigger than Larue's fish. Tien picked them up with a pole with a hook on the end and tossed them over the side. By the time the sun was low over the water the bin was full of shrimp.

"They're big ones," Tran said. "We'll make plenty off them."

The boat headed past Horn Island bound for home. Gulls hovered about, still hopeful of easy pickings. A flight of pelicans flew low across the water toward the island. Larue thought of Miss Ella. She could've landed on any of the small islands. A voodoo woman could do anything. He might see her or he might not, but he was hopeful that his father was in Gulfport.

The Liens were happy. While Tien took the wheel Mr. Lien cooked fish and rice over a small stove. Then they ate, the men drinking beer and Larue and Tran cokes. Some of the fish the men and Tran ate raw, cutting thin strips from the fresh fish and then squeezing lemon juice over them. The brothers had taken Janis Joplin off and had put on the "B-52s." Larue liked living with the Liens. But he feared that if they did not find some trace of his father in Gulfport, they would take him to the police. Then Mr. Wendell and Anse Carter would find him and he'd be finished. It would be nice if they'd stopped on one of the islands and there was Miss Ella, dead but alive. Larue wondered if it was possible to live with a dead but alive person. They could live on the island. They'd have a garden and he could fish. Anse Carter would never find them.

Back in Biloxi they sold the shrimp to the wholesaler at the dock. Larue watched him pay Mr. Lien in cash, peeling the bills off a roll of money. He had two big dogs in the building. Larue guessed that was to protect all that money he had.

At the house the men all drank more beer. Mr. Lien kissed Mrs. Lien. Then everyone went off to sleep.

Larue sucked on his cut hand. That was what Mr. Lien had told him to do. He still couldn't sleep. He lay in bed thinking of what was going to happen if they went to Gulfport and his father was not there. He woke up Tran.

"Do you think my papa's in Gulfport?" Larue asked.

"I don't know," Tran said. "People disappear sometimes. We thought my uncle was in Hong Kong but nobody can find him. It's

A Song For Alice Loom

best if you know they're dead. Like all those pictures on the wall."

"He's not dead."

"I didn't say he was. I was born in America. But my brothers have friends who just disappeared. It's what happens sometimes. But that was because of the war."

Larue wasn't quite sure what war Tran was talking about or even where Vietnam was. He meant to find a book of maps and look it up or look on a globe like the one they had at his school in Pine.

"He wasn't in no war," Larue said.

"People get killed, they die, they disappear," Tran said. "Pop and Mom talk about it all the time. It can happen here too."

Larue thought of his mother and Tiffany. He thought of Miss Ella. The image of Anse Carter holding her in his arms formed in his mind. She was falling, falling into that machine. And he thought of the voice that had appeared out of the night.

"Some people can't be killed," Larue said.

Tran laughed.

"Larue, you are talking crazy. Most of our family is on that wall. When people die, they go to heaven or hell. The priest talks about it in church."

"They fly up when they go to heaven," Larue said.

"Their souls," Tran said. "Let's go to sleep. I'm tired. We'll find your father in the morning."

Larue lay in bed and stared at the dark ceiling. Soon Tran was asleep, breathing heavily. Larue got up and went to the shrine in the room with the TV. Then he went to the kitchen and got a box of matches off the stove. One by one he lit the candles. He looked at the pictures on the wall and tried to imagine his mother's and Tiffany's and Miss Ella's there. He wondered exactly what Mrs. Lien was doing as she knelt before all those pictures of dead people, the Virgin and the baby Jesus looking down on her. People came and paid Miss Ella money for things she did with the rag doll Virgin. But that was when they lived in New Orleans, across the river in Algiers. He blew out the candles, thinking of a birthday cake as he did it.

Back in bed he lay on his back and waited for sleep. Tran mumbled something about the sea. Then he was quiet.

"Larue, you get out of the Chinaman's house," the voice said.

Scott Ely

Like the first time, the voice came out of the air, not loud enough to wake Tran, but clear, as if the speaker had his lips to Larue's ear.

"They ain't no Chinese people," Larue whispered. "They's Vietnamese."

"*Get out, Anse Carter is coming,*" the voice said.

Larue thought of Anse Carter, who'd been so close to him that night on the river.

"I want my father," Larue whispered.

Larue was so scared he could hardly talk. Even on the river he hadn't felt like this. If Anse Carter could find him here, he could find him anywhere. There was no safe place to hide. Not in the whole world.

"*I don't know about your father,*" the voice said. "*You get out of there. You help yourself.*"

Saki and Ernie are helping me. Something they've always been afraid to do. I know their fields are sparkling and popping just like mine is. But I've now got the power to talk, to send my voice to Mississippi.

It's coming apart, Saki says.

The sea is turning purple, Ernie says.

"Help me," I say. "Help me."

And they do, although I know they're scared. They concentrate hard and we all together send my voice to Larue.

"Anse Carter," I say. "You've got to get away. Go now."

"Where?" Larue asks. "He can see in the dark."

"It doesn't matter," I say. "Get away."

"Anse Carter," Larue says. He—

And that's all because Ernie starts screaming that his field is collapsing.

Wait, I say. Try a little longer.

But they're too scared and I'm almost as scared as they are. I stop talking and lie very still. My field changes to a narrow cylinder, contracting around me. I stretch out and try to make myself thin. Then the colors began to fade and the sparks subside. It expands so I'm comfortable again.

Ernie, are you all right? I ask.

Fine, he says.

Saki?

A Song For Alice Loom

Lying still, Saki says.

Let's not talk for a while, I say.

So Saki and I lie still and quiet beneath the black sand and Ernie beneath the blue sea. After a while I'll try to talk with Larue again. To see if he's done as I've asked. I can't bear to think of what will happen if Anse Carter finds him. Ever since my talk with him I feel as if something unclean has touched me. I wish I could lie out there in the water with Ernie where the currents would wash the sound of Anse's voice out of my ears.

Larue quietly dressed. He still had money left out of the hundred dollars he'd taken from Miss Rosalind. He couldn't take the chance that his father was not in Gulfport. By morning he could be there, even if he had to walk.

Larue went out of the house and down the steps. When he reached the bottom step, he saw Anse Carter's white straw hat going across the street. He ducked under the house through an opening in the lattice work. The house set up on brick piers.

He lay very still as he heard Anse Carter walk up the driveway, his feet crunching in the oyster shells. Then he went past, going around back where the screen door was fastened with just a hook. Larue lay very still and didn't move even though the mosquitoes had now found him. He wasn't going to move until Anse Carter was gone.

Larue lay still a long time, longer than he had waited for the first net to break the surface of the sea. A dog began to bark at the house next door but then was silent. He heard the front door open and someone going down the steps and footsteps in the oyster shell driveway. And then nothing. Finally he raised his face. He lay there and waited for the voice to speak to him again, to tell him what to do. But there was nothing.

He slipped out from beneath the house and brushed the sand off his clothes. Then he went inside. He carefully made his way in the darkness to Tran's room. He shook Tran gently to wake him up. When Tran didn't even groan in his sleep or roll over, Larue shook him harder. Tran lay still, limp under his hands. Larue turned on the lamp by the bed. Tran looked like he was in a deep, peaceful sleep except his eyes were open. There was a small hole in his head above his right eye. Larue closed Tran's eyes, the lids warm under

Scott Ely

his fingers. One stayed closed but the other popped open. Larue closed it again, and it stayed closed. There was not much blood, just a little around the edges of the hole. Larue put his hand flat on Tran's chest, not hoping to feel a heartbeat, but just wanting to touch him one last time. Tran now felt a little cold but still warm enough so that Larue could imagine waking him up with a good shake. Larue picked up his arm and let it flop back on the bed. Tran was heavy, heavy, heavy with death. This was what it was like for his mother and Tiffany. And then there was Miss Ella. She'd never appeared as he had expected her to. He was beginning to doubt that even she with her magic could overcome such heaviness. He went from room to room and found the rest of the family, all shot in the head. Larue stumbled into the bathroom and threw up, smelling fish as he did it. He sat on the tile floor and cried for the Tran and his family and for Miss Ella. Afterwards he wiped his face on a towel.

He started out of the house, first pausing at the darkened shrine, the scent of burning candles still in the air. The Virgin held the baby Jesus, but he had no impulse to light a candle, no desire to place any trust in them. They only did things after it was too late. The Lien's kin were still dead, the lost still lost. He wondered how the baby Jesus could look so happy with all that going on. But things were hard for him later. Larue thought of the figure sprawled out on the cross above Tran's bed. Even he had looked calmly on while Anse Carter had killed Tran. He thought of how people didn't want anything much to do with the rag doll Virgin after they left Algiers. The power of Virgins and baby Jesuses might have something to do with geography. This pair on the shrine before him might have stopped Anse Carter in Vietnam but not here. If they'd stayed in Algiers, the Virgin might have kept Miss Ella safe from Anse Carter; now she was dead. From now on he wouldn't think of Miss Ella or his father. He put all his trust in the voice of that spirit, who could save him when all the others had no power at all.

Larue left the house. The dog next door began to bark again. At first he walked slowly, fearful of every car that approached, but then, thinking of the dead people, he began to run, his arms pumping and his tennis shoes hitting the pavement with rhythmic splats, as he ran through the darkness toward the Gulf.

Rosalind woke up just as Anse's car pulled out onto the highway. It was still dark. As Anse drove west toward Gulfport, she followed at a safe distance. But when he turned north at Gulfport, just as the sun started to rise, she was surprised. She'd thought he'd drive on up to Pass Christian. If he were checking shrimp boats, there were plenty left on the coast. She'd learned how much time it took to stop and ask questions.

It was when he crossed interstate 95 that she realized he was headed back to Pine. So he'd failed in his hunt for Larue. She decided that she'd follow Anse until the FBI had located the boy. So she drove up along the highway, soybean fields stretching off in the distance on either side. Irrigators, looking like huge metal bugs, moved slowly on rubber tires across the flat land, rainbows sometimes caught up in their spray. Larue was going to live, she thought. Larue was going to live.

Scott Ely

Chapter 25

Wendell hoped Anse would settle the business with the boy soon. He thought he might sell the big house and enlarge his apartment at the office. But there was that troublesome clause in his father's will about keeping the house for Alice to live in as long as she was alive. A good lawyer might find a way to break that.

It was payday, time to be collecting rents, which was Anse's job. He expected Anse back at any time. He'd told him not to call. Wendell had never considered a telephone a secure means of communication. It was too easy for someone to overhear a conversation, poking their nose into his business. Dawson Smith, the black detetctive asssigned to the case, could be listening in. He had been around asking questions about the old woman and the boy. He expected Dawson was looking hard for the boy. If the boy was in Biloxi, Anse would get there first. But Wendell was beginning to doubt that the boy had even left town. How would a ten-year-old boy with no money get to Biloxi? Dawson had been polite and acted like he was embarrassed about asking the kinds of questions he had to. Wendell had told him he had worked at the office and then gone to the Leather & Lace Club. He expected Dawson had gone out there asking questions.

All afternoon he'd been collecting rent money. But many of the people weren't home, and Wendell knew he was going to have to go back at night. You had to get the money when their paycheck was in their hands, before it ended up in the hands of the liquor store owner or the crack man.

That suited him just fine. If the boy was in town it was a perfect way to be on the lookout for him. Wendell carried a .45 in a shoulder holster. If he ran into the boy he'd take care of him. He could claim someone shot at him in a dispute over rent and he shot back in self-defense, or someone tried to steal the money he'd collected. Which story he used would have to depend on the circumstances. In either case he'd claim the boy had gotten in the line of fire, had been killed by mistake.

As he ate dinner at a restaurant, he felt slightly nauseated. All day he'd been driving the streets of French Town and out into the suburbs, driving up and down the grids of streets. He'd even made a trip out to Sunlight Estates. It was all that driving that had made him sick. He ended the day by going down to the river where they were still dragging it for the boy. If he had seen that waterlogged body being pulled in on one of those hooks, he could have enjoyed his dinner. Now he'd go collect rent the rest of the night.

He got in the car and laid the pistol on the seat beside him. His method was different than Anse's. Anse would walk those narrow alleys, hang out across the street from one of the three liquor stores or the two cash and carry grocery stores. Wendell drove up to a house and blew the horn until they sent someone out, usually a child. Sometimes the child had the money. If not he would demand that it be sent out. He always made sure the pistol was in plain view. But lately with all that crack, which turned ordinary niggers into crazy niggers, even this method might not be safe. He promised himself he would not get out of the car, that he would be careful.

Wendell had the names and addresses on a list. Once he had known all the houses by heart, but since Anse Carter had been doing the work, he'd forgotten. New people had moved in and the old ones out. He'd bought and sold houses when he was only dimly aware of their locations.

He drove down Bull Street, which split French Town in half, past a store which sold fish. BUFFALO FISH 49 CENTS LB was written in soap on the store window. Two men walked out of the store with packages in their hands. One of them might owe him rent. Anse

Scott Ely

would have known immediately, and the bill would've been settled right there on the street.

He was lucky and right away checked off five of the names. It was like the old days. They sent a little girl out to investigate, to see who was in the big car. Then the girl came back with the money. Out of the five, there was just one instance in which he had to go inside.

When he got out of the car, the heat rising around him thick and heavy, he put the pistol back in the shoulder holster. It was too heavy and pulled at his shoulder under his coat. He was glad he wasn't prone to arthritis like Alice, but his back hurt from driving around all day.

There was garbage piled in the alley. All the fault of the old woman, he thought. It would be weeks before Hudson's crews got to all of it. He'd heard they were all back at work, the foolishness over voodoo finished with the old woman's death. There was a streetlight next to the house, but the lamp had recently been broken out. The glass crunched under his feet. It was a good-sized house, now split into three apartments. He remembered buying it. He found number two, the hallway smelling of something bad he couldn't identify. Then he knocked on the door with his flashlight. Inside he heard the TV. They could afford to have a TV but couldn't afford to pay their rent. He knocked on the door harder this time. Someone was moving inside. He stepped back from the door and put his hand on the butt of the pistol.

Someone giggled on the other side of the door. They could be drunk or wild on crack. He gagged on the bad smell in the hall.

"Rent!" he said. "Rent!"

He knocked again, hitting the door with the palm of his hand to make a louder sound. The door swung open and there was a child standing before him, a girl.

Behind her were two other very young children. He slipped the pistol back in its holster, thinking how if he' been lucky it would've been that boy who opened the door. He imagined himself telling the story to Dawson Smith. How shots were fired by an adult, the boy in the line of fire. How sorry he was that he was dead. She held out money in her hand, crumpled bills.

"You tell Mr. Carter we paid," she said.

He took it without counting and went out of the house. Outside

A Song For Alice Loom

195

the air felt fresh even though it was tainted with the scent of rotting garbage. He heard water running. A man was urinating against the side of the wall. Drunk. After all it was payday.

Then he turned a corner and there was Alice's Lincoln.

Wendell got into the front seat beside her.

"You didn't even have the front door locked," Wendell said. "What are you doing down here?"

"Looking for Larue," she said.

"Why?"

"Because he's lost."

"He's dead. Voodoo people carried him off or threw him in the river. Boys like that disappear all the time and nobody ever finds them."

Wendell wished that he knew it was true.

"I have a responsibility to that boy," Alice said.

Alice regarded Wendell. She could see him clearly in the dashboard lights. Her eyes were still excellent. She'd never worn glasses.

"You can imagine whatever you want," Wendell said.

Alice wondered how Wendell would react if the hairs on the hat turned out to be from Miss Ella. Jack hadn't called and wouldn't return the calls she made to his office.

"I'm taking him home with me if I find him."

"You're not going to find him. What's going to happen is that someone is going to stick a knife in you and steal this car. Or worse."

"Worse than dying?"

She watched Wendell fidget uncomfortably in the seat.

"Oh, that," she said. "I don't think so. I've been careful. I'll find that boy if he's here."

Wendell sighed.

"Sister, you do what you want," he said. "I've got rents to collect."

As Alice drove off, she wondered if she should have confronted him. It was hard not to spit the words at him, but it could turn out to be dangerous. Better to wait and see what Jack found out about the hat.

Wendell considered Alice's search for the boy. If Alice got herself killed driving around at night in French Town that was just too bad. But if she happened on the boy, what then? Anse Carter had already looked. Nobody could look like Anse. The boy was someplace else. At this moment Anse might be taking care of that problem in Biloxi.

He made the rest of the collections, having to get out of the car only one more time. This time the lights were all on in the house, the yard neat and tidy. A woman paid him the money. He reflected it was easy because Anse Carter had done such a good job for him, laid the ground work for people paying.

Then he thought of Alice searching for the boy. Wendell started driving the streets again. It was almost ten o'clock. The fish store was now closed. The chain-link screens were over the door and the plate-glass windows. He drove past the liquor store on River Street. It was filled with people making a last run on the whiskey before it closed. They'd still be selling bootleg and crack the rest of the night. He drove past the Sabine house. The police had finished with it and said he could rent it again. Right now it was costing him money sitting there empty.

He began to drive French Town again, past the fish store, the two grocery stores, the three liquor stores, the piles of garbage. He drove a pattern that took him into the heart of the section where the streets were barely wide enough for the big car. He never saw the Lincoln again. People appeared in the lights from time to time, fading away into the shadows. He saw the bluish glow from TV screens through the open doors and windows. Then gradually the screens began to go out one by one as people went off to sleep.

Wendell used the fish store as a landmark, trying not to approach it from the same direction twice. It was like a charm he was working to make the boy appear in his headlights. He thought of the boy hiding in an alley, waiting for the car to pass by. He began to feel sick again, dizzy from all the turning and driving in circles. He wished he were driving the big car fast on the interstate, the cruise control on, the radio playing, and there in his headlights the boy would suddenly appear, transfixed by the lights like a deer, and he would run him down, a slight bump in the big car as it passed over him. Once he'd hit a hog like that, going at the animal at an angle at the last moment to save himself so that it was struck a glancing blow, rolling away from him into the ditch. The only damage had been a slightly bent fender.

He had turned up a street a block from the fish market when he saw the boy dart across in front of the headlights. Wendell swung the car into the alley where he ran, but it was blocked by garbage. He got out of the car, smelling the sweet scent of a nearby mimosa tree mixing with the stink of garbage. He ran ahead, the pistol in one hand and the flashlight in the other. The light picked up the boy's white T-shirt just as he turned into a narrow passageway between two houses. He followed at a run, knowing the boy would outdistance him soon. He'd have to get lucky. If Anse had just been there, the boy would already have been dead.

Wendell wandered through the maze of passageways between the houses. Dogs were roused and barked at him. Once he slipped and fell in garbage. Then he rounded a corner and lights were shined in his face.

"Don't move!" a voice said. "Police!"

He stopped, blinking at the lights.

"Put that gun down!"

He started to put the gun on the ground.

"Slow! Do it slow!"

He eased the gun toward the ground.

"Wait, it's Mr. Loom."

The lights were removed from his eyes and there before him was Dawson Smith along with two officers in uniform. One of them was holding a boy by the arm. They were in the dark so he couldn't make out the boy's features. Dawson turned his flashlight on the boy.

"You know this boy?" Dawson asked.

Wendell was relieved it wasn't the Sabine boy. This one was heavier and taller.

"He says you were chasing him," Dawson said.

"I'm collecting rents," Wendell said. "They want to spend it on whiskey. I thought he lived in a house I own. He ran when he saw me."

The boy said nothing.

"Does he have crack on him?" Wendell said. "Are you out here after crack dealers? Anse checks on my renters. I don't rent to crack people."

"Anse not working for you anymore?" Dawson asked.

"Visiting his mother," Wendell said.

Scott Ely

The two uniformed officers, one white and one black, laughed.

"It's dangerous around here late at night," Dawson said. "You should know that."

"Rents got to be collected on time," Wendell said. "Don't do that and the good ones start to be late. I've got bills to pay."

Wendell wasn't sure how all this was sounding to Dawson, who was not dumb. At least the boy was keeping his mouth shut.

"You find any crack on him?" Wendell asked again.

"I'm not down here looking for crack," Dawson said. "We still haven't found that boy."

"I expect you'll find him in the river tomorrow," Wendell said.

"Boy, you get on home," Dawson said to the boy.

When the officer released him, the boy walked off down the street. He turned a corner under a streetlight and was gone.

"I don't think we're going to find him in the river," Dawson said. "If I did, I wouldn't be here. You got a permit for that pistol?"

"You know I do," Wendell said. "Like you said. It's dangerous. I've got to protect my rent money."

"You be careful chasing people with that pistol," Dawson said. "That permit doesn't give you the right to do that. It happens again and you'll lose it."

"You're right," Wendell said. "I guess I lost my head."

Dawson had one of the officers escort him back to his car. As Wendell drove out past the fish store he knew he'd been lucky. He might have shot the boy and then he could easily have gone to jail for shooting the wrong person. He wondered what made Dawson think the boy wasn't in the river but decided Dawson was guessing. Besides, if the boy was in Biloxi, Dawson was wasting his time. Yet if the boy was here, in the city, Dawson stood a good chance of finding him. He wanted to drive the streets until morning but was afraid he'd run into Dawson again. Besides he had to sleep. He drove toward his office through the deserted streets, the nausea still with him, as if this were that day in June when he'd stumbled up through the cold water onto a beach at Normandy, his men dead and dying around him.

A Song For Alice Loom

Chapter 26

Alice called Jack at home. His wife Katie answered the phone. Alice heard the sound of the TV in the background. Katie told her Jack had gone to his study to take the call.

"Hello, Alice," Jack said.

"Have you talked with Chief Stone?" Alice asked.

"I talk with him almost every day," Jack said. "We do Bible study together."

"Have you taken the hat to Chief Stone? Found out about those hairs on it?"

Jack laughed.

"Alice, you must have meant to call someone else," he said.

Alice wondered if she'd heard Jack correctly so she asked again.

"Ella Sabine's hat," she said. "Anse Carter killed her."

Jack laughed.

"Voodoo people killed her," Jack said. "Alice, are you all right?"

"Where is the hat?" she asked.

"It's all going to end in fire."

So what they had been saying about Jack was true. She'd entrusted the hat to a crazy man. She was furious with herself.

"The hat?" she asked.

"The fire is already here," Jack said. "I saw it at the landfill."

"The hat?"

"Fire took it. But it don't matter. It's gonna take all of us."

Alice hung up the phone. Drusila was working in the kitchen. She heard her chopping something. Alice's thoughts were chaotic now, her mind lighting on first one thing and then another. She thought of Lou joining the Marines. She was sure that if she'd tried she could have persuaded him to join one of the other services. He could have played in an Army band. They would have been glad to have him. She thought of the dead man on the lawn. This time she was not going to stand by like those ladies at the garden party and shriek in disapproval while men like her father and Wendell did as they wished.

The hat could be anywhere. At Jack's office or his home. He'd spoken of the landfill fire. She decided that would be the easiest place to start. She tried Hudson at home and the office but he wasn't there.

Alice was stopped by Moses at the gate and paid her ten dollar dumping fee. Hudson was there overseeing the pumping of water onto the fire. She asked Moses about Jack and the hat.

"Do you remember a hat?" Alice asked. "A straw hat with a green visor."

"No, ma'am," he said. "He wasn't wearing no hat. Been out here twice today. Mr. Hudson said not to let him in no more. Never thought a man could get so worked up about a fire. We're putting water on Charlene."

She found Hudson on the landfill. She stopped the car by the yellow barrier tape. A plume of smoke rose out of the ground. Men were laying plastic pipe across the top of the bare ground, the pipe ending at a tripod which held a piece of pipe aimed at the vent. The moment she got out of the car the flies were on her. She never imagined there could be so many flies. The stink of garbage filled the air. The heat made her feel dizzy. Off in the distance she heard the clank of a bulldozer's treads and the throb of the engine.

Hudson came up to her. His face was covered with dust and he wore goggles against it.

"Mama, what are you doing out here?" he asked.

"Anse Carter killed Ella Sabine," she said.

"We've already talked about that."

She explained to Hudson about the hat.

Now it truly seemed to Hudson that this was the day people had decided to go crazy. Jack had come out twice to complain about the plan to put water on Charlene. When he asked him why, Jack had spouted Bible verses and said that God had promised no more water. The second time, Hudson had made a joke about how he wasn't going to put Pine under water. Jack got mad and left.

"Moses says Jack has been out here," Alice said.

"The hat's gone," Hudson said. "He threw it in the fire. Why didn't you tell me? You knew Jack was sort of crazy. How could you trust him?"

"He told me not to tell anyone," she said. "I was afraid what you might do to Wendell or Anse. I didn't want you to go to prison."

Hudson couldn't understand why they'd thrown her in the machine. That wasn't necessary. Killing her that way wasn't like Anse at all. He wished that he'd been able to stop Jack from destroying the hat. Wendell was going to get away with yet another crime.

"Wendell told him to do it," Hudson said.

"I know," Alice said.

Alice stared at the vent.

"You come sit in my car," Hudson said.

Hudson took off his goggles, leaving a racoon-like mask of white skin. He was sweating, the sweat cutting tracks through the dust on his face.

"Are they still dragging the river for that boy?" she asked.

"No, they stopped today, he said. "But they'll find him somewhere downstream. I'm sure of it."

"That poor lost boy," she said. "Just like Lou."

"Mama, I want you to go home," he said.

She didn't reply, just sat there, her lips pressed together.

A worker rapped on the window.

"Mama, I've got to go," Hudson said. "Do you want me to have someone drive you home?"

She thought of the house vacant of Looms. Hudson and Rosalind might live in it for a time but then they would be gone too. There would be no grandchildren. And then nothing would continue. It seemed as if the Sabines were being killed almost as fast as they were born.

Scott Ely

"No, I'm fine," she said.

"You go home," Hudson said. "But you say nothing to Wendell. Promise me."

"I'm at Drusila's."

"Good. You stay there."

Hudson took her in his arms.

Alice felt small and frail, as if she were one of those pieces of wind-blown paper that might sail across the landfill and get caught up in the trees.

She got in her car. He wondered what he was going to do the next time he saw Wendell. And Anse. He'd enjoy squashing Anse like a bug. A worker called out to him and he returned to the fire.

Alice drove across the landfill, the taste of dust in her mouth and the smell of garbage in the car. She thought of Wendell as a child again. She remembered him lifting the edge of the canvas where the dead man lay and their father yelling at him.

She was going to keep looking for Larue. And when she found him she was going to take him to some place where Wendell could never touch him.

Chapter 27

Hudson drove to the landfill to check on the fire, the sun already high in a cloudless sky. A dust devil wandered across the field of young pines, plucking the bits of paper off some trees and dropping a piece here and a piece there on others. At the gate Moses told him it was still burning and that Jack Tisdale had been there all night watching it.

"He paid his ten dollars," Moses said. "He came in just before I shut down the gate at six. Just like I'm supposed to. I went down and talked to him about ten. But he said he was in charge of garbage. And I know he is. I told him."

Hudson drove off, leaving Moses talking to himself. Out on the landfill he saw Jack's white city car. Jack was taking down the yellow barrier tape. A brown stream of water gushed out of the pump. It was not supposed to be running. Hudson had shut it down himself. He remembered standing and watching the steam rise from the vent. But there had been no more dark, oily smoke.

A new vent had formed to the south of the old from which issued the same black smoke. Hudson parked the car a good distance away, suspicious of the unstable ground. Jack walked along, his head bent, winding up the rest of the barrier tape.

"Jack!" Hudson yelled at him.

A couple of crows sailed overhead, cawing to each other. Another dust devil, maybe the same one that had been in the field of pines, meandered across the southern end of the landfill, the whirlwind thick and swollen with the fine brown dust.

Jack looked up and grinned, then waved at him. He was dressed in a suit covered with dust and patches of mud. He walked around the edge of the old vent, now sunken several feet below the level of the rest of the landfill, the depression filled with garbage bags and pieces of paper, some charred by the fire. Jack made the circuit of the old vent and walked up to him, the bundle of barrier tape in his arm, flies swirling about his head.

"Did you turn on the pump?" Hudson asked.

"Sure did," Jack said.

"Goddamn, you!" Hudson said.

That explained the patches of grey river mud on Jack's pants.

"Hudson, I'm putting it out," Jack said. "We're gonna be saved."

"Go home, Jack," Hudson said.

Hudson turned his back on the man and walked fast along the plastic pipe across the landfill, feeling calmer as he put some distance between Jack and himself, walking slower and slower as he felt the anger drain out of him. He arrived at the river calm but covered with sweat. He stepped into the grey mud by the river's edge and switched off the pump.

Suddenly it was quiet, the only sounds the gurgle of the water against the bank and birds singing from the timber across the river. The crows, a gang of them now, circled above the river and then dropped down onto the landfill. He walked back to a stretch of sand and sat down. He wanted to give Jack time to leave before he returned.

He thought of Larue and how maybe today a fisherman downstream would find his body caught in some willows or washed up on a sandbar. The boy would not be pleasant to look at, his body swollen and wrinkled by exposure to the water, his flesh eaten by turtles. That was what they usually looked like after several days in the river.

One of those big woodpeckers the black people in his youth called Lord Coming flew across the river, giving its sharp call.

Hudson felt like crying. He could hardly remember the last time he'd cried. It had been when he was a boy and had discovered his father was not the owner of the Japanese swords and flags like he'd told the boys at school. His mother had taken him up to her room and explained to him slowly and carefully the difference between his father and Rosalind's. Then he'd cried because it wasn't fair. Rosalind didn't give a damn about the sword or the flag or the fact that her father was a Marine.

"Hudson?"

He looked up. It was Jack.

"You start the pump again, Hudson," Jack said.

Hudson turned his head and stared out at the river. He hoped that Jack would just go away.

"Hudson?"

"Go home," Hudson said.

"I'm your supervisor," Jack said. "I'm the city councilman in charge of garbage."

"Your bad luck."

"I'd hate to have to fire you."

"It still wouldn't get that pump started."

"I'm putting it out. To save us all."

"You are undermining the landfill," Hudson said slowly.

"But it's still burning."

"Landfill fires are like that. You put too much water on 'em, it undermines the fill. That opens up new pockets of methane."

Hudson wondered why he was wasting his time arguing with Jack.

"Go home and get some sleep," Hudson said. "You look like you need some sleep."

"When it comes, it'll come down on your family," Jack said.

Hudson ignored Jack.

"Turn on the pump," Jack said.

Jack walked to the pump, the mud sucking at his Italian loafers. Hudson watched him adjust the choke and then pull the starter cord. He had to pull it three times before it caught. Hudson got up and turned it off, the river suddenly silent again. The crows swooped down low overhead, talking to each other. Jack put his hand on the starter cord. Hudson reached down and took it off. Jack struggled but

Hudson was the bigger and stronger man.

"Let go," Jack said. "You're hurting my hand."

"I want you off my landfill," Hudson said.

Jack in his craziness had destroyed the only chance to make Wendell pay for what he'd done.

"You forgot," Jack said. "You're fired."

"Not without a city council meeting," Hudson said. "And I get a hearing before it. You go call a meeting. See if they'll listen to you."

"I signed the requisition for that pump."

"So you did. That's your job."

"Hudson, you don't understand. I'm putting out that fire that's gonna fall on all of us. Your family especially."

"What about my family?"

"Anse Carter killed that old woman."

The crows swung overhead. Off against the blue sky was black smudge which was smoke from the vent. Hudson didn't want to talk about the hat.

"And he doesn't make a move unless your uncle tells him," Jack said.

Hudson listened patiently while Jack explained about Alice's visit and the hat. And then Jack told Hudson he had dropped it in the vent.

"Don't matter what anyone's done," he said. "The wicked will be punished soon enough. I'm one of 'em. That's why you've got to turn on that pump."

Hudson took the spark plug out of the pump. Jack stood on the bank and complained.

"If that boy's alive, he can't go to the police," Jack said. "Wendell will find a way to get to him."

"You told anybody else?" Hudson asked.

"Just you," Jack said. "I don't trust many folks in town. But I trust you Hudson. I told you. Now why won't you fix that pump so it'll run."

Hudson took Jack's arm and pulled him up the bank. Then he walked across the landfill with Jack in tow behind him, as if he were a runaway child being returned to school. Jack complained all the way, but Hudson paid no attention to him. He put Jack behind the wheel

A Song For Alice Loom

of the city car, full of flies because Jack had left the door open.

"Go home," Hudson said. "And don't you speak to anyone about this. I see you on this landfill again and I swear I will break your leg."

Jack started the car and drove off fast. Hudson breathed a sigh of relief. Short of beating Jack senseless and putting him in the trunk he didn't know how he would have gotten rid of him if Jack had refused to leave.

The section around the old vent had further collapsed. They'd give it a couple of more days to dry out and then put fill in it again. Until then he'd leave the fire alone.

At the gate he told Moses the landfill was closed to everyone but city crews until further notice and especially closed to Jack Tisdale. He drove into town, uncertain of what he was going to do. Jack was unreliable, no fit witness at a trial. They'd believe Alice, but what she said wouldn't matter much without the hat. Larue was the key. The boy may have seen everything.

Hudson had a meeting to attend so he planned to shower first and change clothes. The police chief and the other heads of city departments would be there. He could ask Chief Stone if he'd turned up anything new about where Larue might be.

At the department, he unlocked the door at the rear of the shop. The place was deserted, the drivers all out on their routes. The showers were simple, with just a concrete floor. The layout always reminded him of the showers in his high school gym. Sometimes after football practice he'd be so tired that he'd walk into the shower wearing his uniform. He took off his clothes and turned on the water.

He was drying himself when he heard footsteps in the shop. It was probably Tom Guess, come to check on the open door. Then Dawson Smith appeared in the doorway.

"You been working on a truck yourself?" Dawson asked.

Hudson laughed.

"No, it ain't got that bad," Hudson said. "Besides I'm too old to be pitching garbage."

"You find the boy?" Hudson asked.

"No," Dawson said.

"Would you tell me if you had?"

Smith hesitated and then said, "Probably."

Scott Ely

Hudson sat down on a bench and ran a towel through his hair. He liked Smith, who had a reputation for being a good detective. No one had promoted Smith just because he was black and scored high on the exams. He got results.

"You been talking to voodoo folks?" Hudson asked.

Smith laughed.

"I don't know where to start with that," he said. "Maybe I should go to New Orleans. Study up on it. Or you could teach me. You did good with that truck."

"What do you want, Dawson?"

"I'm getting a bad feeling that I'm not going to ever find out who killed Ella Sabine or what happened to the boy. I've got a bad feeling that lots of people won't care as long as I look hard. After the election they won't even care if I look."

"You should be in politics."

Smith grinned.

"I like to work for a living." Smith paused for a moment and Hudson felt the man's eyes on him. "Now you tell me everything you know."

"I don't know anything," Hudson said.

"We got a bullet out of your boat," Dawson said. "Lodged in the floatation under the seat. Came from a .38. No blood. Just that bullet hole. I wonder what that means?"

"So do I," Hudson said.

Anse, Hudson thought.

"I own one," Hudson said. "Is that why you're here? I'll bring it in to the office in the morning if you want it."

"No, that won't be necessary."

"Can I have the boat back now?"

"I don't see why not."

"What do you want?"

Dawson hesitated a moment before he spoke.

"I want you to help. Something you know that you're not telling. Or that you don't think is important."

"She wanted me to take that boy into my house," Hudson said. "She had me mixed up with Wendell or just thought any Loom would do. That old woman was crazy. I wish I'd done it. Might not have done her any good. But that boy'd be alive today."

A Song For Alice Loom

209

"We've dragged the river," Dawson said. "He didn't show up in any of the usual places."

Hudson thought that maybe Larue was alive. The boat could have been a decoy for Anse. Would the boy have been that smart? Hudson knew he couldn't just wish the boy alive. Anse didn't miss. But if there was no blood, then the boy might have escaped. If he hadn't drowned, he might be hiding in the swamps bordering the river, afraid to come back to town.

"Hudson?" Dawson asked. "You got something to tell me?"

"Just thinking," Hudson said. "You looked in the swamps?"

"With dogs," Dawson said.

But Larue might be hiding from everyone. The boy might have considered the police and all searchers an extension of Wendell.

"Then he must be in the river," Hudson said.

"I'm not going to stop looking," Dawson said. "You call me if you think of anything."

Hudson said he would. Dawson went out of the building. The boy was the key, but first he had to find him.

Scott Ely

Chapter 28

Hudson took a .44 magnum Ruger Trooper and a box of ammunition from his gun rack. He sat at his desk and slowly and carefully filled all the chambers except one with the short thick cartridges. For a time he sat and tried to think where he'd have gone if he were the boy and what Wendell might be doing. But for these questions he could come up with no definite answers. The weight of the gun felt good in his hand. It made him feel safe.

Hudson unloaded the gun and put it back on the rack. He took the autographed baseball bat off the mantel. He could break bones with the bat. One, two swings and Anse Carter would be helpless. The bones would heal. He'd not have blood on his hands.

If he got lucky and found Larue, he'd take the boy out of Mississippi. All the way to FBI headquarters in Washington if he had to. Some place beyond Wendell's reach. He went out of the house.

He went to the shop and opened a closet where he kept a set of fishing and camping equipment. He filled the gas cans and bought some ice and drinks along with cheese and sardines and crackers at the River Street store. Then he drove to the boat and loaded his gear. As he came down the hill by the office he saw Tom Guess watching him. Hudson still thought Larue could still be hiding in the woods or might have taken up with some cat fishermen. The best way to find him was to get out on the river.

It was very hot on the river. By the time he had finished loading the gear, he was covered with sweat. At least Anse Carter would not be out looking for Larue in the heat. He'd wait until night to do his looking. He pushed the boat off and started the motor.

Once he'd cleared the railroad bridge, going down the river was like traveling back to a Mississippi before there were cities and towns. Turtles, which lined the logs, slid off at his approach, and snakes made wavy marks as they swam the river. It was difficult to find a channel sometimes. At a few places he had to get out and pull the boat over a sandbar or a fallen log.

All afternoon he ran the boat up into creeks. Sometimes he got out and walked the banks, shouting Larue's name. He remembered stories of how lost children sometimes hid in the bushes while searchers walked past, the children afraid to cry out. And this child had watched his cousin die horribly and had himself been pursued and shot at. He thought of Larue drifting downstream in the boat. When Anse Carter had opened fire, Larue had probably gone over the side and swum for shore. It would be easy to get lost in the swamps along the river. By now, if that had happened, the boy was hungry and mosquito-bitten. Hudson walked through the woods calling Larue's name, his voice echoing among the cypresses and gums. He walked carefully, the woods alive with snakes, mostly harmless ones; but once he almost stepped on a moccasin, the snake holding its ground and displaying its white mouth. He hoped Larue had found a place to sleep at night and hadn't tried to move around much. It would be almost more than he could bear, he thought, to come upon the body of the boy, dead of snakebite.

At mid-afternoon Hudson stopped and tied up in the shade of a big poplar where there was a deep pool below some shoals. He had a drink from the cooler and ate a can of sardines and a fried pie. He sat very still and watched soft-shelled turtles rise to the surface of the pool. Before he started the motor and left, he called for Larue again, his voice echoing through the trees.

Around the bend from the deep pool he came upon a commercial fisherman checking his turtle traps. Soft shell turtles were a delicacy. They had already trapped out the alligator snapping turtles, their capture or sale now illegal.

The fisherman was a little man who looked like he could use a swim in the river and a good scrubbing with a wire brush. And even that might not get him clean. Despite the heat he wore a camouflage duck-hunting hat and a canvas coat. Hudson was covered with sweat, but there wasn't a drop on the little man's face.

"You been hollering?" the fisherman asked.

"That's right," Hudson said. "I'm looking for a lost boy. A little black boy."

"Ain't seen no little nigger boys."

"You do, you let me know."

The fisherman dropped a turtle trap back in a pool and tied it to a tree with trotline cord.

"They been dragging the river for a little nigger boy," the fisherman said. "He'll be rising soon. Some bodies they stay down three or four days. Expect he'll be rising soon. They drug up some of my turtle traps. I told'em he's still down on the bottom of the river. Just wait. He'll come up."

"I'm not looking for him," Hudson said. "This is another one."

The fisherman laughed.

"Lot's of people looking for little nigger boys these days."

"He was down here fishing. Got lost in the woods."

"I come upon a dead man once. I was checking my traps and there he was. Floating face down. Turtles had chewed up his face. Couldn't tell if he was a white man or a nigger. Skin had turned kinda grey. That's what that boy'll look like when he rises. Lying down there on the bottom with the turtles eating him."

"You got any turtles or catfish for sale?"

"Not as big as the ones you're after. Gonna hit 'em over the head with that baseball bat?"

The man pointed to the bat lying in the bottom of Hudson's boat.

"Could be," Hudson said. "You got any little ones?"

The man grinned.

"A few," the man said. "Business has been bad ever since that boy drowned. I hope they find him soon. I may find him myself tomorrow. Folks don't like to eat things they think been feeding on dead people."

A Song For Alice Loom

213

Hudson paid the man for a catfish. He had plenty of canned food but he wanted something fresh for supper and didn't want to take the time to fish.

"What's that boy to you?" the catfisherman asked.

"Just a lost boy."

"Why's a white man hunting a little nigger boy? He steal something from you? Little nigger boys are bad to steal."

"He doesn't steal."

"What's that boy to you if he ain't stole nothing?"

For a moment Hudson couldn't think what to say to the man. He almost decided it would be simpler to agree with him, but then he changed his mind.

"He's kin," Hudson said.

The cat fisherman laughed again.

Hudson pushed the boat off and started the motor. He couldn't hear the laughter anymore but could see the man's mouth was open and he was laughing, displaying his rotten teeth.

Until it was near dark, Hudson searched for Larue, walking the riverbank woods and calling his name. But he found nothing, not even a tennis shoe track in the soft mud of the riverbank. He made camp, determined to search a tract of timber where he came in the fall to hunt squirrels. If the boy had done a lot of walking he could have reached this far downriver by now. The river itself would keep him from walking in circles if he stayed close to the bank.

Hudson made camp on a low bluff above a sandbar. He cleaned the catfish. After dipping it in egg and rolling it in corn meal, he cooked it over the fire in an iron skillet. If Larue was about, there was a chance he might be attracted by the fire. Hudson sat up until well past midnight, keeping the fire built up.

Then he strung the jungle hammock between two trees. It was the simplest method he had found of camping on the river. The hammock had built-in mosquito netting and a rain tarp. He'd bought it at the war surplus store years ago and had grown used to sleeping in it. It was very good for places where there were snakes and insects. He climbed in and zipped up the netting. This was the time Anse Carter might be out in these same woods and swamps conducting his own search for Larue. Hudson resolved to spend the day walking two more stretches of woods he knew about a little way downstream. He couldn't conceive of the boy traveling farther than that.

Hudson lay in the hammock and listened to the whippoorwills calling and the hum of the insects in the trees. It pained him to think of the boy spending another night in the swamp. He hoped he had walked to the house of a black family someplace and they'd taken him in. They wouldn't reveal his presence to Anse Carter or Wendell, not once Larue had told them the story of the murder of Miss Ella. They'd take care of their own.

In the morning, if he found Larue, they would go downriver, not up. At Monticello they would go ashore and take a bus to Hattiesburg where there was a U.S. district attorney, someone who owed no allegiance to Wendell. Then Wendell and Anse Carter would go to jail for what they'd done.

Hudson thought of pitching a baseball with the boy on the lawn of his grandfather's house. He imagined the pop of the leather as the ball hit his glove, the way it stung his palm, and over and over he listened to that imaginary sound as the cicadas hummed in the trees and the whippoorwills bore him off to sleep.

Chapter 29

Larue slipped through a break in a chain-link fence and crawled between some azalea bushes to sleep. Up across a lawn covered with pines and one big live oak tree was a large house, its facade lit by floodlights. He hoped they'd not turned a big dog loose to roam the grounds at night. Up among the plants, he pulled some pine straw, which had been used as mulch, into a pile and curled up in it. From the nearby highway came the sound of cars. He couldn't hear the sea. He buried his face in the straw, put his arms over his ears in an attempt to keep the mosquitoes away, and tried to sleep.

He finally did and dreamed of Tran. They were climbing on those booms the shrimp boats lowered like wings over the water, and Anse Carter was at the wheel of the boat, a pistol in his hand. Larue shouted at Tran to dive. They went down together, both trailing bubbles. Tran was ahead of him and reached the bottom first, a bright and sunlit floor of pure white sand. There shrimp swam up in rose-colored clouds around them, their tails beating. And when he looked up through the shrimp he saw Anse Carter's face peering down at them as if he were looking through the wrong end of a telescope. Just at that moment Larue saw his father in a diver's helmet, trailing air bubbles, come walking over the sand. Larue looked toward the surface. Anse Carter was gone.

Larue, wakened by the mosquitoes, kept returning to that same dream over and over. Then he slept a dreamless sleep. He woke up when the birds began to sing. A car drove by, and someone tossed a paper over a gate onto the driveway. He got up and crawled back out through the fence. Then, after checking up and down the highway for Anse Carter, he walked west toward New Orleans. That was where they said his father had gone. He wished he still had his Mississippi map, but he had left it at Tran's house. When he thought of Tran he started to cry, so he pushed the thought of him out of his mind by thinking of what he would eat for breakfast. He still had plenty left out of Rosalind's hundred dollars.

Larue wished that the voice would talk to him again, tell him what he should do. Maybe the spirit could only talk with him at night. But there was no real reason to think that was so. It would be good to sit on the beach and listen to that voice while seagulls sailed overhead.

"Where's Anse?" he asked.

He said it a few times, but there was no reply. A mockingbird was singing in a magnolia. Then a pair of bluejays began to scream at a cat crossing the yard. The voice had been right, Larue thought. He was going to have to help himself.

He abandoned the idea of walking along the side of the highway. It would be too easy for Anse Carter to locate him there. He walked inland until he came to a road called Irish Hill Drive, which paralleled a set of railroad tracks. He followed it to the west. He passed a sign that read Keesler Air Force base and saw the tops of barracks and buildings beyond a wire fence. Then he saw a restaurant. He ordered breakfast: scrambled eggs, sausage, and a biscuit along with a large coke. He sat at a table away from the window and ate slowly as he tried to decide what he was going to do.

He thought of his father, who months ago had left Biloxi to look for work. Pine was only a couple of hours away, and his father had not even bothered to visit before he left. He hadn't written, had sent them no money. He thought of Tran's father. Mr. Lien wouldn't have gone off someplace without telling his family, even if he was not married to Mrs. Lien any longer. He started to cry again as he ate the last of his sausage. And he forced himself not to think what happened in the house. If someone saw him crying they would begin to ask questions. Soon the police would come, who might be, as Miss Rosalind had pointed out, friends of Mr. Wendell. He considered buying a bus ticket to New Orleans but was afraid Anse Carter might be watching the station.

Larue finished his breakfast without deciding what he was going to do. It had been much easier when he had the goal of finding his father at Biloxi. He thought he could find his way to Algiers where his father might be living in their old apartment. But his father, he decided, might not even be in New Orleans. He went to the bathroom and washed his face and hands and brushed the few remaining bits of pine needles out of his hair. Then he went out onto the street again. He decided to follow the street west, for that was the direction of New Orleans.

Larue felt nervous walking on the street. At any moment Anse Carter might pull up beside him. He'd see him briefly for an instant and then it would be over, that pistol coming out from beneath his blue suit coat. He thought of the Lien family again, and now that no one was watching he started to cry. He walked down the street crying, making no attempt to wipe away the tears. Miss Ella was dead, his mother was dead, Tiffany was dead, the Liens were dead. Larue cried for all of them. He felt foolish that he'd believed Miss Ella had flown up out of the machine and that he expected to see her when he reached the sea. When you were dead you didn't fly up. You were still, and they put you in the ground. A car like Mr. Wendell's approached, and Larue stepped behind a tree. It passed. A blond-headed woman was driving.

He continued down the street, the houses all neat bungalows with palm trees in the yards and driveways of crushed oyster shells. Sometimes there were white people in the yards, sometimes black. A train carrying cars and pickup trucks moved slowly along the tracks and stopped. Larue wondered if the train was going to New Orleans, those cars and trucks soon to be on the lot at some dealership. He left the street and going between two houses walked up on the embankment that held the tracks. A dog barked at him from a fenced-in yard. A woman, watching two children swim in a small above-ground pool, stared at him but said nothing.

The right-of-way smelled of diesel fuel and hot metal. A few gulls sailed overhead, playing in the breeze that brought him the smell

Scott Ely

of the sea. He looked up and down the tracks. They were deserted. He climbed up onto one of the cars. First he tried the doors of the trucks, but they were locked. He'd planned on stretching out on the seat and listening to the radio. Instead he climbed into the bed of a pickup, shaded by the trucks on top. He stood up and watched the kids playing in the pool. They danced about as the woman sprayed them with a hose, their shouts and laughter drifting up to him.

Larue lay down against the cool metal as the train started to move. After the train picked up more speed, Larue felt safe for the first time that day. He wondered where Anse Carter was. He hoped he was still looking for him in Biloxi. He was sorry that he'd run away from Miss Rosalind who was going to take him to the FBI. Then he'd have told them how Miss Ella had flown up out of the machine. Now it would be different.

He stood up and watched the backsides of houses pass. He'd like to have lived in one of those houses with his father and mother and Tiffany and Miss Ella, to have his mother spray water on him while he swam in a pool. He thought of finding his father in New Orleans, thought of the dream in which his father had on a diver's helmet. He thought of the Lien family. The same thing could happen to his father if Anse Carter tracked him to New Orleans. Even being an airborne ranger wouldn't do his father any good if Anse Carter came in the night while they were asleep. He wanted to cry for all of them again but found that he couldn't. He ached for them as if their deaths were some enormous weight pressing down on him.

He lay back again, the wheels of the car clicking at the rail joints. He wouldn't go to New Orleans. If his father wanted him, then he could come seek him out in Pine. That was where he was going. Anse Carter would be looking in every direction but that one. He'd find Miss Rosalind. The FBI would put Anse Carter and Mr. Wendell in jail.

But if the train didn't slow down or stop in Gulfport, he might be on his way to New Orleans. He'd seen people jump off trains on TV. As he watched the crossties flash by, he knew he wasn't going to attempt it. He couldn't tell where Biloxi ended and Gulfport started. The train began to slow, a cluster of taller buildings coming into view, which he hoped was downtown Gulfport. He imagined Anse Carter following the train in his car. When the train stopped, Anse Carter would start looking for him.

He got out of the truck bed and went to the edge of the car on the side away from the ocean. The train still felt like it was going very fast, too fast to jump. Then it slowed some more, the brakes squealing, and he caught the scent of hot metal. He climbed down on the ladder. Several cars away a man with a walkie-talkie in his hand was holding onto the ladder and waving his free arm at him and shouting something. Larue turned his back on him, thankful it wasn't Anse Carter. If it had been he'd be dead.

The train kept up its speed, a little too fast to make him feel safe jumping. He looked at the man who was still yelling and waving his arm at him. They were passing a school where there was a playground with monkey bars, seesaws, and swings. Ahead was a more level place on the roadway as they approached an intersection. The train slowed some more. He heard the clang of the warning bell and saw the flash of the red lights. He took a look at the man again, still waving his arm. Larue jumped.

He tried to keep his feet but tripped, rolling in the sand of the road's shoulder. When he got to his feet again he saw the man still hanging onto the ladder. He was no longer waving his arm but shaking his head. Larue turned and ran from the man hanging onto the car and from the idea of Anse Carter on the other side of the tracks, blocked by the passing train, but waiting. Larue could imagine him at the wheel wearing his cowboy hat and those dark glasses.

He didn't stop running until he had turned the corner toward the town. Then he walked west on Old Pass Christian Road until it intersected with Highway 49. Once he reached the highway he retraced his steps and sat in the shade behind a dumpster in a parking lot.

Larue heard the sound of children's voices from across a fence. He pulled back one of the green plastic strips woven into the chain-link and saw a group of children coming out of a building. There were two buses in the lot. They were blue and had Sunlight Estates AME Church painted on the side. The long name took up most of the side of the bus. Sunlight Estates was a part of Pine. And all the children were black. Many had on T-shirts which read Sunlight Estates AME

Scott Ely

Church in blue letters.

Larue went around the fence and into the parking lot. The children had divided themselves into two groups: one girls and the other boys. Larue, trying to act casual, walked over and stood with the boys. He was glad to see that he was bigger than most. A boy a little taller than Larue came up to him.

"You a Gulfport boy?" he asked.

"No, I'm from Pine," Larue said.

He was tired of telling lies to people, even other children, and wondered what he was going to say to the boy.

"He ain't from Pine," another boy said.

"I am," Larue said. "I live on River Street. Across from the garbage department."

They all laughed. Their clothes were much better than his. Only their basketball shoes were the same. They were rich kids who never had their power and water cut off.

Larue told them he had run away from his father who was a drunk to go live with his mother in Pine. The story had worked before. He was tired and it was the only thing he could think of.

"You come with us," another boy said.

The children all agreed. Larue exchanged his airborne T-shirt with another boy his size for a church T-shirt. They gave him a new name: Clifton Smart. His father was a doctor who lived in Sunlight Estates. Clifton had gotten sick and was unable to come but the counselors didn't know that. They had been calling his name off their list. The boys had been taking turns answering for him to confuse the counselors.

"They'll never know," the biggest boy said, whose name was Charles.

They were there on the first day of a two-day church trip and were on their way to a barbecue. Larue liked the idea of going back among the other children. Anse Carter could drive right by the bus and never know he was there.

Larue spent the afternoon with the children, who all soon knew about him. They delighted in keeping it secret from the four young men and women, also dressed in church T-shirts, who were in charge of them. The counselors called him Clifton.

A Song For Alice Loom

The buses drove to a lake out in the country where there were cabins. Charles had two bags, and he let Larue carry one of them. After an hour spent listening to preaching on wooden benches set on the side of a hill in a grove of pines, they were allowed to go swimming in the lake. Larue passed his swimming test easily. All they asked him to do was swim the length of a dock and back. But he had to lie again and tell them he had forgotten his swimming trunks. He had swum much farther in the river where there was a current, and snags to worry about. Charles failed his test and was condemned to wear an orange life preserver.

He tried not to think of the Liens or Miss Ella. Miss Rosalind would take him to the FBI when he got back. They would settle all of it, settle Anse Carter and Mr. Wendell too. After the barbecue, followed by more preaching and hymn-singing, they had a bonfire down by the lake and all sang songs. Larue hadn't ever cared much for preaching and singing. But it was good to have plenty to eat and children to talk with and no chance in the world that Anse Carter was hanging about in the woods on the other side of the lake.

Larue liked going to sleep with the other children, Charles in the bunk under his. It was almost like sleeping with Miss Ella again. He tried not to think of the dead as he lay in the bunk, listening to the giggling of the children.

"Where's Anse?" Larue asked softly.

There was no reply. He said it again, over and over.

"You talk to me," he said.

The children had quieted down now. Outside the cicadas were trilling. Somewhere, maybe as far as the other side of the lake, a whippoorwill was calling. Larue thought that he could listen to the bird and it would make him fall to sleep, but it didn't. He remained wide awake.

He imagined himself as Clifton Smart and wondered what Clifton's house looked like and what kind of bicycle he rode. He wished he could turn himself into Clifton so that even if Anse Carter slipped into the cabin sometime before dawn and stared at their sleeping faces in the dark he would depart frustrated, harming no one. And it was as he was thinking of Clifton that he dropped off to sleep.

The children spent a large part of the morning listening to more

Scott Ely

preaching and people singing hymns. But they still got to swim in the lake. Late in the afternoon they boarded the buses again. Even though Larue didn't have his map, the names of the little towns were familiar: Wiggins, Seminary, Magee, Mendenhall, and on into Pine.

They drove under an arch, which had Sunlight Estates written on it. There were big houses set on lots with tall trees around them. They stopped in the parking lot of the AME Church where there was a basketball goal set up and Larue could see the screen backstop of a baseball field. If he were really Clifton Smart, he thought, he'd just walk down the street to his house. Clifton probably had his own basketball goal in the driveway. Many of the houses they had passed had them.

Some of the children were met by their parents, but others took their overnight bags and walked home. When Larue tried to give Charles back his bag, Charles refused it, saying there were some T-shirts in it he'd gotten tired of wearing. Besides the bag belonged to his older brother, and Charles didn't care what happened to it.

Larue walked down one of the smoothly paved streets, passing the houses where water sprinklers were on to keep the lawns perfect and past the basketball goals and the big cars parked in the driveways and out under the arch. Down the road he stopped at a gas station and used the payphone to call a cab. He would use the rest of Miss Rosalind's money on it. He wondered how long it would take to pay her back.

When the cab arrived, he directed the driver to take him to a playground on the edge of French Town. Anse Carter was still looking for him in Biloxi. Miss Rosalind lived in a house not far from the playground. When it got dark, he was going to walk over there and wait until he saw his chance to present himself to her. They would go to the FBI. He would be safe. No more people would die.

Chapter 30

Wendell sat behind his desk. It was late afternoon and his secretary had gone home. Anse Carter, whose nose was sunburned, the skin peeling, sat across from him. Anse had just finished telling him about killing the Lien family.

"And what good did that do?" Wendell asked.

"That boy told 'em," Anse said. "Now they won't tell."

"That boy could have told half of Biloxi by now," Wendell said angrily. "You gonna kill all of them? There's only one person you need to kill and that's the boy. You should still be down there looking for him."

"I run out of money. You said not to call."

"You had him and you let him get away."

Wendell watched Anse pick a piece of dead skin off the bridge of his nose. He dropped it, the skin falling lightly onto the carpet.

"I couldn't ask around for him," Anse said. "No way of knowing which way he went. I looked everywhere, even the beach. I took a chance going out in the sun like that."

"You just think about that sun at Parchman."

Wendell explained to Anse how everyone was looking for the boy.

"But all of that don't mean a thing if *we* can find that boy," Wendell said.

He thought of how bad their luck had been. If the boy had been in the house with the Vietnamese, he'd be dead, and their problems would be over. Wendell thought how he'd like to open the morning papers and discover some pervert had killed Larue. That would be the best luck of all. They found the skeletons of children from time to time off in some isolated patch of woods. But that was wishing for luck and he'd never done that before. He'd always made his own luck.

"In the morning you're going back down to the coast," Wendell said. "You'll find that boy."

"That motel I stayed at had roaches."

"Then find one that don't. But you're not staying in some fancy hotel. You might as well take an ad out in the paper that you're down there."

"I don't like them roaches."

"Don't you care about going to jail? They're executing people in this state again."

Wendell discovered he was frightening himself. If the worst happened, he planned to make it clear to the jury who dropped the old woman into the machine. He was sending Anse back to Biloxi, but just in case the boy had fooled them all and was in the city, he was going to keep looking hard for him while Anse was gone.

"I didn't have no roaches at Parchman," Anse said. "They sprayed for 'em."

"Have you still got the pistol you used on those gooks?" Wendell asked.

Anse smiled and took a .22 automatic out of his pocket. Then out of the other pocket he pulled a silencer almost as large as the pistol.

"Don't make hardly no noise at all," Anse said.

"Goddamit! What are you doing with that?" Wendell said.

"Didn't know nobody down there," Anse said. "Didn't have a way to get another one."

"Get rid of it. This time use a knife. Or your hands. He's just a boy."

"He's lively. And besides, I ain't touching any of 'em. That bite she gave me is festering."

Wendell noticed Anse had replaced the small bandage with a

larger one. Before Wendell could stop him, Anse peeled it off. The wound was swollen and had turned yellow around the edges.

"I put iodine on it," Anse said. "But it didn't do no good. Just stung like hell."

Wendell got up and looked at the wound.

"I'll take you to the Medi-Quick Clinic," he said. "They'll give you some pills."

"I don't believe in no doctors," Anse said.

"You get blood poisoning and they'll have to cut your damn head off to cure you."

Anse was a valuable man, but sometimes, Wendell thought, he was worse than a child. Despite Anse's protests Wendell took him to the clinic. There Anse was treated by a young doctor, who gave him a prescription for antibiotics.

Then they got back in the car and with Anse driving went out over the new river bridge. Wendell wiped the pistol and silencer clean with his handkerchief. They had to make three trips over the bridge before it was empty of cars. As Anse slowed the car Wendell tossed both pistol and silencer into the river.

"You think about using a knife," Wendell said. "And I don't want you around the house anymore. You get Alice and Rosalind all upset. You sleep in the office tonight."

"I need some things from the cabin," Anse said.

"What things?"

"Clothes and such."

"You go to Wal-mart and buy you some new ones."

Wendell was feeling better now that the pistol and the silencer were on the bottom of the river. He was taking control of events again. Anse had come so close to the boy last time. This time he'd be successful and all that would be left was some family unpleasantness to straighten out. Alice and Rosalind might decide to leave and live elsewhere. He'd sell the house.

"You take me to the cabin," Anse said. "I got some things I need."

Wendell reluctantly agreed.

"If those women are back, I'll park out on the street and you can slip in quiet," Wendell said.

They drove back through town and along River Street. Wendell was still searching the yards and sidewalks for Larue. If he saw the boy he'd give the .45 to Anse. He could say that Anse went crazy and took the pistol from him, that he tried to stop him from killing Larue. They drove past the shack, still unrented. He was going to have to hire some one to clean all the voodoo stuff out. Right now it was just sitting there costing him money. And it even had a brand new toilet bowl. He had the plumber's bill for the installation sitting on his desk. One night, not long after he had it installed, they showed a picture of it on TV. That was Ed Luck at the TV station trying to make up for all the trouble he had caused by giving Miss Ella and her demonstration coverage. After the election he planned to come up with a way to pay Ed back. Putting that toilet bowl on TV wasn't enough.

They left French Town and drove into Wendell's neighborhood. When they went by the house Wendell saw the driveway was empty, the house dark. But he was taking no chances and parked down the street.

Anse went up the drive and around back to his cabin. Wendell got out of the car and, leaning against it, smoked a cigarette. He liked the big trees, the houses set far back from the street, the same families living in them year after year. Too bad the Yankees had burned the entire town down doing the war or the houses would have been even more impressive.

As Anse came around the side of the house from the back yard, carrying a sack on his back, Wendell saw the boy walk across the driveway under the security light. Anse and the boy almost ran into each other. Helpless, Wendell watched Anse drop the sack and reach into his coat pocket.

"Get him, get him," Wendell said under his breath.

Then incredibly, instead of giving chase, Anse came running down the driveway, the sack on his shoulder. Halfway to the street he lost it, the sack falling to the ground, dirty clothes spewing from the open top. Anse stopped and stuffed them back in while Wendell, frozen into inaction by the absurdity of the scene he was witnessing, had stood and watched, the half-smoked cigarette smoldering at his feet, waving his hand at Anse to give chase to the boy.

But by the time Anse stumbled across the street, Wendell had opened the door and grabbed the pistol. Anse tossed the canvas sack into the back seat.

"Dammit," Wendell said. "You had him."

"You threw my pistol in the river," Anse said. "I ain't touching one of them Sabine niggers again."

Wendell shoved the .45 into his hand.

"He'll head for French Town," Wendell said. "You go over to the next street. I'll meet you at the end."

"Shoot him here?"

"Yes, dammit. We can say we caught him breaking into a house."

Anse went off at a run. Wendell doubted that Anse had enough speed to run the boy down. But once in French Town Anse knew the network of streets and alleys. He'd find him hiding there and kill him. If Anse went to jail for killing the boy, that would just be too bad.

Wendell drove slowly down the street, looking for Larue. The canvas sack of clothes had a musty smell to it. He reached the end of the street and turned right and halfway to the parallel street stopped and waited for Anse. As he stood by the car again and smoked another cigarette, he longed to hear the sound of the big pistol.

It took a long time for Anse to appear and when he did it was at a walk. He came up to the car breathing hard.

"I told you he was lively," Anse said.

Wendell was so angry he found it difficult to breathe, the thought of speaking out of the question.

They got in the car and Wendell drove. Anse, instead of looking for the boy, had pulled the sack of dirty clothes into the front seat and was going through it, shaking his head as he did it.

"What is it?"

"Her hat," Anse said.

"What?"

"That old lady's hat. Didn't see no reason to waste a good hat like that. Had an eye shade."

"You took her hat?"

"Yes, and I put it in this bag. Was gonna wash it."

"Forget about the hat," he said. "You look for the boy."

Anse grinned and said, "That boy has run to French Town. I'll find him easy. Too bad we threw that little twenty-two in the river. Wouldn't have made no fuss at all. This thing is gonna wake up the whole town."

"You just make sure you only have to shoot it once then."

They were on River Street. Suddenly, miraculously, the boy darted across the street in front of the car lights, going down the hill to the garbage department. Wendell stopped the car and backed up to follow. Now it could be done away from people. He hoped the boy was making for the river. He wished he could persuade Anse to drown him, but doubted if Anse would go along with that.

It was going to soon be over, he thought, as he went down the hill.

"He's gone to ground," Anse was saying. "He's gone to ground."

Chapter 31

Larue had climbed the fence at the rear of the house and then gone behind the cabin and around the back of the garage. He was going to wait there in the darkness until Rosalind drove up. If it were Mr. Wendell, he'd just fade away along the side of the garage and be over the fence and gone before he even got the car stopped. But he couldn't see the street as well as he wished, so he decided to cross to the other side of the garage where there were some azalea bushes. There he could hide and not have to keep poking his head around the corner of the garage to see the street.

Instead of going around back, he decided to cross the front of the garage. The security light up on a pole threw a circle of light on the concrete, but the street was clear and it was just a few feet. To cross around the back he'd have to climb the fence twice.

So he stepped from darkness into light and stood looking at Anse Carter, who had just walked from the grass onto the concrete, carrying a canvas bag in both arms, his cowboy hat pushed back on his head. For a moment Larue couldn't move. Anse Carter dropped the bag, which hit the concrete with a thud, and fumbled at the pocket of his jacket, his hand emerging empty. Larue bolted, his shoes squeaking on the concrete, and turned the corner of the garage. The fence came up on him, tall and covered with ivy. He imagined Anse was right behind him, and he jumped for the top, his hand around a post, the toe of his right shoe fumbling for and then finding a hold on one of the open spaces in the chain-link. As he rolled over the top, he expected to feel Anse Carter's hands on his legs, dragging him back, but there was nothing, no shouts after him, and dropping to the ground he ran across someone's back yard, headed for the familiar streets of French Town.

But when he reached French Town again, out of breath and exhausted, he considered that the next time he saw Anse Carter it would be here, and he'd have a pistol in his hand. Now he was in the center of the town. Around the corner was Mr. Pascal's fish store. He decided to hide out in the woods across the river. In the morning he'd try again to find Miss Rosalind.

He crossed the street. Mr. Pascal was closing up the place, putting a lock on the screen over the window. He made his way through alleys and over fences to a position two houses down from Mr. Hone's store on River Street. Then he worked his way from back yard to back yard, passing the house where his mother and Tiffany had died. Finally he was opposite the entrance to the garbage department.

He crouched in some bushes waiting for the street to be clear of cars.

"Hey, you," a voice said.

He looked at the front of the house behind him and saw a man sitting on the steps. The man was barefoot, his shirt off, and he held a can of beer in his hand.

"Boy," he said. "You—"

But Larue was already running, darting behind a passing car. And then, as he heard the car's tires squeal as the driver applied the brakes and smelled the burning rubber and saw the smoke in the streetlights, he realized it was Mr. Wendell and Anse Carter.

He ran desperately now, his arms pumping, listening to his own jerky breathing. Behind him he heard the squeal of tires as the car came down off the street behind him. He didn't look back; he just kept watching the dark line of trees along the river get closer and closer. The gate to the parking lot was closed and chained, so he went over it, tearing his shirt on the barbed wire on top. At least now they'd have to follow him on foot. Then he ran between the parked trucks, not even looking back when he heard the car stop at the locked gate.

A Song For Alice Loom

He went over the levee and expected to see Mr. Hudson's fishing boat again, but it was gone.

Larue took off his tennis shoes, tied the laces together, and hung them around his neck. He entered the river, letting the sluggish current carry him downstream. The water was warm. The moon was not up yet, and he stayed in the channel, wanting to be as far downstream as possible when Anse Carter reached the levee.

He heard the report of the pistol, the splash in the water beside his head coming at almost the same instant. He dove for the bottom of the river, which at this point wasn't far, the mud soft under his hands. His shoes had fallen off.

Larue held his breath as long as he could, his body sliding against moss-covered snags. Then he came up and snatched a breath of air, hearing at the same time the report of the pistol and the splat of the bullet, this time much farther from his head. He went under, the river deepening, and swam out of the warmer water into a cooler zone, holding his breath until his lungs were burning. When he surfaced for air, there was no accompanying shot. Just to be safe he dove again but ran head-first into a snag. Stunned and disoriented, he struggled to the surface. The river had bent away from the levee. Unless Anse Carter was in the river with him he was temporarily safe.

He swam on the surface now, the bank above too high to climb. The bank gradually dropped off, the river becoming shallow again. He stood up and waded to a sandbar. The sound of the motor and the light seemed to come at almost the same instant and for a moment he was frozen, shielding his eyes against the glare with one hand. He bolted for the safety of the trees.

"Boy, wait!" he heard a voice call.

It was Mr. Hudson.

Hudson had seen the figure emerge out of the river. He'd been sitting in the slack water next to the bank, drinking his last cold drink, and thinking about all the places he had looked for Larue, when he heard the shooting. When the boy emerged from the water, he'd started the motor and crossed the river.

Larue's face sprang up out of the darkness, the boy momentarily transfixed by the light. For a moment, even after Hudson spoke to him, he thought the boy was going to run for the trees.

Scott Ely

"Wait," Hudson said again. "It's Hudson Loom."

He turned the light on himself so the boy could see who it was. Larue stopped and came to the boat. He climbed in, and Hudson had him lie down in the bow.

"Who's shooting?" Hudson asked.

"Anse Carter," Larue said.

Larue lay curled up, thinking that at any moment he was going to hear bullets hitting the boat. He remembered the sound the bullet had made when Anse Carter had shot and hit it while he lay hidden in the willows. The bottom of the boat was cool beneath his cheek. He sucked in gasps of air, catching the scent of fish and dried river mud. He hoped Mr. Hudson could protect him. Larue was tired of running. His eyes filled with tears as he thought of all the dead people. He wanted to stay curled up on the bottom of the boat forever.

But gradually Larue calmed down, his heart beating slower and slower and his breathing becoming more regular. He didn't think that Anse Carter would be able to follow once the levee ended. The bank was a tangle of briars, cane, vines, and small trees. But that possibility was gone when Mr. Hudson twisted the throttle of the motor, and they shot down the river, the bottom of the boat slapping against the water. Larue hoped Mr. Hudson knew what he was doing because there were plenty of snags.

Hudson realized running fast in the dark was risky, but he had a good outline of the river in his head. He didn't want to take the chance of Wendell or Anse following along the bank and getting ahead of them. Once he had made a couple of bends he slowed the boat.

"Sit up, boy," he told Larue.

He handed Larue the big flashlight.

"We'll run slow now," Hudson said. "You watch for snags."

They went slowly, Larue occasionally signaling that a snag was ahead and playing the light on it. Hudson tried to decide what he would do if he were Wendell. One thing Wendell and Anse could do would be to wait for them at the railroad bridge. There'd be nobody around to witness what went on. And he wouldn't even know they were there until it was too late. He decided to try to get off the river through the landfill. Wendell might think of that, but Hudson thought it was their best chance. And he didn't want to play hide and seek with Anse Carter in the woods at night. They might even decide to divide their forces, in which case he might have to deal with only one of them at a time. Once across the landfill he could use Moses' truck to get Larue out of town. In the morning he'd take Larue to the federal district attorney's office. The boy could make a statement and Wendell would be finished.

Hudson stopped the boat at the pump. He explained to Larue what they were going to do.

"You ain't got a gun?" Larue asked.

"No," Hudson said.

He was beginning to wish he'd not left the revolver at home.

"We'll be fine," Hudson said. "They'll never find us."

It did not seem possible to Larue that Mr. Hudson had been out on the river without a gun. Mr. Hudson had known he might run into Mr. Wendell and Anse Carter.

"This bat has got Murphy's autograph on it," Hudson said.

"He hits the long ball," Larue said. "Hits the long ball and the Braves still lose."

Hudson gave Larue the bat. He wanted to take the boy's mind off guns and Anse Carter. But Larue couldn't see the writing in the dark.

"You can see it later," Hudson said. "We'll get us a couple of hamburgers. Someplace where there's plenty of light."

They went up the bank and followed the plastic pipe across the cleared ground. One thing Hudson liked about the landfill at night was that there were no flies. Hudson noticed the moon had started to rise over the trees across the river. He urged Larue to walk fast before its light caught them on the exposed ground. They went past the sunken hole where the fire had been. The light from Moses' guard shack made a glow just over the hill.

Hudson heard the car before he saw it, coming with no lights across the landfill, its tires making a tearing sound in the soft dirt, the moonlight glinting off its roof. Suddenly from the car a spotlight swept across the landfill, catching first the tripod that held the pipe and then sweeping past them.

He pressed Larue to the ground, shielding the boy's body with his own. The light paused and then returned. There was nowhere to hide.

Scott Ely

It centered on them. He shielded his eyes with his hand against the glare. He prayed they didn't have a rifle. But that wouldn't have been Anse Carter's style.

The car's headlights snapped on, fixing them. He sat up and pushed Larue behind him.

"Don't you run, boy," he said. "I can't save you if you run."

"I won't," Larue said.

The car came on and on, seeming to take forever to cover the three hundred yards that must have lain between them. He put the flashlight at arm's length from them and switched it on.

A bullet plowed into the ground by the side of the flashlight. The second one shattered it. Damn fine shot, he thought. He felt foolish holding the bat in his hand.

Hudson thought of the revolver. How good it would feel in his hand right now.

"I'm going to run," Hudson said. "When they start shooting at me, you run. Don't look back. Don't stop. You go to the FBI office. It's in the post office downtown."

Hudson leaped to his feet, digging hard, the bat in his hand. For a moment he expected to hear the voice of some coach screaming at him to drop the bat. If he could lure them into the brush that bordered the landfill, he might have a chance. There was the sound of pistol shots. He ran, twisting and bobbing to give Anse a poor target. The car had changed course and there on the edge of the fire a figure stood firing at the car. Anse returned fire and the figure dropped to the ground. The car disappeared, followed by a very heavy sound like a dragline dumping a load of dirt.

Hudson stopped.

"Larue?" Hudson shouted.

The boy got up. He hadn't moved.

Hudson heard a kind of ticking sound. Then there was an explosion, a plume of flame spiraling up into the night sky. Hudson ran for the boy. He reached him and swept him up in his arms.

Charlene, Hudson thought. They drove right into Charlene. The barrier tape Jack removed had not been replaced.

"They gone?" Larue asked.

The flames shot up into the sky. There was another explosion, the ground shaking under their feet as a pocket of methane gas went up.

"Gone," Hudson said.

With the boy at his side, Hudson walked toward the fire.

Scott Ely

Chapter 32

Hudson found Rosalind standing on the edge of the fire. Sparks and flames still shot up into the night sky. The car had opened a hole. Now there was plenty of oxygen for Charlene.

Rosalind hugged Larue.

"Anse Carter missed," Rosalind said. "How could that be?"

He hoped she hadn't shot Wendell.

"The bullets came so close," Rosalind said. "I fell." She thought of that afternoon she'd gone to kill the sergeant.

"I hit a headlight," she said.

"That's right," Hudson said.

They all went up to the guard shack. When they were twenty yards from it, Hudson, fearing what he would find there, made Larue stop. But what they found was Moses asleep on his cot, an empty pint bottle of Four Roses on the floor beside him. Whiskey had saved Moses' life.

After he woke Moses, who was too drunk to talk coherently, Hudson borrowed the keys to his truck. Then he called Chief Stone, who agreed to meet them at his office and take their depositions. Hudson and Larue and Rosalind got in the truck.

"I stole a hundred dollars from Miss Rosalind," Larue said.

He said the words without looking at Rosalind, speaking them as if she were not even there.

"She can afford it," Hudson said.

Larue wasn't sure exactly what Hudson meant by that. Miss Rosalind laughed.

"They won't put me in jail?" Larue asked.

Now Hudson and Rosalind laughed.

"Nobody is going to jail," he said. "Those that would've gone are dead."

"I could work for you and pay her back," Larue said.

Hudson looked down at Larue's bare feet.

"Her kin cost you a pair of shoes," Hudson said.

"My mama bought 'em," Larue said. "Paid more than a hundred dollars."

"Don't seem that a pair of shoes for a boy should cost that much," Hudson said. "But I guess that makes it even with you and the Looms."

Larue was relieved he wasn't going to have to pay Miss Rosalind back.

"You can jump higher in 'em," Larue said.

Larue thought of jumping up just like the players in those commercials on TV, soaring past the rim of the basket.

Hudson decided that the next day he'd take the boy out to the mall and buy him a new pair of shoes. They were on the highway now and began to meet the police cars. One, two, three, four of them Larue counted and then the rescue squad and a fire truck. Hudson knew they were going to have a hard time retrieving the car and the bodies. The firemen would pour more water on Charlene, and it wouldn't do any good at all. But tomorrow he'd worry about the damage they were sure to cause and would come up with a new plan for Charlene. Right now, for the first time, he felt weak, his arms and legs sluggish and heavy. They'd been lucky.

At Chief Stone's office they gave their depositions. Alice didn't answer the phone. Maurice showed up, Joe Wallace with him. Hudson knew that Sydney Cable was going to make much of the murder. He was glad he had made such a solid contribution to Sydney. Then Chief Stone announced that social services would take care of Larue and find him a foster home.

"He's coming home with us," Hudson said.

Scott Ely

"Yes," Rosalind said. "He's our kin."

"Sydney Cable might make something out of that," Joe Wallace said.

"And what would that be?" Hudson asked.

"It'd be safer if you didn't," Maurice said.

"We're responsible for him," Hudson said. "It's just like Miss Ella said."

"You want to go with Mr. Loom?" Chief Stone asked Larue.

Larue looked around the room at the faces of the men. He looked at Miss Rosalind.

"He took me off the river," Larue said.

"But do you want to go home with him?" Chief Stone asked. "Stay at his house for a few days."

"Yes, sir," Larue said.

Larue felt better now that he had decided. He took a step closer to Hudson. He put his arms around Miss Rosalind.

"There's an election coming up," Maurice said. "We have to move carefully."

"I agree," Hudson said. "But where this boy sleeps tonight is not part of that."

Hudson took Larue by the hand and they walked out of the room.

"Hudson—" Maurice called out after them.

They went down the hall, Joe Wallace right behind them.

"Maurice thinks you should reconsider," Joe Wallace said.

Hudson reached the elevator and punched the button. The door opened; they all stepped inside.

"Whose side are you on?" Joe Wallace asked.

"Nobody's," Hudson said as the door closed.

He drove home. Hudson had Larue strip off his dirty clothes and sent him to take a shower. He put the boy's clothes in the washer and gave him an old set of sweats to wear that had belonged to one of his girlfriends. Before long the driveway was going to fill up with reporters and television crews. Rosalind called their mother. Drusila said Alice had gone to Biloxi.

"She figured it out too," Rosalind said.

Rosalind wondered if she'd run into the people from Mendenhall.

A Song For Alice Loom

Hudson was going to make the TV people stay out there and wait until morning. He was not planning on answering the door. His mother would read about what had happened in the paper and come home.

In the refrigerator he found half of a frozen pizza and put it in the microwave. Then he opened himself and Rosalind a beer and poured Larue a coke. The boy appeared wearing the sweats, which swallowed him, the shirt coming to his knees, the pants rolled up in huge cuffs.

"You like pizza?" Hudson asked.

"Yes, sir," Larue said.

Larue thought he wanted to stay in this house. It didn't matter if Mr. Hudson was a white man. Hudson handed him the Coke.

"You like baseball?" Hudson asked.

"Yeah, the Braves are on tonight," Rosalind said.

The boy looked nervous and kept casting his eyes at the floor.

"Yes," Larue said.

Hudson put the bat in Larue's hands. Larue examined Murphy's autograph.

"It's real," Hudson said. "You can have it. We'll all go to Atlanta real soon and get us another one."

"Mine?" Larue asked.

"That's what I said," Hudson replied.

Larue took a few swings with the bat. It was too big for him.

The bell on the microwave rang.

Hudson found a Braves' game still on. They were playing Oakland. Now it was going into extra innings with the score tied.

"You like the Braves?" Hudson asked.

"Sometimes," Larue said. "They always lose."

"Not this year," Rosalind said.

Larue ate all his pizza before Hudson even got started on his. He went to the kitchen and put another pizza in the microwave and opened another beer. He heard the roar of the crowd as he returned.

"They got a hit?" Hudson asked.

"Long fly ball," Larue said. "I expect they'll get a hit."

"I hope so," Hudson said.

"They got two men on base," Larue said.

"We're hopeful," Rosalind said.

Scott Ely

"And only one out," Larue said.

"They lose that way a lot," Hudson said.

"That's true," Larue said.

Hudson listened to the announcer giving statistics about the player at the plate and the pitcher and the last times the Braves had won a game in extra innings. A seagull appeared on the screen, sailing about over center field.

They all sat together in the darkened room, the glow of the TV screen on their faces, no longer talking as they watched the game spin itself out in its leisurely way.

Chapter 33

The voices of Anse Carter and Wendell Loom come sailing into my ears. I'm glad they're dead. That means Larue is safe.

"You let him trick you," Wendell says.

"How was I to know?" Anse says.

"You should have known," Wendell says. "That's what I pay you for."

I chuckle at that. They've still got one foot in the world of the living. Soon they'll be buried. Soon they'll stop talking.

"It's sparkling all around," Anse says. "Like the Fourth of July."

"You better damn well be still," Wendell says. "You're making all these lights go crazy. I know it's you who's doing it."

On and on they go, arguing about getting tricked by Hudson Loom and worrying about their unstable fields. And I'd talk to them, tell them that the time for hating is past, except that those Japs are too close. I don't want to do anything to set those metal detectors off.

I listen to the detectors humming and to the hiss of the steel rods as they come sliding down through the ash. The Japs are probing for bones. At least they won't get Ernie out in the ocean. I look down at my dogtags tied around the bootlaces of my left boot, the right one gone God knows where, and at my belt buckle. Lucky for me my rifle's not there. That would send the detectors buzzing.

Now I'm curled up, assuming that fetus-in-a-womb position, if I can be said to lie inside anything. One of those steel rods is going to come sliding down through the ash pretty soon, and I'll find out what comes after this. They'll ship my bones home to the States for Alice to bury. I can imagine my child standing above the grave, watching them lower me into the ground. I'll never get to hold her in my arms. Even if my child were lying here beside me, we could never touch.

Love, I said Love. And save them. Save the Looms and the Sabines. Somebody had to save them. Nobody has really been saved, although Larue is alive and Anse and Wendell are dead. New Anses and Wendells will appear unless all of them learn to love.

I hear the metal detectors humming. They're homing in on Saki's helmet. He's been worried about that helmet. I listen to them talking excitedly. But now they're getting distracted by a couple of ammo boxes and have moved away. I talk quietly with Saki, giving him encouragement. But he's still worried about that helmet lying right under his field.

I think of Alice, how much I love her. I was beginning to play better music because of her. That's what we told each other, that our love made the other's work better. I was riding that high from her that was better than any kick dope ever gave me. But I practiced hard too, practiced until my fingers were sore and my chest ached from blowing. Who knows how good I might have become. Saving the Looms and the Sabines is the same as saving me. I like the sound of that thought so I repeat it. How can that be true? I'm not even sure what is me and what is not me. Those bones are not me. But what am I? Something like that cold glow at the end of a firefly's tail. What will I be if they find me?

A Song For Alice Loom

The Japs have found the ammo boxes. I know what's written on them—BALL-30 CALIBER. I was carrying them just before that naval shell hit, running at a crouch through that damn ash. It must have been a naval shell because the Japs didn't have big stuff like that up on the volcano. If they had, they would have used it against the fleet. I hear them talking. Very excited. I hope they move away up the slope where there's more metal junk buried in the ash: part of a jeep, a box of C-rations, rifles, K-Bar fighting knives, the leather handles rotted away, the rusty blades plenty to set a detector buzzing.

Saki is talking to me and I talk back despite the fact that the effort makes the field shift. Lots of unstable shit in it now. He's afraid. But again. I stretch out. I think it's not fair to have to die twice. And I'm worried about what happens after they destroy the field. What then? Will I hover above my bones for eternity or will there be something else. Ernie thinks that it will be something else. Not heaven or hell but something else. Then the field starts to contract and I repeat the words over and over, Save them. Save them.

The Japs have dug up an ammo box. I can hear their disappointment. They want bones. Now they start working the slope and home in on the transmission. I'll bet all that metal just lights up those metal detectors. I hope there's not an unexploded naval shell tangled up in that junk.

Ernie is laughing at me again. He always does that when I try to talk with Alice. How can the living be saved? he asks. But he's always been like that, secure from the Japanese under twenty feet of water. Everything is always cool with Ernie.

"Love," I say.

Ernie laughs that deep underwater laugh of his. The field shifts and I curl what is me up inside it.

"Love," I say again.

Scott Ely

The field quivers, drops of light falling off it like I'm wrapped up inside a rainbow. Saki starts talking fast. The Japanese have worked their way back down the slope. I talk calmly to him. He says he's lying there looking at that helmet as if he were alive and it's a frag with the pin pulled. I think I could play that rainbow if I had my saxophone and hands and lips to play it and a good pair of lungs.

Now they're directly over him. I tell him to be cool. But Saki is crying he's so scared. I'm scared too. I think of playing my sax, running those notes together. The Japanese dig closer and closer to Saki. He says it's strange to see the shovel blades slicing through the ash. They put the metal detector on him again. The helmet lies a little to one side of his bones. There's always a chance they'll not find him. That's happened before. The slope is so full of metal that sometimes they get careless. But they'll be sure to dig some more when they find something personal like a helmet. The only thing worse would be a belt buckle. They'll dig a hole in the ash big enough to hide a tank if they come upon a belt buckle or a set of dog tags.

They find the helmet. Saki is by now almost too scared to talk. Ernie and I talk to him. I wished they hadn't found that other Japanese guy, Numo, in the cave up on the mountain. Saki knew him and Numo could always calm him down. We tell him to be calm, but it must be a scary thing, lying there watching the blade of the shovel come down, the field dancing around, all the colors glowing.

"Saki," I say, "they'll take the helmet. No one will ever find you once it's gone. Think of that."

The Japanese pull the helmet out of the hole and spend some time examining it. We all wait to see if they dig more or start sifting the ash for bone fragments. Once they decide to search they are very thorough. They get every sliver of bone. Instead, they dig another hole ten feet beyond the end of Saki's field. The detector homes in on a canteen.

Ernie starts telling Saki a story about when he was a boy in Iowa. It's about hunting pheasants. Their plumage, Ernie says, was like the roof of his field. Sometimes he tells us about the fish, how they glide through the field. And sharks. Sometimes there are sharks out there. Probably the kin of those who did so well in '45. Saki doesn't want to hear about pheasants. He wants to hear about those fish so Ernie tells him.

The Japanese dig fast and find the canteen. It's an American canteen. Then they get out the wire screens and all of us know that Saki is finished.

"Too bad, buddy," Ernie says.

And I say, "Be cool, man."

I also say that maybe they'll only go down a foot or so and stop. Saki is worried about the shovels but we tell him they can't hurt him. "You should have sharks swimming through you," Ernie says. "I could tell you stories about those sharks."

The Japanese screen out the ash as they go down but find nothing. They pass right through the field. Saki tells us he doesn't feel anything when they screen the field, so if they don't find the bones he'll be all right. But they do. And it's like when you switch off a radio. Suddenly he's gone. That's the great mystery to us. We like to think he goes with the bones to be buried with them in Japan. But who knows?

"Too bad," I say.

"He was a good man," Ernie says. "Let me tell you about those sharks, Lou."

So I listen to Ernie telling me about all the sharks he's seen for the past forty years or so. And although I've heard most of the stories before, I get interested because it's so different out there in the ocean. I first notice the Japanese when their metal detector

Scott Ely

starts doing weird things to my field. You'd think they'd be satisfied for the day with Saki's bones.

"Man, those Japs have got their shit together," Ernie says.

"I'm cool," I say.

That dog tag is not a helmet. It might not even register on that detector. I think of the dog tag tied to my boot, still bright and shiny, the aluminum incorruptible. It was the right place to put it because that big shell chewed me up pretty bad. If it had been around my neck, it would have been lost forever. I think of my name and religion and blood type stamped on it. Nothing in the Bible or anything I heard in the Methodist Church ever prepared me for this. At least they'll send the bones home to Alice.

The shovel blades slide down through the ash. I hear Ernie talking to me. He's telling another shark story. The blades pass through me, but the field remains in place as the ash is sifted by the Japanese. Then they find the first bone. I see one of them put his hand on it, all of them talking excitedly. The field begins to dissolve, the colors all running together. Ernie is still talking.

"Be cool," man, he says.

I smell cinnamon. The field collapses in a rain of orange and blue and green. Then all is not me.

A Song For Alice Loom

Scott Ely was born in Atlanta, GA, and he moved to Jackson, MS when he was eight. He served in Vietnam (somewhere in the highlands near Pleiku). He graduated with an MFA from the University of Arkansas, Fayetteville. He teaches fiction writing at Winthrop University in South Carolina. His previous book publications include STARLIGHT (Weidenfeld & Nicolson); PITBULL (Weidenfeld & Nicolson, Penguin); OVERGROWN WITH LOVE (University of Arkansas Press); THE ANGEL OF THE GARDEN (University of Missouri Press); PULPWOOD (Livingston Press); EATING MISSISSIPPI (Livingston Press). His work has been translated in Italy, Germany, Israel, Poland, and Japan. There were also UK editions of the novels published.